For Genieve Wilson

AMPED

General Biologics™

Neural Autofocus MK-4®

User's Manual—*US Version*

The Neural Autofocus MK-4® Brain Implant

The Neural Autofocus MK-4® Brain Implant is used to send electrical impulses to specific parts of the brain as well as to sense brain activity.

The implant consists of an **electrode array (A)** placed on the brain surface, a subdermal **processing unit (B)**, a biologically charged **capacitor (C)**, and a **maintenance port (D)** that is located above the ear (adjacent to the temporal lobe).

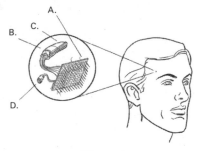

Figure 1.

The central purpose of the Neural Autofocus MK-4® is to increase your ability to concentrate on mental and physical tasks by sensing brain wave states associated with inattention and stimulating the brain wave state toward beta one (focused attention).

Figure 2.

In addition, the unit can serve as a Brain-Computer Interface (BCI) for users who wish to operate an externally worn medical exoskeleton device, powered prosthetic limb (or limbs), or microelectric retinal implant device.

In the first months of use, your Neural Autofocus MK-4® Brain Implant will develop an accurate model of your brain function. In response to the unit, your own neural circuits will adapt, strengthening existing pathways associated with concentration and motor function. This feedback process will continue throughout the lifetime of the implant device. Please note that these changes are irreversible, even if use of the implant is discontinued.

Monthly application of bio-gel® via the maintenance port is crucial to prevent infection or foreign body rejection. Our patented bio-gel® is also guaranteed to minimize the incidence of neural scarring, which can degrade electrode efficiency.

Congratulations! With proper care, your new Neural Autofocus MK-4® Brain Implant will improve your life for years to come!

Note: As with all types of surgery, neural implantation carries some risks. Talk to your physician about warnings, precautions, and possible hazards. Viral or bacterial infection is a life-threatening condition. Call your doctor right away if you experience symptoms of infection, including stiff neck, confusion, fever, local redness, swelling, discharge, or seizures.

We can change ourselves.
Think of the possibilities.

—CARL SAGAN

Supreme Court of the United States

No. 09-1153

SAMANTHA BLEX

v.

BOARD OF EDUCATION

ON WRIT OF CERTIORARI TO THE UNITED STATES COURT OF APPEALS FOR THE NINTH CIRCUIT

MR. CHIEF JUSTICE ANFUSO delivered the opinion of the Court.

The question in this case is whether users of implantable technology (e.g., Neural Autofocus® units) are guaranteed a right to education under the Fourteenth Amendment. The respondent Board of Education asserted that implanted students wield an unfair intellectual advantage over nonimplanted students and faculty, interfering with the fair administration of education.

The case of *Brown v. Board of Education*, 347 U.S. 483, established that public institutions may not discriminate against students based on their immutable characteristics. We hold that the use of implantable technology constitutes an *elective surgery,* and that there is therefore no protection for implanted citizens under the Fourteenth Amendment.

Therefore, we hold that implanted citizens are not a protected class.

It is so ordered.

1
THE FIRST STEP

I'm standing on the steep slate roof of Allderdice High School, gripping a rain-spattered wrought iron decoration in one hand and holding up my other hand, palm out.

"Don't," I'm saying to the girl in front of me. "Please don't."

My hand wavers, tracing incantations of fear and panic in the air. Just beyond my outstretched fingers is something that has been spiraling out of control for years. Only I shouldn't call her something. Should *never* call her a thing.

Somebody is what I mean.

It's the technology, see? We can't get away from it. Anywhere you find people, you find *it*. Clever little contraptions. Cunning strategies. We're toolmakers born and bred; and even if you don't believe in anything else, you'd better believe in that. Because *that's* human nature.

It's the tools that make us strong.

And it's the tools that put a girl on the edge of this roof. I crawled out here against all advice the second I heard who it was. I owe this girl a debt and I can never repay it but I'm doing my best to try.

Samantha is just fifteen. The wind is smearing her brown hair against gray skies, pushing her tears in streaks across her blank, emotionless face. Allderdice is a massive school, built during the industrial genesis of Pittsburgh. Sam stands on the precipice, six stories up. The rain is spitting at us through afternoon sunlight, and the dull stone building seems to be bleeding or crying or both.

I can't believe she's really going to jump. Not after all she's been through.

You make a tool to fix a problem, right? But—and I've thought about this—it's the boundaries that define us. Bold, black lines that can't be crossed—the limits of human ability. Lately, the edges have been torn off the map.

Now we're all getting lost.

Eight years ago a little kid named Samantha Blex missed a week of class. In the first photos on the news, you could see Sam was a little cross-eyed. She smiled a lot through her kid-sized purple eyeglasses. Cute. The kid was all slobber and grubby fingers and grins. Had a habit of putting blocks in her mouth.

That's why, when Samantha walked back into school after her weeklong hiatus, a lot of the other kids' parents were scared. Terrified is more like it. A textbook case of fight or flight, with a serious lean toward fight.

See, Sam wasn't cross-eyed when she came back to class. She didn't put blocks in her mouth anymore, either. In fact, Samantha Blex pretty quickly demonstrated that she was now the smartest kid in third grade. After a few breathless rounds of testing, Sam turned out to be in the top-hundredth percentile on citywide intelligence tests.

The kid had one hell of a week away.

In an interview, Sam's teacher told a reporter in a shaky voice that he wasn't sure if Sam was still the same little girl, now that she'd visited her doctor and been given a Neural Autofocus implant. That quote grabbed a lot of airtime. I felt really bad about it later. Should have known better than to say it.

And that's how it started. With sweet little Sam walking back into my classroom, looking me right in the eye with a new spark of intelligence—a new electricity altogether.

Where'd the spark come from? It's simple enough. An aspirin-sized piece of conductive metal, an *amp*, carefully placed in the prefrontal cortex of the kid's brain. A baby squid pulsing with an exquisitely timed series of electrical stimulations, gently pushing her mind toward the beta one wave state. Focused concentration, 24-7. This sharpened focus massively amplified her intelligence, bulldozing away the dim, mild, slobber-mouthed little girl I knew.

And only a little nub of dark plastic on her temple, like a mole, to show for it. A maintenance port.

Just like mine.

"I know how you feel, Sam," I call to the coltish teen on the roof. "I get the stares. I hear the whispers. We can make it through this."

I'm flawed hardware, like anybody. Have been for a long time. Epilepsy. My doctor says it's a Tower of Babel in my head and I believe him. Of course, I would. My doctor is my father.

But the nub on my temple doesn't lead to anything as hot shit as a General Biologics Neural Autofocus unit. It's just a simple stimulator designed to treat epilepsy and keep me from swallowing the old tongue. Proverbially. Dad has always said that doesn't really happen.

Still, turning my implant off is not an option. And that's the bitch of it. These tools we love so much have burrowed under our skin like parasites. They're in our brains now, our joints and organs. Crouching behind our eyeballs and clinging to our sinuses. Making us smarter and stronger and always, always more dependent.

"You don't know how it feels," says Sam. "You're medical. Not elective. You've got no *inkling*."

Sometime in the past, in some sterile office, a doctor said Sam had a problem. She had a little trouble concentrating, that's all. But there was a solution available. And her parents chose to use it. They had a little bit of money and they wanted the best for their daughter and they were willing to take the risk. Any parent might have done the same.

"You didn't choose this, Sam."

"Tell me about it," she mutters, eyeing the ground.

It was my first year teaching. Age twenty-two. Those chubby faces with their quick eyes sent me packing to teach high school the very next year. But I was *there*. I watched it all begin. Now, I'm crouching on the roof and inching away from the safety of the window and I'm watching it end.

"Stop that, Mr. Gray," Samantha warns. She sounds slightly irritated, as if she'd caught me picking my nose. "Don't come any *fucking* closer."

I'm creeping across the spine of the building toward her now. A shivering, cowardly twenty-nine-year-old turtle on a slippery log. My knees and crotch and chest are blotched with water, my cheeks sprinkled with drops. *Please, please, please,* I'm thinking. Please don't let me slip and fall and die this morning with my water-splotched crotch and my goddamn useless pencils in my shirt pocket and my soft clean hands with no calluses on them. This roof is slicker than ice. Slicker than a fucking waterslide and there's no going back, so I hump it forward and ignore Sam's annoyed voice.

She gives up protesting, and waits.

It was the Pure Human Citizen's Council that pressured schools across the country into barring implanted kids. They said the few modified kids were taking precious resources away from the vast majority of *human* kids. It was true and Allderdice agreed, but Samantha's parents were passionate and that's how she ended up before the Supreme Court. A poster child for the inevitable future.

The lawyers picked Sam because she was a straight Neural Autofocus job. The nub on her temple wasn't connected to the minnow's flash of a retinal implant in her eye or a gleaming prosthetic limb. She was just a little girl, pretty and pure—save the one inhuman flaw buried inside, the truth of it flickering out into her IQ score.

Finally, my face crosses over into shadow. I see a knee-length skirt snapping in the breeze. Samantha stands with her hands on her hips, resigned.

I realize that she hasn't jumped yet because she is trying to figure out how to make sure I am safe. A relieved breath hisses out of me, a whimper. We both hear it and think about it for a second.

"Jesus, you're a pussy," says Samantha. She glowers down at me like a ship's figurehead sprouting from the peak of the roof. Too hard to be made of wood. Made of metal. Little flecks of it, anyway.

"I'm jumping," she says. "Trust me, you'd have jumped years ago."

"No, Samantha—"

"Shut your mouth," she snaps. "You don't know shit. I'm smarter than you, remember? You couldn't teach me back then, so why try to talk to me now? Just shut up. I'm jumping. The impact is going to kill me instantly. It'll take about two seconds to fall."

Immediately I think of how she looked in those little purple eyeglasses. The memory of her floats like a haze over this teenage girl in front of me. It was too much, the gap between the old Samantha and the new. Something broke in that week she was gone. A piece of her must have got lost in the transition.

Samantha glances down. "It looks like I'll hit damp grass, which doesn't mean I won't die. That's inevitable from this height. I'll have accelerated to about forty miles an hour. But the grass is good. It means that when I hit, there's a solid chance my guts won't spray out of my mouth and asshole."

I just blink. Her words are a rock wall and I've rammed into it going full speed with all the momentum gathered by an idealistic career teaching mostly docile students. I mean, I know that the obedient kids I teach are different from the ones who stream out into the world at the end of the day. But I never fathomed this kind of talk. *This* never showed up from eight to three. It was trapped inside the desks and books and held back by, what? The threat of detention, I guess.

Samantha doesn't seem worried about detention.

"And don't think that nub on your temple makes you anything besides a spaz, Gray. Sorry. I meant to say autosomal dominant frontal lobe epileptic. Yes, we all know."

She taps the mole-sized nub that protrudes from her right temple, clear hazel eyes shining in the spotty sunlight.

"This, Mr. Gray. *This* is really something. You know, right after I got this, I was actually looking forward to coming back to school. I didn't see things so clearly then."

"You can't listen to other kids," I say. "They're only jealous."

"Kids?" she asks. "You think this is Algernon syndrome? That dumb little Samantha woke up and realized the other kids were *mean*? I haven't worried about children since the third grade. It's the rest of the world, Mr. Gray. Allderdice is a microcosm. And the larger world hates us. To quote the Honorable Chief Justice Anfuso, 'The existence of a class of superabled citizens threatens to pull apart the fabric of our society.' There's no place for me here. Or anywhere else."

"That's today. But what about tomorrow? What about the Free Body Liberty Group? We don't know what might happen," I urge.

"The world has been changing, Mr. Gray. People have been waiting for permission to hate us. Now all the evil is going to come out. There are too many of *them* and not nearly enough of us. This has all happened before. It will end the same. In labor camps. Mass graves." She looks at me with pity. "You're a dead man walking. How pathetic that you don't even know it."

Somehow, I find the courage to crouch on cramping legs.

I reach my wavering hand out to her, feeling the warm lick of rain on it.

"Please, Samantha," I'm saying.

"You were right," she says.

"About what?" I ask.

"What you told those reporters. You said you didn't know who I was when I came back. It's true. I'm not the same girl."

"Don't do this. We'll fight them. I promise you, Sam."

"Sam's gone. I'm somebody else. Somebody that never should have existed."

I'm shouting and standing up and I've forgotten to be afraid. As I reach for her, I see her tear-streaked face between my fingers for a frozen instant. Her eyes are wide open when she steps off the roof.

Eight years ago, a little girl named Samantha Blex missed a week of school. When she came back, she changed the world. And this morning, she left it.

Washington DC: Bomb blast rocks Pure Human Citizen's Council

A massive bomb blast has torn through a building in the US capital of Washington DC, killing three and injuring eleven.

CNN said no arrests have been made and no group has claimed responsibility for the attack.

Local news footage showed a plume of smoke floating over a two-storey office building that had been largely reduced to rubble. The street was cordoned off by police investigating the bombing, even as firefighters continued to suppress the flames.

All roads into the city centre have been closed, said radio network NPR, and security officials evacuated people from the area, fearing another blast. A spokesman for the Washington Hospital Center said the survivors had been taken there for treatment, many with serious injuries.

In a telephone call to a DC television station, Eric Vale, assistant chief of Washington DC police, said the leadership of the Pure Human Citizen's Council was safe, including Pennsylvania senator Joseph Vaughn, head of the PHCC. An investigation is ongoing, according to Mr. Vale. "We urge people not to point fingers until all the facts are in. We've got experts taking the scene apart in order to determine who is responsible for this attack."

The names of the dead have not been released.

2

NO SIRENS, NO LIGHTS

Boom.

I didn't see Samantha hit the ground. But I heard the sound of it. The blunt impact is still looping through my brain, ringing like a concussion. It's a blurry haze that settles over everything: my crawl back to the window, the sharp looks from late-to-arrive cops, and the concerned questions from my students in the hallways. I can barely speak, much less answer. Principal Stratton takes one look and tells me to take the rest of the day off.

Now, I'm walking fast and aimless through downtown. Headed on a loose path toward my dad's office. The rain has let up and I'm searching the gleaming streets for something sane to latch onto. Some thought, some sight. I'm not finding anything.

The city of Pittsburgh is in the middle of a major course correction. The rest of the nation is, too. The Supreme Court's ruling has slapped about half a million people in the face. This morning, everybody with an amp in his head is standing, blinking into the light of a new day. Wondering what it all means.

I'm starting to get the gist.

Legalized discrimination. Around a hundred thousand amped kids being sent home from school across the nation. Nearly half a million amped adults wondering if they've still got a job. And a couple hundred million normal people, celebrating.

Sirens wail as a column of dark SUVs hurtles past me, long antennae seesawing over potholes. At one point, a tubby, middle-aged guy sprints by, barefoot and panting and with one metal-laced plastic leg. His real foot hits the sidewalk, then his fake one.

Slap, clink. Slap, clink. Slap, clink.

I stop and watch the man until he is gone. The shock of what I saw this morning is starting to fade around the edges, tickling and stinging. An acid knot of anger and sadness has wormed its way into the back of my throat and cornered itself there.

From somewhere nearby, I hear the repetitive, booming calls of a rally.

"Pure Pride," they're chanting. "Pure Pride."

The Pure Human Citizen's Council is reveling in the decision. The organization grew up organically in the last decade, responding to amps like a foreign body rejection. At first the PHCC was a religious nonprofit. Sanctity of the body, love what God gave ya—that sort of thing. But then they got support from all over and they got it fast. Middle-class families who worried their kids wouldn't be able to compete in the new future. Labor unions with an eye on keeping jobs for their human members. And politicians who knew a good bandwagon when they saw it.

Pure pride. *Pure pride.*

Following the chants, I find the Cathedral of Learning jutting out of the university lawn like a broken shard of some fairy-tale castle. Out in front, a crowd surrounds a hastily constructed stage with a solid-looking podium on top. These people are all smiles, victorious. Less than a mile from here someone is rinsing blood off a high school lawn.

Everywhere I look, I see bare temples.

Crossing into the park, I slide half behind a tree and watch a girl wearing a short skirt and a pair of sunglasses with frames that dip to intentionally expose her smooth, unmodified temples. Hairstyles, sunglasses, hats—all designed to make sure that one important patch of undisturbed skin is visible. Proof of your humanity.

I don't remember when the style became popular. A year ago?

Two? Maybe when people first started boycotting amp-run businesses. Or when the first Paralympian broke an Olympic record. It was a gradual erosion. Always something small enough to shrug off. And besides, none of it should affect me. I'm not an amp like Samantha.

The neural implant in my head only kills seizures. That's it. Boring. No intelligence amplification or prosthetic memory or body diagnostics—just a run-of-the-mill medical implant. Amazing for the minute after it was created, then made stupendously mundane by mass proliferation and daily use.

I'm a normal guy. I was a normal kid. Normal as anybody. That's the speech I practiced for so many years. A litany I repeated so many times I'd even convinced myself. Until this morning.

Now I'm starting to understand that I stood right in the middle of the train tracks until it was too late. I convinced myself things were fine, even while the steel rails were vibrating under my feet like jackhammers and that great big steaming black mother of a locomotive was inches away, whistle shrieking, barreling down on me faster than God's thoughts.

The nub on the side of my head feels like a conspicuous pimple. I let my hair hang loose over it, but it won't fool anybody. And I see it hasn't fooled the three well-dressed guys with radio earpieces who roam the crowd. Nobody allows his hair to hang this way by accident. Not unless he has something to hide.

Some weakness. Some deformity.

My first seizure happened when I was thirteen. I was hanging with some older kids from school. We skipped out to lunch and I rode in the back of a real manual-driven pickup truck. Dumb typical teenager shit. I remember standing up and leaning into the wind. My hair lashing my face numb. That old truck rattling with speed, really galloping.

And then the bump, of course.

I didn't feel the impact. Just the cold hand of a ghost running down the back of my neck. Saw trees flashing by. Body skipping over asphalt and rolling to a stop like a puppet with cut strings. The smell of grass and the burned-rubber scrape of my sneakers on hot pavement. Limbs quaking. Those strange funny moans in my throat. I remember the eyes of my friends as they leaned over me, scared and guilty and confused.

Those same eyes were there when I came back from the hospital. Amped. My own dad, Dr. Gray, put the bug in my head and he always said he did it just right. I didn't come back any smarter. Didn't move any faster. Still had all my fingers and toes. Just left the seizures and brain trauma behind me.

I thought I came back normal. Thought I could pull it off.

But a medical maintenance nub looks the same as a Neural Autofocus one. No matter what you say to yourself, you get the same stares. The technology has made it inside your body and contaminated you. *Outsider,* say the eyes that flash my way. *You don't belong here.*

I flinch when the applause begins.

"I am incredibly honored to introduce the president and founder of the Pure Human Citizen's Council, based right here in Pittsburgh . . . our very own senator Joseph Vaughn," announces a reedy-voiced woman from the podium. Rapturous applause radiates from the crowd.

Vaughn. Self-appointed watchdog for the human race. As a second-term senator from Pennsylvania and a news pundit, he doesn't promote hate but calls the struggle between amps and "pure humans" a war. Never condones violence but supports self-defense for any person whose way of life is under attack. Claims only to target extremist amps, but says that among amps, well, extremism is mainstream.

This is the man who is responsible for pushing Samantha's case all the way to the Supreme Court.

The crowd vibrates to Vaughn's thousand-watt smile. The politician is shaking hands and making eye contact with each person he greets. Everywhere he looks, his smile is reflected in the faces of his supporters. Watching him move among the crowd is like watching a fire spreading.

By the time the head of the Pure Human Citizen's Council bounces onto the stage, the crowd is buzzing. Signs bob in the air: "PURE PRIDE!" "LEVEL THE PLAYING FIELD." "HUMANS FIRST!"

"The highest court in the land has spoken. . . . Welcome to the first day of the future of the United States of America!" shouts Vaughn, pumping his fist to violent applause.

A shadow falls across me and I'm staring at a red tie. It is wrapped around the neck of a large, friendly-looking man. His suit is crisp but his fingernails are filthy. A tattoo marks the web of his right thumb. Two tiny capital letters: *EM*.

I frown at the tattoo and he casually folds his hands to hide it.

"Maybe you want to move along?" asks the security guard, smiling down at me like he was my best friend's dad. *That's okay,* I think. Maybe I'll just stay and hear this rally out. Learn something about my enemy.

So I smile right back and sit down cross-legged in the grass. He takes a measured breath and mutters something into his collar. Then he smiles wide again and walks around behind me. I feel his palm on the top of my head. His meaty fingers drum against my skull a couple times.

"That's fine," he says. "Just be a good little amp."

I rest my chin in my hand and listen to the senator.

"Today, the Supreme Court upheld what we knew was right all along—this country needs a *level* playing field!" he shouts. The crowd's hands blur in applause.

"Yes, the courts have ruled in our favor," Vaughn says, "but the fight is not over. Just this morning, our offices in Washington, DC, were bombed. I know we're all praying for our brothers and sisters who were murdered in that cowardly attack, and we sure won't rest until the guilty parties are brought to justice!"

The energy feels manic. People spew ragged shouts of approval.

"And there are plenty of guilty parties. As I speak, doctors trained at this university are turning more people into amps. Federally funded researchers are not just curing disease but going further—tearing the humanity away from regular people. Our soldiers. Our parents. Our children.

"The federal Uplift program promised that, with a wave of a magical wand, our disadvantaged youth would be implanted and cured forever. They made promises. Said their legs will run faster, their minds will think more clearly, and their eyes will see farther. The doctors came and turned whole communities of people into amps overnight," says Vaughn, his vowels falling like snow on the crowd.

Strictly speaking, it wasn't overnight. The changes crept in around the edges, too slow to be noticed, like mold on bread. Fixing serious medical problems first but always moving closer to the simple trials of daily life.

It started with kids. The blind kids, the ones crippled by disease, and the stone-faced kids with low IQs. Kids with attention-deficit/hyperactivity disorder so bad they couldn't sit still long enough to wipe their own asses.

I remember seeing those kids after school was out, climbing inside a wheezing government bus with the words UPLIFT PROGRAM written on it. Its windows were painted over with the silhouette of a little boy reaching hopefully for the sky. Diagnosed and evaluated and treated in one afternoon. The kids came back to school the next day with a nub on their temples and a wicked case of the smarts.

It was a new life for kids in need. Until one day an amp kid threw a football hard enough to snap ribs. A high school debate championship got canceled when the judges realized two-thirds of the participants had amps. A new generation of children was arriving, smart and fast and strong enough to send chills down your human spine.

"But what if *you* are not ready?" asks Vaughn. "What if you see the risk as too great, the cost as too high, or if you are comforted in the knowledge that your child is perfect in God's eyes, as all children are? Ask yourself, how long will you be able to hold the line against this new wave of parasitic technology? Because we are on the verge of an arms race. One child upgrades and leaves for an amp school. Then another. And another. Soon, your child will be the *only* normal child. Left behind. And even if your community doesn't upgrade, *others will.* So if you don't live in a flashy place like Los Angeles or New York City, why, you just might watch your whole town get left behind. How then will you protect your *children?*"

Vaughn's voice breaks with emotion on the word. He pinches the bridge of his nose and wipes his eyes. Very convincing.

"Amps are going to work together. Amps are going to find each other. And if we don't stop them *right now,* these amp communities will continue to grow like a cancer that will rot out the heart of this great nation.

"We are balanced on the edge of a cliff, my friends. When we step off that ledge, things will never return to normal. There are now nearly five hundred thousand amps. Once these implants become even more widespread, the technology will accelerate faster and faster until we are in a future spinning out of control. Our society—the one our forefathers fought and died for—will be ripped away from its heritage, cast out of the orbit of human civilization that stretches back for thousands of years. And we must not let that happen."

Joseph Vaughn rakes a sober gaze over the crowd and then looks down at his pages, waiting until the adulation subsides.

"What can we do? How can we stop the destruction of our nation, our society, and our children's future? Well, I'll tell you how. We've got to *separate* the amps. *Regulate* the amps. And *obliterate* the technology that turns human beings into amps. Together, we stand as the last generation of pure human citizens. And so we must act as a collective instead of as individuals. We must fight for our nation instead of for ourselves. And we must win. Because if we fail, ladies and gentlemen, the world of humankind—our world—will come to an end."

The crowd's wild response is like proof that Samantha was right. Everything changed today. The most terrifying part is that Sam was smarter than me. Her eyes were open so wide at the very end—open for such a long time while mine were squeezed shut. She saw this coming and she chose to step away. Chose to have her dead body shoveled onto a gurney and pushed into an ambulance waiting quietly in the parking lot with its goddamn engine off.

No sirens, no lights.

In a final orgy of applause, the rally moves on. The smiling faces and unblemished temples march out of the park, singing, headed downtown for the next stop. They leave behind muddy footprints, crumpled flyers, and tiny plastic American flags.

The litter of patriots.

I sit in the damp grass and absorb the numb quiet for fifteen minutes. Soon, the Cathedral green is abandoned. Even my friendly bodyguard with the strange little tattoo has ambled away. Now there is just the stage and the podium sprouting from it like a tombstone.

Curious and alone, I mount the stage and stand behind the podium. Looking out onto the green expanse shaded by the slat-windowed cathedral tower, I try to imagine the power Vaughn must have felt standing here.

But I don't feel powerful. I feel empty.

My enemy stood on this spot moments ago and declared war

on people like me. His vision of how the world should be seems so stark. Now that he has the momentum of the nation, I doubt Senator Vaughn and his Pure Priders will stop at words.

A piece of paper still rests on the podium. Just an extra page that must have fallen off the end of the speech. I pin it against the wood, hold it quivering in the breeze.

The letterhead is marked with an official seal: a coat of arms with the words "Pure Human Citizen's Council" on a circular banner, wrapped around the bas-relief image of a smiling little girl with a clean temple. Beneath her face, the word "Elysium" is embossed. Faintly, I notice the first and last letters of the word are bigger. Somehow familiar.

I've seen those two letters before, in a tattoo: *EM*.

Pittsburgh Post-Gazette

Federal Agents to Seize Research

*** *FOR IMMEDIATE RELEASE—BREAKING NEWS* ***

PITTSBURGH—In another blow to implanted citizens, agents with the FBI have been tasked this morning with seizing research equipment and documents from federally funded laboratories in Pittsburgh and throughout the nation.

The seizures are part of an ongoing ethics investigation that took on sudden urgency with the announcement that the federal government would not consider implanted citizens a protected class. As a result, the federal committee on research and technology issued a nationwide freeze on government research into neural implants and announced a recall of all related equipment from federally funded laboratories.

According to the FBI, this first series of seizures will likely be without incident. Since last July, federal research dollars have been restricted to medical studies that center on curing serious neurological disease, such as refractory epilepsy or Parkinson's disease.

"We don't like to call our people in on such short notice, but we were instructed to take action immediately," said Tanner Blanton, supervisory agent for the FBI's Pittsburgh southside office. "There is no criminal investigation at this time, but based on careful examination of seized evidence we will determine whether federal funds were used outside the mandate of government contracts."

3

SOMETHING EXTRA

I must have noticed the white van parked just outside my father's office on some level, but the meaning of it doesn't hit me until about thirty minutes later—right after the detonation.

I'm standing in the sunlight outside my dad's medical practice, a government satellite office two blocks from the University of Pittsburgh School of Medicine where Neural Autofocus was invented. Vaughn's speech is finished, but I can still hear the roar of his crowd from where it has gathered on the school steps just around the corner.

My dad answers the door. I open my mouth to tell him what happened and he doesn't let me finish the sentence. Grabs me and folds me into a bear hug.

"It was on the news, Owen. I'm sorry," he says.

Then, oddly, he scans the street. Pulls me into the waiting room and locks the front door. I give him a look, and my dad says something that puts a cold sweat on my forehead: "The police are looking for you. Just for questioning. But there are things you need to know."

We march past familiar photos of my father's happy patients: a toddler with his prosthetic carbon fiber arm clasped around his mother's neck, preteens with their maintenance nodes coated in rainbow colors they chose from a thick binder, and an elderly man standing straight and proud with the skeletal metal of an artificial calf and foot shining below his khaki shorts.

You can't separate the body from the mind. In the last decade, the Neural Autofocus became elective with every upgrade, from artificial limbs to medical exoskeletons to retinal implants. Autofocus makes the communication between mind and body seamless. Sharpens you up, they say. Every one of those smiling faces on the wall has that subliminal gleam of intelligence. Overclocked brains and shiny new limbs.

My dad ushers me through the empty waiting room and down an antiseptic corridor toward the back offices. Most of the lights are off. An office window is broken. Papers are strewn around the floor, marked by boot prints.

"We were raided this morning," Dad says. "The feds seized everything."

"Because of the ruling?"

He nods. "A research freeze. Vaughn's rallies have them in a frenzy."

My father cocks his head and listens to the eerily quiet hallway. Then he opens the door to his cramped office. Cheap venetian blinds chatter as the door swings. He squeezes into the squeaky chair behind his desk. A blank square marks where his computer used to be. Emptied file cabinets gape.

I sit down across from him.

As a kid, I played with toy cars on the floor under this desk. After my mom passed away, I hung out here for countless hours before and after school. I grew up under these fluorescent lights, but now the place seems strange, broken.

"What's going to happen?" I ask.

My father just shakes his head.

"It's too much to tell and I waited too long. I am sorry."

"Sorry?"

He clears his throat and looks away, blinking. I realize how much older he looks today.

"Sorry for what?" I ask.

"You have to understand, Owen, when we started this research all those years ago, we were excited. The potential to do so much good. Curing diseases, making people better. But when you got hurt . . ." He takes a deep breath. "I'm sorry I never told you."

"Never told me what?" I ask, my voice hollow.

The answer is already nibbling at the back of my mind. Little memories of life here at the shop: playing, working, even sleeping here when my dad worked late. And every once in a while, after the nurses left and the front door was locked, Dad called me into the operating room to check on my implant. He wanted to make sure the seizures would leave me alone, he said. I'd stare at the anatomy poster on the wall while he put on his mask and pulled his magnifier lens over one eye. The last time he tinkered with my implant was in high school, when I was about Samantha's age. The age she'll always be.

Frontal lobe. Temporal lobe. Motor cortex. Sensory cortex.

"You're an amp," he says.

My father watches me absorb the words, desperate for forgiveness. Grasping at it. But this new reality is too shocking to digest.

"I'm not medical?" I ask, reeling.

His lip twitches involuntarily and I realize he is holding back tears. "You were hurt so bad, Owen," he says. "My baby boy. Falling off that truck hurt you worse than you knew. Worse than I ever, ever let on."

"But you said I had a simple brain stimulator. That I'm not like the elective kids. Not an amp." I mumble the words like an incantation. Like a prayer. "You told me I was *normal*."

"Understand that I used every possible means at my disposal to repair the trauma. You didn't need to know. Stigma does terrible things to children. You've heard those demonstrators outside. I needed to give you a normal childhood."

"So you lied."

"Until you have a child of your own, you cannot comprehend how much I love you," he says flatly.

"Do I even have epilepsy?"

"You do. But the hardware you've got is special. It does much more than prevent seizures. The insult you suffered to your brain was . . . devastating. The implant had to shoulder the burden while you healed. It became a part of you, Owen."

There is something else. Something worse. Some shiver of guilt in my father's shoulders gives it away. "Neural Autofocus can't do that," I say.

He fixes his eyes on mine and replies instantly. "I gave you something extra."

I press my palms against my eyes until dark pinwheels lace my vision. I've had a head full of lies all of my life. This thing my father put in my brain does more than stave off epilepsy. It must accelerate my mind, sharpen my intellect, insinuate itself into every thought I have.

Every thought I've ever had.

For an instant, I envy Samantha Blex. At least she saw herself for who she was. It occurs to me that my own father killed whoever I am, or might have been, with the implant he chose to put in my adolescent skull.

"Things got out of control so fast," says my father. "Joe Vaughn and his Pure Human Citizen's Council—they came out of nowhere. You can never underestimate the fear that drives humankind."

"I need to think," I say.

"You don't have *time* to think," he says. "The federal government already has my research. There were things in there I couldn't erase. Parts requisitions. Lab time. Once they figure out what I did, I'll be arrested. Then they're going to come for you. For what's inside your head. They are likely already on their way."

I'm touching the nub on my temple, prodding it compulsively with my fingertip. "What did you do to me?"

"The hardware I gave you was stolen," he says. "At the time, there was no other choice. Nothing off the shelf was powerful enough to compensate for the damage."

"This is crazy—"

"You need to go right now. Through the side office. The police are looking for you about your student's death. Do not speak to them under any circumstances. Try to close your bank account."

He starts scribbling notes on a piece of paper, frantic. "Listen to me, Owen. Get your things and go west, to a place called Eden. It's a trailer park in Eastern Oklahoma," he says, handing me the paper.

I stand up and open the office door. "A *trailer park*?" I ask.

"Eden is where all of this began—the original Uplift site. We chose to test Autofocus there because it was isolated and rural. The population was in need. A perfect setting for our experiment. Only now, it's become an enclave. Full of other people who are like you. Your own kind, Owen."

He reacts to the look on my face. *My own kind?*

"You've got to find a man named Jim Howard, an old colleague of mine. He'll guide you through this. There's a lot you need to learn about yourself."

"Dad?" I ask. "Dad, come with me. I can't—"

"Go!" he barks. The force of his exclamation jolts me into the hallway. "Find Jim Howard. Don't tell me how you're getting there. They're coming for me *right now*. When they take me in, I will have the opportunity to obfuscate the situation. At the very least, I may cause a delay. It is the best chance you've got."

My father is suddenly small and old and feeble behind his desk. Like someone I've never met. Never would want to meet.

"I risked everything to give you a life," he says. "Don't throw it away."

I know the thing I'm about to say isn't fair and that I can never take it back, but I say it anyway. That's just how it goes, sometimes. "You didn't give me a life," I say. "You stole it."

My father is quiet for a long second. When he speaks, his voice is without emotion. "You've got to realize, Owen, that without the amp you would have died. It is a part of you, but you have to give it permission. I gave you something *extra*. When the time comes, you have to activate the amp willingly."

"When the time comes for what?"

"To do good, Owen," he says, standing. He softly pushes the door, eyes never leaving mine. "I'm sorry that I waited until it was too late. Find Jim. The old man is the only one who can help you now."

Click.

The door shuts and the hallway is silent save the far-off roar of demonstrators. I follow my dad's advice and walk on dull legs out the side door. Through the adjoining offices. Out into the alley that runs alongside the building. Run my fingers over rough brick. Look at the world without seeing it. After a half minute walking through the familiar backstreet, I get a funny feeling. For some reason, I stop and look at the sky.

A block away, a bomb detonates.

The guttural roar engulfs me and a shock wave brings my knees to the pavement. Dark smoke pours into the street behind me. The concussion has erased half my father's building. Pieces of brick and concrete are still spinning away.

It takes a little while for my legs to listen to me.

A harsh ringing in my ears already combines with a cacophony of sirens. Fire trucks, ambulances, police. I stagger toward the smoke, an urban zombie. Flames are eating the rind of the building. Its heart is a burned-out mess. The parking lot is wiped empty, the pavement cratered where the white van sat.

The realization gently nudges into my mind: my father could not have survived.

A heap of smoking gray rubble smolders where his office was. Nothing recognizable, just twisted rebar and concrete and ash. I don't stop advancing when the surging heat starts to prick my face or when my throat goes raw and stinging from the smoke.

I stop when I see the flashing blues and reds.

Under no circumstances, my father said. Tears well in my eyes as I survey the wreck. I blink them away, searching for some sign of life. The clouds of smoke throb with police lights, ring with sirens. The silhouette of a police officer drifts through the haze and comes into focus.

"Hey," she calls.

I turn and stumble away. Ignore her shouts as I duck around a corner. Eyes leaking, I accelerate until I'm sprinting down the alley—running blind, breath rasping, away from the noise and turmoil and death.

In the United States District Court for the Western District of Pennsylvania Pittsburgh Division

STATE OF PENNSYLVANIA, by and through
Attorney General Sam Pondi, et al.:

Plaintiffs,
JOHN SIZEMORE

v.

Defendants,
TAMMY ROGERS, representing

ORDER GRANTING SUMMARY JUDGMENT

In this case, we define capacity to contract to exclude individuals
with artificially enhanced intelligence.

As has long been established, those with diminished capacity
(e.g., minors and people with mental disabilities) lack the capacity to contract as a matter of law. Similarly, we find that individuals
with artificially enhanced intelligence possess an *enhanced* capacity
to contract, which necessarily creates an unlevel playing field.

We saw evidence that these enhanced individuals may prey
on those with inferior "natural" intelligence of the sort belonging
to what we have known heretofore as the "average man." In other
words, individuals with artificially enhanced intelligence implicitly
confer diminished capacity to others.

In an effort to remedy the growing disparity between natural
and enhanced levels of intelligence, and in an effort to create a
level playing field, we hereby find that individuals with artificially
enhanced intelligence lack the capacity to contract as a matter of law.

As a result, we thus find that the contract entered into between
John Sizemore and Tammy Rogers is considered null and void.

4

THE RULES

The toaster misses my face by about a foot, then explodes into shards of white plastic on the sidewalk. I blink at it once or twice before a wooden napkin ring clips me across the bridge of my nose.

I catch sight of a scrawny forearm lurking in the second-story window of my apartment. Charles, my landlord, is throwing my belongings out the window in neat little parabolas. He's already packed and dragged out a haphazard pile of cardboard boxes that rest on the grass next to the sidewalk. A couch and a chair sit incongruously in the yard.

"Charles!" I say. "What the hell are you doing?"

He pokes his gaunt face out of the window and glares down at me, breathing hard. He swallows and his Adam's apple bobs. Muttering, he flings a handful of silverware at me and ducks back inside.

The front door flies open as I reach for the handle. Charles, all hundred and twenty pounds of him, charges out. He slams the door shut, locks it.

The lock is bright as cut copper, new.

"I don't have to talk to you," says Charles in the clipped, broken accent of a lifelong Pittsburgher.

"What?"

"Back up. To the sidewalk. You're trespassing."

Charles advances, eyes narrowed. Confused, I put my hands

out and step back. "Charles, I don't know what's going on. What happened, man?"

"Thought you were so smart. Well, who's smart now? Score one for the Yinzers, asshole."

Charles kicks a box, and what looks like my college textbooks spill out onto the wet lawn. I stoop down to push the books back into the damp cardboard box. A young guy walking up the sidewalk carefully inspects a pile of my kitchen stuff.

"Hey," I say. "This isn't a garage sale."

The young guy doesn't respond, looks past me and makes eye contact with Charles.

"That means take off," I say.

Charles taps his temple. "Don't have to listen to him," he says.

No reaction. No sympathy or anger. The guy just stands there, watching me warily, the way you'd watch a crazy person at a bus stop.

It hits me that something fundamental has changed. Whatever empathy glues society together is somehow drying up, becoming cracked and brittle. This guy standing over my stuff—he's looking at me and what he sees is person shaped, but I don't think he's seeing a person.

Charles is all pumped up. His face is flushed with blood and I can see a vein in his neck throbbing. His hands are shaking from adrenaline as he speaks. "Joe Vaughn's been on the TV, warning us about you people for years. Taking our jobs and messing up the schools and blowing up buildings."

"You can't kick me out. There's still five months on my lease."

"Not no more. State law says you amps can't go into contracts with normal people. Just like I can't sign no contract with a retard, you can't sign one with me. You're too *smart*."

"That law is being challenged, Charles. It's not official."

"Highest court in the country thinks it is. The Supreme

goddamn Court of the United States of America says you ain't protected. So I guess it *is* the law."

The word "law" rings in my ears. Dominoes are falling. No contracts? Meaning no lease, no marriage, no job. No life.

A few more people have stopped to rubberneck. A couple. An older guy. Most are just curious. Others are scrutinizing my stuff, sizing it up.

Charles curls his hands into fists, lets them hang by his sides like rotten fruit. Through clenched teeth he says, "You gotta go *now*."

I lean over and scrabble through the box, dig out an old duffel bag. "Give me a damn minute—"

Now a couple of people are just grabbing stuff. Others watch, blinking slowly. The thieves walk away without looking at me. The old guy carefully steps over my hand like it was a crack in the sidewalk, holding my lamp.

"I'm calling the goddamn cops," says Charles.

I drop to my knees and start shoving things into the duffel bag. Clothes, shoes, a box of granola bars. Appliances are too heavy to carry. Laptop is gone. Forget the furniture.

As pedestrians gawk, silent people carry away the puzzle pieces of my life. They see through me, hear past me. The expressions in their eyes are unreadable. I wonder why this is. Do they pity me? Or are they afraid? Is it possible that they really feel nothing at all?

I hope this scene isn't playing out all over the nation. People like me struggling to grab what they can. Whole families, even. Grasping at the leftover shards of their lives. If that's the case, it doesn't really matter what these vulture people around me are thinking or feeling. Whether I'm less than human or more than human—animal or god—it's all the same.

I'm not a real citizen anymore. Rules no longer apply.

When my bag is full, I move on. Leave Charles on the sidewalk, staring at me with clenched fists and a tight grin. I push past the onlookers and get myself on down the road.

It's all on little pieces of paper. Thou shalt not. Thou shalt. The rules are there so that we can remember them and follow them. If the rules were obvious, we wouldn't have to write them down.

I let my hair hang over the nub on my temple and step inside my bank and wait in line. I can feel the stares like cigarette burns on my skin. A security guard watches me, his back to the wall, beefy hands resting on his belt. I look around without seeing anything, push my breaths in and out through my nose. The teller is cautious but she lets me withdraw everything in my account. She stuffs about eighteen hundred dollars into an envelope.

I walk out of the bank, forcing myself not to run. Keep walking. Thinking.

In a frigid fast-food restaurant, I take my phone out of my pocket and call Allderdice High School. The administrative assistant tells me that all amps, I mean implantees, have been placed on unpaid leave. And the police called to speak to me, again.

"Hey, buddy, let me see your temple," calls a chubby guy a few seats over. He and his friend wear painter's caps and overalls, eat burgers with stained fingers.

I ignore him, hang up my phone. Then, I methodically dial my friends. Nobody answers. Must be a busy morning.

"What's the matter? You can't hear me, buddy?" asks the painter.

It's the Joseph Vaughns of the world who have given regular people license to act like this. Talking heads on television who have repeated the incendiary words again and again until the insane has become commonplace. This guy sitting here wearing his work clothes isn't a monster, he probably has a wife and kids and—

"Hey!" he shouts.

The cashier walks over, shoes squeaking on tile. Puts a hand on my shoulder. "We don't want trouble. You got to go," he says quietly.

"I'll go when I'm ready," I say.

"Let's see your temple, buddy," calls the painter again.

I hang my head lower, studying the meaningless TV-fuzz design on the countertop. Looking for a pattern in noise. This day has been coming for years and I had front-row seats but I never let myself see. Samantha bounced around the courts, trying to find a legal ground for her own existence, but every time things took another turn for the worse, I convinced myself it was someone else's problem. Well, it's sure as hell my problem now.

"You a fucking amp or something?" asks the painter, voice rising.

The cashier puts his hands on his hips, motions with his head toward the door.

I get up and leave.

My friend Dwayne lives a few minutes from here. I've known him for a few years and he's the kind of guy who can see things from another person's perspective. I sling my duffel bag over my shoulder and walk in his direction. Cars blow past me, scattering candy wrappers and damp paper cartons of iced tea. A crucifix of sweat stains my T-shirt by the time I trudge through Dwayne's toy-strewn yard and knock on the door.

"You're on TV, Owen. That sucks about your dad," he says.

I swallow salty tears.

"But did you kill that girl?" he asks, half hiding behind the door. *"What?"*

"News said the cops want to talk to you. They got your face up there with a bunch of other guys. Soldiers or terrorists or something."

"She was a student—"

"That's what they said on the news. She was a former student of yours. What was going on between you two, man? This is serious."

I don't even know how to respond. "I need a place to stay for a couple nights. My dad . . . I've got no place to go."

"I don't know. I think you need to get on the move, man. Let this all blow over."

"Tomorrow."

Dwayne orients his body to block the door. "Owen, man, I've got to think about Monica and the kids," he whispers urgently. "Your face is on the news. I can't let you in here."

"How long have I known you, Dwayne?"

He pauses for a second, then answers, "No."

"What?"

"No. I'm sorry, Owen. You have to find someplace else to go."

Dwayne is standing there, chin set, blocking the doorway. I get the strange feeling that this is all a joke, that we're together onstage and any minute he's going to burst out laughing and welcome me inside.

"It's a mistake. A mix-up," I say, taking a step forward. "I'm still me."

Dwayne doesn't move, but his eyes get hard. The door swings open a little wider and I see he's got a splintery wooden bat clenched in his other hand. The one he keeps in the umbrella stand by his front door.

"It's my family. There's a lot of bad shit going down—what am I supposed to do?" he asks.

I've got no answer to that question. Until now, the rules were written down on paper, neat and legible. But a judge tore the fucking paper to shreds. The rules are gone. All that's left is the grass-stained baseball bat in Dwayne's fist.

"I'm sorry," says Dwayne.

I turn and hurry down the porch steps.

"What am I supposed to do?" he calls after me. "What can I do about it, Owen?"

CNN.com

Live Blog: Former Echo Squad Soldiers Suspected in Bombing Plot, One Suspect Killed

Report Timeline:

[Posted at 8:12 a.m. ET] A bomb blast has torn through the heart of Washington, D.C., destroying offices of the Pure Human Citizen's Council. Local hospitals reported that three people were killed and eleven more injured seriously. As of now, no arrests have been made and no group has claimed responsibility for the attack.

[Updated at 6:06 p.m. ET] A spokesman for the Washington, D.C., metropolitan police department has announced that authorities believe an amp separatist organization called Astra is to blame for the bombing. The spokesman declined to comment on what evidence led police to this conclusion. "Our nation is officially under attack by the radical amp minority, just as I have long warned that it would be," Senator Joseph Vaughn, head of the PHCC, said in a statement.

[Updated at 7:32 p.m. ET] A suspect detained near the site of the bombing has been shot and killed by police officers. Witnesses described a scene of panic as officers approached an onlooker who was exhibiting suspicious behavior. "The guy was moving weird. Like, too fast," said a witness who asked not to be identified.

[Updated at 9:42 p.m. ET] The suspect killed earlier today has been identified as Lawrence Krambule, a former member of the infamous Echo Squad. The group of twelve Special Forces soldiers was disbanded ten years ago after it was determined they had been willingly and illegally implanted with classified, militarized Neural Autofocus implants.

5

SPEEDING METAL

Hitching west. I tell myself that there is no shame in running away. It doesn't matter if fear fuels your flight. Just so long as you're running *toward* something. There is a device in my head that my father paid for with his life and only one person who can tell me what it is: a stranger named Jim who lives in a damn trailer park.

I should have known this day was coming.

The pressure built silently, month after month. Court cases. Protests. The strain growing until it was unbearable, hidden in silent interactions between amps and regular people. I felt it in the burnt-eared shame of falling eye contact. In the rippling shift of elbows at the lunch table when an amp student sat down. By the end, the pressure was pushing in so hard that I wanted to pop my ears or scream or curl up and hide.

And then, boom. Pressure released. Enter free fall.

Every second now takes me away from the broken remains of my life. A job I've been effectively fired from, apartment I've been evicted from, and friends who've turned their backs on me. For the last twenty-four hours I've been running away from nothing— the life of a ghost.

The cab of the semitruck pulsates with rap music, the bass low and loud. I can smell fast food and lotion and sweat. But only barely. The air-conditioning is gushing icy odorless air into this oasis of life support, this pod wrapped in a ten-ton pile of hot speeding metal.

The autonomous rig looks a lot like the old-school trucks from the movies. A few more video screens, maybe. There's a steering wheel and gas and brake pedals. The driver, Cortez, leans back in his seat, pudgy arms crossed over his stomach, hands lightly resting on puffy touch pads embedded in the steering wheel. His tiny pinkish fingernails list lazily with the wheel as it adjusts itself.

As we roll, my thoughts turn to the machinery that I carry inside my skull. Something special, my dad said. *Something extra.* Leaning my head against the cool window, I let the hum of the road vibrate through me. I imagine that I can *feel* the anonymous black plastic inside as it sends feathery pulses of electricity forking away into my gray matter.

Fwish. Fwish. Fwish.

Like a clock counting down, a time bomb wedged in the meat between my eyes. How long until it explodes? If the biocapacitor fails, the implant will lose power and I could die fast—lights out. If the clock falls too far out of sync, then the implant will send bad commands to my brain and I could die slow. And if the temperature or vibration or current fluctuates, or my bio-gel runs out or spoils, there's a chance I'll die and, honestly, who cares how fast or slow it happens?

There is no separating me from the amp. Our fates are grotesquely interwoven—a tree grown through a chain-link fence. Live or die, it's a part of me.

I must have reached up and stroked the nub of plastic jutting from my temple without knowing it, because Cortez swivels his great head toward me. He watches my face for a long second, his three-hundred-pound frame quivering in his seat, settled in there like a scoop of chocolate ice cream.

Shit. How stupid can I be? I burrow deeper into my cushioned seat and nonchalantly press a palm against the tinted window. Outside, relentless sunlight acid washes the highway, sending up dazzling heat lines that make the horizon dance. Shadows of clouds skate across rolling green hills. Nothing else moves save the glinting of far-off traffic.

I can't remember ever being able to see this far.

"You coming from out east, huh?" asks Cortez.

"Yeah."

"Good luck."

"Why?"

"These rednecks out here don't like people being too smart," says Cortez, tapping his temple. "Pure Priders are always preaching that y'all will steal their jobs, you know? They probably have a point."

The dash-mounted video screen chirps, stutters on.

The thudding music recedes on an automatic quick fade and an emergency alert tone squawks. A fuzzy, nasal voice reads: "All-points bulletin. A BOLO has been issued for Covenant Transport vehicles. Operators are instructed to be on the lookout for the following persons of interest. Be advised these suspects are former military and should be considered highly dangerous, even if unarmed. On contact, please report immediately to your regional coordinator. Operators are advised to verify information before taking action."

A grainy video appears. A title card reads: Echo Squad Conspirators Sought. A series of faces flash by—each of them young and hawkish, aggressive. And oddly similar. These are military portraits taken during boot camp. Each has a name underneath. Valentine. Crosby. Stilman. Daley. Gray.

Oh, shit. The next face blinks onto the screen and there I am.

My school photo, lifted from the Allderdice Web site. Starkly different from the others. Softer. It stares at me and Cortez for a second and a half, then disappears.

Cortez snorts, wide nostrils flaring. "Thought I knew you. Seen you on the tube, pardner."

This has to be a mistake. *Why the fuck am I on a bulletin?* How could I be swept up in a manhunt with real criminals? I keep my face pointed forward, panic rising in my chest. "What are you going to do?" I ask.

"Turn you in, man. I'm responsible for this truck. Anything goes wrong in here, it's my fault. This is a good job. I don't want to lose it."

"Look, they've got me confused with somebody else. You can see I'm not military. Just let me off anywhere," I say, my voice going hollow with fear. I'm staring at a button on the steering wheel. It has a phone on it. With a touch of his finger, Cortez can send me to jail or worse.

"I won't tell anybody you picked me up," I say. "No harm, no foul."

"Sorry," he drawls. "Company already knows somebody in here. This truck is wired to the tits."

It's true. If the big man's hands leave those pads on the steering wheel for more than a few seconds, the truck will pull itself over and cut the engine. This is because years ago an original model autonomous tanker with a sensor malfunction and no driver rolled off the road and smashed into the side of an office building. Wouldn't have been a big deal if the truck weren't hauling a double load of gasoline. The trucking company was sued out of business. And the rest of the industry realized they needed an insurance policy. Someone to take the blame.

In other words, a human driver.

"Why not turn yourself in?" asks Cortez. "You look like a damn schoolteacher or something. You don't want to be on the run from the cops."

I could stop running now, minimize the damage. I didn't push Samantha Blex. Let them arrest me and I can set the record straight. It's the sane thing to do. But I can't forget the edge of panic in my father's voice. Naked, ugly fear was on his face, the kind you never show willingly—the kind that's contagious.

I turn to Cortez.

"You heard amps are going to steal your job? Well, guess what? I couldn't drive your truck if I wanted to," I say. "No amp could steal your job after today."

"How come?"

"I can't take the blame for a wreck. Legally. In the eyes of the law I don't exist. You'd be better off having a three-year-old drive this thing."

Cortez snorts again, his deep-set bluish-gray eyes scanning the featureless, blazing road ahead. I can't read his expression. Can't tell if it's good or bad. But discrimination is legal now, and from what I've seen the regular people are getting the hang of it real fast. If this guy sends me back to Pittsburgh, it's all over.

"That's messed up," he says finally. "They're saying you're not even a person."

"It's what they're saying. I can't get picked up by the cops. I don't have any rights. They can do whatever they want to me. *Will* do."

The emergency alert squawks again. A tinny voice from the dash speaks: "Come in, Cortez. Come in."

Eyebrows up, Cortez paws a button on the dash and responds. "This Cortez."

"Cort. It's Jason. I'm doing the BOLO follow-up. Fleetscan indicates you took on a passenger in Nashville. Can you confirm?"

Cortez frowns at me. "Yeah."

"Okay, can you let me get cab video?"

Cortez blinks, as if he's just woken up. He takes one hand off the steering wheel and scratches his unkempt beard. A light begins to blink on the dashboard, and his chubby hand flutters back to its roost almost unconsciously.

"Jason . . . it's my cousin. Giving him a ride to Tulsa to see his momma."

"That's nice, Cortez. Now let me get cab vid."

"Nah," says Cortez.

"Dammit, Cort. Are you smoking weed in there again?"

"Man, get out of here with that. Check my environmental."

"Then give me video."

"Do I come to your work and stare at you?"

"I'm trying to do my job here, Cortez. I don't have time for this shit. If you don't grant me vidrights, I'm engaging the override and flagging you for law enforcement inspection. Now, are you going to do it or not?"

"This is bullshit. It's called *privacy*, Jason—" responds Cortez, and then the whole dashboard flashes red. The doors *thunk* as they lock themselves. We start losing speed.

"Must be kidding," mutters Cortez, leaning on the steering wheel. He glances at me and shrugs, shakes his head. The gravel shoulder crunches under the truck tires. My stomach drops.

"Uh, hold up," I say, leaning toward the dash. I'm doing my sad best to sound like I could be Cortez's cousin. "Cortez shaved his head, all right? It's nasty. All shiny and shit. Head looks like a bowling ball with cuts all over it. Said he'd get fired before he lets you see it."

Thin laughter tinkles out of the dashboard. "What?" asks the voice. "Seriously?"

Cortez smiles at me, nods. "Barber in Nashville messed me up," he says. "Came at me like a ax murderer. I had to shave it all off. Laugh if you want, but you not gonna be seeing my mug for about two weeks."

The laughter slowly dies away. There is a long pause. Static.

"So, that's your cousin?" asks the voice.

"Yeah," says Cortez.

"He sounds white."

"What'd you say? Oh, we done," says Cortez. "Done, done, done." And he punches the cutoff button.

The truck crawls over the gravel shoulder, slowing until it

finally stops. Blistering cold air rasps across my face and the dash burns bright red in my eyes. We sit together in silence for thirty seconds.

"Cops come," says Cortez in a whisper. "I'm saying you held me hostage."

"Fair enough," I say.

The dash flickers and goes dark.

Then, the lights power up and the dash returns to normal. The engine rumbles, starts. A smile spreads across Cortez's bearded face. I take a deep breath and collapse back into my seat. We're safe.

Cortez pulls back onto the highway. We roll together toward the western horizon for about ten minutes before he speaks.

"What people been saying about amps," he says, "I heard all that shit before. If they're not calling you a monkey, then they're calling you a superman."

"So . . . are we good?" I ask.

"We be all right," says Cortez, never taking his eyes off the road. "Cuz," he adds, breaking into a wide grin. He playfully shoves me in the shoulder. "You know I gotta shave my head now, right?"

After eight hours in the truck we pull in for gas outside Sallisaw, Oklahoma. I grab my pack, lean over, and shake hands with Cortez. When I crack open the hermetically sealed door, a razor's edge of dusk sunlight briefly stripes his face.

"You pretty close to where you going. Motel is over there. Should be an okay one for you—guy who owns it is blind."

His amused chuckle is lost in the low bass line and profanity-laced lyrics. I thank Cortez and leave him in his rolling den. Step around the gas station's automatic fueler, avoiding the patterned light that it sprays as it blindly searches for a gas cap. Cortez never has to leave the truck, not even to fuel it.

Taking the blame is a full-time job.

Walking toward the motel, I hear a chime from the idling truck as it acknowledges the pump. I pretend to scratch my forehead, blocking the sight of my face from the two subtle lumps on that hulking hood as they twinkle with laser light, scanning the environment and matching the truck's local map with what's up there in the satellite. Even way out here, the world is thick with cameras.

Just another link in the supply chain of human civilization.

It used to be people who drove the trucks and airplanes and boats. Things still look the same from the outside, but the core is always changing, always being upgraded. And the role of technology is under constant renegotiation.

As the big rig hauls itself out of the parking lot, engine hissing, I keep my head down and wonder what would happen if we rolled everything back ten years. The computers would go a little slower, I guess. The factories would make a little less, and the farms wouldn't produce as much. These seem like such small things, but we depend on each new advance.

Millions would die. Because once we have the tech, we can't let it go.

Fwish, fwish, fwish goes the implant in my head. It is inscrutable and mute and God knows what it does. But it doesn't seem like a clock ticking down anymore. More like a heartbeat. Steady and dependable.

At least, I hope so.

I have seen
The old gods go
And the new gods come.

Day by day
And year by year
The idols fall
And the idols rise.

Today
I worship the hammer.

—CARL SANDBURG (1914)

The Washington Post

Disbanded Echo Squad Vets Under Investigation

FORT COLLINS—This morning a spokesman for the US Army confirmed that members of the so-called Echo Squad, made up entirely of "amped" soldiers outfitted with prototype neural implants, were under federal investigation for plotting terrorist crimes. Four federal warrants were issued, although records indicate there were twelve original members.

Echo Squad was dissolved a decade ago in the wake of a scandal. Documents exposing the existence of the squad were leaked by an online coalition of hackers known as Archos, and published simultaneously by three collaborating newspapers.

An Army spokesman said, "In the interest of national security we cannot comment. These men are walking weapons. People's lives are at stake here."

Army officials have come under criticism for failing to track the soldiers after Echo Squad was decommissioned. Head of the Pure Human Citizen's Council (PHCC) and U.S. senator from Pennsylvania Joseph Vaughn argued that the effort was bungled. "How could the U.S. Army allow dishonorably discharged veterans with militarized neural implants back into society? These members of our service personnel volunteered for an illegal and immoral program, and there should have been a system of tracking put in place before these animals were discharged into the general public," he said.

6

EDEN

Jim Howard lives in the Eden trailer park in Eastern Oklahoma. About a four-mile walk from the motel. I can't sleep, so I hoof it at first light. My legs are soaked by the time I arrive, lashed by the dewy grass that grows knee-high along the roadside. I'm shivering as the sun teases the horizon, a reluctant lump of warmth and light that seems to want to let me freeze in the dark a little bit longer.

Birds are starting to sing, and the list of questions in my head is growing.

I find the dirty white trailer on the edge of Eden. The trailer park is the size of a couple football fields, wrapped in a fence and strewn with trailers in loose rows connected by meandering dirt paths. The ground is carpeted with sticks and stems from a sprawling canopy of pecan trees. Jim's trailer is up on concrete blocks, weeds sprouting under it. A haphazard wooden deck has been built alongside a small porch, with the remains of old paper lanterns strung over the gaping carcass of a hot tub.

The porch light wavers in the dawn, powering through mildewed plastic and crusted layers of insect corpses. As I climb the steps, I hear creaking from over my head. It's a stealthy, careful sound.

I step back until I can see the roof.

A dark figure stands on top, thin and crooked. It's a man with his hands out, elbows bending as he takes an exaggerated slow-motion step. The roof of the trailer complains as he moves through some kind of tai chi routine. Silhouetted fingers splay and his head turns toward me. He slows and then stops. Stands up straight.

"Howdy, kid," says a firm voice.

"Jim?" I ask.

There's a long pause. If this doesn't work and Jim turns me away, well, I saw an overpass on my walk over here. I guess that's where I'll be living.

"Owen," says the old man. "Your pop told me you might be coming."

"Is he . . ." I trail off, voice breaking.

Jim shakes his head, mouth in a line.

"How did you know him?" I ask.

"We worked together, a long time ago. Good man."

"Oh," is all I can say.

"I'm headed out to work about now. You can come along, I guess. Long as you ain't scared of getting yelled at a little bit."

"Pure trash," snaps the old man. "That's what I call 'em. Not Pure Pride. Joe Vaughn can kiss my wrinkled old ass."

White hair sticking out from under a ball cap, Jim hooks a thumb at a group of young men standing across the street. The demonstrators watch us silently, heads cocked, squinted eyes swimming in shadows. One of them spits on the ground. Standing with crossed arms or perched on pickup truck tailgates, none of them reveals the slightest expression.

The old man takes off his cap, tosses it to me. "Put this on and don't talk to anybody. Nobody should be out here looking for you, but better to play it safe."

I shuffle ahead to keep up with Jim as the bent old man humps it across the street. With only a piece of toast in my belly and virtually no sleep, it's a struggle to keep my footsteps in his shadow. He's got a heavy-looking duffel bag over one shoulder, but he hobbles quick and steady in the dry morning heat, like an old camel.

Jim has a strong chin and high, weathered cheekbones. On the drive over, he told me he's a full-blood Cherokee but his hair went pale after his life hit a rough spot. I don't have the gall to ask what that was. I imagine it involved a war.

"Fuckin' gray hair," calls one of the men from across the street as we reach the orange-ribbed fence of the construction zone. "Go home, ya scab amp!"

Jim doesn't even look up, just leads me into the job site.

"Who are they?" I ask.

"Workers we replaced. They're pure human. And young. But I tell you what, every man's got a right to earn a living. Being young don't earn you a damn thing in my book."

A five-story, half-framed building crowds the work site. The rising sun flings skewers of light through its half-renovated steel skeleton. The frame straddles a deep, unfinished subbasement that makes a nauseating drop into crisp shadow. Jim tells me that, in a few months, this steep pit will be a claustrophobic parking garage for auto-driven cars. He says we don't even have to run lighting down there—the cars won't need it.

It's still early. A crusty cement mixer filled with toolboxes swings overhead, lifted out of thieves' reach by the site crane. A few elderly men mill around, drinking coffee. There's hardly a worker here under sixty-five. Each has a maintenance nub, including Jim. Amps. When the old guys pass each other, they nod. Sometimes they give each other halfhearted little salutes. No smiles.

"Not a big talker, are you?" I ask Jim.

He shakes his head.

"My dad said I needed to find you. He said that you could explain why I'm here."

Jim glances at me, eyes sharp and calculating. Chews on the

inside of his cheek, considering. Finally, he shrugs. "Maybe," he says. "Probably not. Anyway, there's work to do."

The old man drops to one knee and fiddles the drawstring open on his canvas duffel bag. In a well-practiced motion, he rolls down the sides of the faded bag to reveal tangled columns of dust-coated metal. Under a frenzied pattern of scratches and dings, I see the thin tubes are light-gold colored. Titanium alloy.

An ID code, like a VIN, is stamped onto one tube.

"My ride," says Jim. "Beats a wheelchair and it beats the living crap out of the goddamn scooters that civilians get. *Semper fi,* kid. *Semper* friggin' *fidelis.*"

Jim grabs the lightweight frame, lifts it out of the bag, and shakes it like a dirty T-shirt. The tubes flop out onto the ground, connected like a skeleton, with legs and arms attached to a backpack-like trunk. Without a pause, Jim plants one boot onto a foot-shaped piece of plastic at the end of one tube. He steps in with the other foot and then shrugs on the backpack part. The skeletal arms hang loose, their unfastened straps lolling like tongues.

"You're a vet?" I ask, reaching out and touching the loose metal wrist of the thing. Jim nods. A pair of dull pincers hang from just above the wrist joint, scarred with shining gashes. I lift the dead metal, and the arm bends, limp. An array of compact tools is folded underneath, ready to be deployed: screwdrivers, files, even a power saw.

The pincer clamps onto my wrist and I jump back. I reflexively wrench my arm away from the cold metal, shake it off like a spider. Jim lets out a hoarse giggle. As both robotic arms settle down to his sides, the old man taps the maintenance nub on his temple.

"Settle down, kid. The exoskeleton is linked to my amp. Works even for a guy with no arms and legs. Mind control. All a vet has to do is claim arthritis and the VA coughs these things up like nickels."

He casually lowers his arms into the arm bars of the device, straps them in one at a time. "Makes us more employable," he says.

Jim is in his late seventies. He says he retired from the military forty years ago and he retired from the workforce a decade ago. Now he's standing in front of me wearing a government-issued medical exoskeleton and about to start another day of hard labor, and this is the reason that those young men across the street are huddled together giving us the evil eye.

The old folks have stolen all the jobs.

Jim speaks to the foreman on my behalf. The Pure Priders outside won't work alongside the old men, so the work site has to bring in extra amps. They could always use one more, according to Jim.

Around the site, a dozen other elderly workers shrug themselves into glinting metallic devices—drinking in the pure, sweet strength of youth. Others sway on prosthetic legs or flex sinuous carbon fiber forearms. All the old men set to their jobs with the grim robotic work ethic that always belongs to the previous generation. And across the street from the construction site, a dark pool of anger deepens.

For the next few hours, I'm setting up scaffolding and breaking it down so these vintage spider monkeys can place chattering rods of rebar. The sun has come up for real now, dull and pounding. Jim tells me I'm making less than minimum wage in cash for this. I'm thankful for the money but mostly for the mindless routine of work.

"Things are changing faster and faster," calls Jim over his shoulder as he lays out rebar for cementing. He talks between the sporadic catcalls that still ring out from beyond the fence. "Change scares people. Makes them dangerous."

"Then why are you here?" I ask. "You've got a pension, right?"

Jim chuckles drily. "You're just a kid. You don't know about getting old. But you're right—it ain't about money."

"Then maybe you should think about getting a hobby."

In a sudden mechanical jerk, Jim hops off the scaffolding and lands hard enough to make me flinch. He holds out his calloused hands, palms up. The exoskeleton motors grind quietly, like a cat purring, as the pincers retract.

"I'm a builder right now. What am I without a job? Without a tool in my hand?" asks Jim.

I picture Jim sitting inside his trailer, alone with a bottle of booze, finishing the umpteenth pointless game of solitaire. Stale, heavy air and the mindless whisper of a television. To him, the exoskeleton must seem like a second chance. Like youth bottled and sold.

"And what if the tool is inside you? What are you then?" I ask.

Jim shrugs an arm out of the machine and wipes sweat off his forehead. Puts his arm back in without looking. He speaks carefully. "It's still only a tool. In the end, a man makes his own decisions. You decide, not the machine."

"Why am I here, Jim?"

Jim reaches for a rod of rebar. He clamps the curved pincers around it, lifts the bouncing metal like it was made of Styrofoam. He stops and looks at the rebar with fresh eyes, as if realizing that every move he makes is a miracle.

"I bet this mess weighs more than I do. And I'm holding it like it was nothing. The machines give us a lot of power." Jim places the rod, continues. "Way I figure, your pop sent you to me, hoping I could tell you what's in your head and what you're going to do with it. Problem is, I don't really know."

My shoulders slump.

"But I got an idea," continues Jim. "And from what I can tell, there are only two bets. Either you're here for Eden to protect you . . . or you're here to protect Eden."

A shrill whistle blows from across the street.

From over the wall, I hear the demonstrators start up a chant. The voice of the crowd is deep, the edges of the words grated off by straining vocal cords. "Pure Pride," they're saying. "Pure Pride."

I imagine those dozens of ragged pink mouths spilling their garbled words and remember Samantha falling between my fingers. Events are still moving out of control. The reins have slipped away and now they're dragging loose, slapping on the ground.

Jim plucks a dusty sledgehammer off the ground.

"How could *I* protect you?" I ask, incredulous.

Jim stares at me, letting his eyes wander to the nub on my temple. "You might be surprised what you're capable of."

The old man is hunched up, leaning over the sledgehammer. A drop of sweat hangs from the tip of his nose and he ignores it. "We've got big problems. And not just here," he says. "Everywhere. Battle lines are being drawn up. Amps and their families are running back to Uplift sites all over the country. Regulars are moving out."

"What do you think is going to happen?" I ask.

"If we don't figure this out quick—find some goddamned way to stop Vaughn and his Pure Priders—well, there's only one thing that *can* happen . . . war."

Then the screaming starts from outside the fence.

The panicked yelling in the street is mixed with strange laughter. The kind of laughter that's got nothing to do with humor. It gets louder as I walk closer.

Through the gaps in the chain-link fence, I spot the laughing man standing on top of his stark shadow in the middle of the street.

He's a shirtless cowboy in dusty black jeans and boots. His lanky arms and slim chest are smothered in tattoos. Crows. Dozens of crows flapping and screeching and tearing their way up and down his body. And a bloody star tattooed across the center of his chest.

Another guy, one of the protesters—and a big one—is staggering away from the cowboy, holding his right hand in his left and looking at it with bugged-out eyes. He is shrieking at what he sees. It strikes me that most of his fingers are pointed the wrong way.

The laughing man takes his cowboy hat in his hand and leans one forearm on his thigh, giggling. He stands and takes a hoarse breath, then doubles over again with barking laughter. Ropes of matted brown hair fall into his face but not before I spot the node on his temple.

The laughing cowboy is an amp.

"Oh, you came *way* too close," says the laughing man. "Paint by numbers, amigo. Saw your game coming a mile away."

A half-formed thought rises. This man looks familiar. I look over at Jim, but he just turns away. Walks back into the job site, shaking his gray head.

"Who is that?" I call.

Jim doesn't stop walking. "Lyle Crosby," he says. "Grew up around here. Gone for a while but now he's back."

A couple of protesters shuffle the guy with broken fingers off the street. The rest watch Lyle with dark expressions, but nobody gets near him.

I let go of the fence and follow Jim. The old man grabs his sledgehammer and gets back to work smashing up a hunk of misplaced concrete. I talk to him between blows.

"Why don't they call the cops?"

"Half of those Priders aren't even American citizens. Just human."

"Then how come they aren't kicking that guy's ass?"

"Won't risk it," says Jim.

"Why?"

Jim stops, turns, and points the twenty-pound sledgehammer at the street, holding it straight out by the tail end. The tube of his exoarm flashes in the sunlight and the hammer goes as level and steady as a girder. "Because they've already seen what happens if they cross him. They know he's dangerous. That he's got a gang of amped kids at his beck and call. What they don't know"—Jim lowers his voice—"is that Lyle is military. Ex-military, anyway."

Now I remember. Those faces flashing across the dash video screen of the semitruck. Crosby. I picture the laughing cowboy in my mind. In the image he was younger, had shorter hair. But it's the same guy.

"Echo Squad," I say.

"It was an experimental group. But somebody tattled. Once the press found out, the squad got disbanded. Lyle was their commander."

"I knew he looked familiar. Our faces were together on the broadcast. They grouped me with him like I was part of his squad."

"Course they did," says Jim, "because technically, you are."

Fwish, fwish, fwish, goes the implant in my skull. My vision blurs for a second and I rest a hand on the cool metal of Jim's exoskeleton forearm. The arm dips, then comes back up, firm as a banister.

"What did you say?" I manage to croak.

Jim continues: "Fifteen years ago, your daddy called me up, crying in the middle of the night. Never heard him like that before. Said you hurt your head real bad. He asked me for a hell of a favor and I helped him. It scared me how much he loved you."

From the street, the chanting has started up again.

"What—" I begin, but my thoughts are moving too fast. My mouth can't keep up. I take a sharp breath through my nose, slow down, and start again.

"What the hell is in my head, Jim?" I ask.

Jim squints at me in the glare of the sun. "It's called a Zenith-class amp. A prototype. There were twelve of them officially installed. A team of handpicked soldiers. Later, when the press found out, they were called Echo Squad. Turns out, the whole operation was illegal. Squad went away and those disgraced soldiers spread to the wind. All that was in the news."

He lowers his voice to a whisper that saps the warmth from the sunlight.

"What never saw print was this: a thirteenth Zenith was made in secret. I made it myself and I copied the encrypted military stuff onto it so it would work. Dropped it into an envelope and mailed it to your old man. He made you the thirteenth. Saved your life, but, like everything, it came with a price. You've got a weapon inside you, Owen. A weapon that's never been turned on. With your pop's office raided, I imagine the government knows all about it by now."

The rail-thin old man watches me, eyebrows low, tired face framed in wrinkles. He's been burned up by the sun and made tough as rawhide, but the intelligence of a scientist still gleams in his eyes.

"That's why I wonder whether I'm supposed to protect you or you me."

I let go of Jim's arm.

"You're a biomedical engineer. Why the hell are you out here working construction?" I ask.

"Once, I designed neural implants for a living. Government R and D. Basic architecture stuff. I quit when I lost sight of whether the Autofocus was a good thing or an evil thing. Still couldn't tell you. So I guess I'll be out here breaking rocks until I figure it out."

"And what about me?"

"You're a Zenith. Like Lyle. They'll either find you, or they won't."

H.R. 1429

One Hundred Twentieth Congress
of the
United States of America

An Act

To authorize the Uplift Program, to provide technological benefits to disadvantaged students and to strengthen education.

Be it enacted by the Senate and House of Representatives of the United States of America in Congress assembled,

SECTION 1. SHORT TITLE

    (a) SHORT TITLE.—This Act may be cited as the "Uplift for Educational Performance Act."

SECTION 2. STATEMENT OF PURPOSE

It is the purpose of this program to improve the educational performance of low-income children by enhancing their cognitive, physical, and emotional development—

    (1) by providing disadvantaged children and their families direct access to implantable medical technology, such as Neural Autofocus®, when such medical devices are determined to be necessary, based on medical evaluation.

7

SPEED CUBE

It's a strange sound. Intense and furtive. A pattern under it. It invades my sleep around the edges, seeping in.

Snick, snick, snick.

Sunday morning. Two days crashing in Jim's tiny spare bedroom. No work today and a damn good thing, too. I'm exhausted. My arms and legs feel stiff under the loose-knit afghan. For the first time in my life, dirt-stained calluses have surfaced on my hands and fingers. I'm sore and glad for the pain, because without it my thoughts slide inexorably back to Pittsburgh. Back to the people I lost.

I've only been in Eden for a couple days, but it's been a blur of work and sleep and failing to wheedle information out of Jim. The old man handed me a forged driver's license yesterday and gave me a short haircut in the living room. Told me I better keep to myself. Stay out of town and never, ever get my numbers run.

Snicksnicksnick.

I force my eyes open. A startled yelp catches in my throat. Something is on the other side of the screened window next to my bed. Some kind of gray-faced monster. Child size. Watching me.

It's a little boy. He must be standing on the hot tub on the deck outside. His hands move rapidly, twisting and swiveling something held out over his potbelly. A Rubik's cube.

He smiles at me, pressing his forehead against the window.

Small sharp teeth flashing. His hands never stop turning and flipping the worn cube.

Something is off about the little boy. His ears sit low on his head like a couple of fleshy lumps. Small eyes, too far from each other. The color of mud. An oddly smooth patch of skin stretches between his upper lip and piggish, upturned nose. Classic fetal alcohol syndrome, the proof of it outlined in his distorted features for everyone to see.

And he's an amp. A nubby maintenance port protrudes from his temple. Faintly I can make out the telltale square outline of a retinal implant on the white of his left eye. The retinal chip floats there like a tattoo, collecting information about the world and ferrying it to the Neural Autofocus embedded in the boy's temple.

There's a lot of hardware in him, but his smile is real. Genuine. It belongs to a little boy and not a monster. And what with the yellowish node on his temple, who knows what might be going on in his head? These days, there's no guessing what kind of mind lurks behind a face.

"Hey," says the boy, voice coming in loud and clear through the window screen. "I'm Nick. You're Owen."

"If you say so," I say, wiping the sleep out of my eyes.

"I'm friends with Jim. Come outside. I wanna show you Eden."

Eden is an island, according to Nick. And it's surrounded by sharks. Real big old gnarly-ass man-eaters.

As we walk, the kid shadows me. I get the feeling I couldn't shake him if I wanted. Eden is too small and Nick's personality is too big. He's telling me his theory now. Theories, actually. The little guy has collected a lot of ideas in his decade or so of life and he doesn't mind sharing.

Nick moves like a puppy. His small brown hands are always in motion, sometimes slow and deliberate, other times making short, eye-blurring bursts.

He can solve the Rubik's cube in under thirty seconds.

"Yeah," says Nick, as he leads me around the trailer park. "I mostly use the Fridrich method. Pretty advanced. With finger shortcuts and triggers I can do four-move bursts. Over ten moves a second. Of course, you gotta lube your cube to go that fast."

Nick bursts into hysterical giggles. Eden is otherwise quiet under the growing heat of the morning sun.

"Eden," he informs me, tongue peeking out of his narrow slit of a mouth, "is all by itself out here. I'm not sayin' you can't venture into shark-infested waters. But you better not be going by yourself. You got to have somebody watching your back every minute. Plus, sharks are worst at night. Nocturnal predators. So, you got to be home before dark."

I ask the obvious question. "Is it shark week on TV or something?"

"Yeah, but that don't change my point," he responds. "The sharks make all of us amps stay together on our islands. To be safe, right? But Eden ain't the only island. There's a bunch more of 'em. Other places where poor people got the Uplift program. And the vets. Plus, out there in Pittsburgh, where they done all the original trials. Lot of test subjects out there with all kinds of crazy junk in their heads."

Is that what we are? A nation of test subjects? Involuntary participants in a never-ending social experiment, exposed to wave after wave of new technology?

Nick points along a row of run-down trailers. "Over there's my house. Earl. Miranda. Jim." The kid stops at a dark trailer on the end. It has an ominous red star spray-painted on its side, paint bleeding from it in dried rivulets. "Lyle and them guys are in those boxes there."

The laughing cowboy and his gang. I try to act casual.

"What do you think of Lyle?" I ask, peering at the rotting, graffiti-covered trailers.

Nick scratches one of his misshapen ears. "Kind of a badass, ain't he? I like that. But mostly I'm just scared of him, I guess."

I raise an eyebrow. "You admit it?"

Nick leads me toward the edge of the trailer park. "Oh, I'm scared of all kinds of stuff. Not the dark or monsters or nothing like that. Stuff I'm scared of is worth being afraid of. Tornadoes. Pure Priders. And Lyle and his friends. Especially Lyle. Sometimes, it's like he can't see you. Like he's got shark eyes."

"I heard the police were looking for him."

"Everybody knows that. But Lyle's got this way of moving. Sneaky fast. Anybody in a suit or a uniform comes around and he's gone. Just leaves us to deal with it."

Nick kicks the dirt, looks away.

"Do you like it here?" I ask.

"I guess. It's hard to leave anymore."

"What about school?"

"My mom teaches out of our house. Hardly any kids go to town for school. It's got where you can't even go out with your port under a hat. If a regular old Reggie Jerkwad finds out, he might mess you up good and send you home."

"Reggie?" I ask.

"They call us amps. We call them reggie. Don't ask me."

Nick keeps leading me around the perimeter of the park, pointing out trailers and cars and pathways through the weeds. I follow, still sleepy, bemused by this hyperactive little creature.

Weeds suffocate the mostly fallen-down wooden fence that surrounds Eden. Through a missing section, I see a brand-new chain-link fence on the other side. Squat and solid, it wraps Eden in shining links. Looks like it was built yesterday.

Seeing me looking at the double fence, the kid goes solemn.

"Not safe to go much past the fence. Mean people live in them houses across the field. At night, they sit out there and drink beer and turn spotlights on us. They call it the neighborhood watch. We call them spotlighters."

"How long has that gone on?" I ask.

"They've come and gone for a long time. But now it's every night. On the news, Senator Vaughn told his Priders they got to watch us at all times. And it's even worse since new amps started showing up here. Spotlighters came out and built that fence without asking. Made a lot of people mad, but nobody did nothing about it."

Together, we stare silently at the shining fence. It looks metallic and alien next to the organic decay of Eden. A grasshopper flitters past and lands on Nick's arm. He brushes it off, breaks the reverie.

"Look," he says, "I ain't trying to get in your business or nothing. But I told you everything about me and Eden, so you've got to tell *me* all about you. Like what you're doing here. Fair is fair."

Nick looks up at me, thrusting out his pointed chin, curious and demanding. But mostly demanding.

"I don't have any other place to go," I say. "Same as the others. Things are complicated right now. Luckily, there are a lot of people in Eden who are like us because of the Uplift program."

"You mean the government cheese?" Nick points at the yellowish nub on his temple. "They came and gave these yellow ones to everybody around here and then they got all mad at us for having them. Pretty stupid."

"I agree."

Nick stands quietly, watching the distant low houses beyond the brown grass. It might as well be the shoreline of another world.

"So that's it?" he asks. "You're hiding, like all the rest?"

"That's it," I say, wondering if it's true.

"I don't believe you," he says.

"Really?"

"Nah. I get the feeling you're here to do something."

I don't say anything. I'm a little taken aback by how confident the kid is. Nick's hands go back to fluttering over the Rubik's cube in little spurts of speed. He solves it, smirks at it. Starts mixing up the squares again.

"Do you ever wish that you were a regular kid? A reggie?" I ask.

Nick snorts. "I could barely see before I got the retinal. Could barely think without Autofocus. And you're asking me if I *want* to have the dumbs? No thanks. I'd rather be weird and know it than be a stupid ass."

I can't help but feel like I'm speaking to an adult.

"What about you?" asks Nick.

"Me?"

"Yeah. You want to be a reggie?"

"It would make life a lot easier."

Nick stops, frowns at me. "Would it?" he asks.

General Biologics to Close US Offices

PITTSBURGH—The General Biologics corporation, makers of the popular Neural Autofocus® brain implant, announced today that it will be closing the main offices in downtown Pittsburgh as well as satellite offices around the country.

A company spokesman indicated that it was impossible to continue in the wake of the Supreme Court ruling, saying, "Recent decisions in the US courts have created an incredibly hostile environment here in the United States—not only for our clients but also for our workers and their families."

Several weeks ago, an explosion at a Pittsburgh laboratory claimed the life of Dr. David Gray, a General Biologics medical researcher. Despite increased security at other research facilities, the threat of violence has become a day-to-day factor for many employees.

The spokesman said the company will likely be moving the bulk of its in-patient operations and production facilities to an as-yet-undisclosed location in Europe. Approximately five hundred employees, many of them highly skilled factory workers, have been invited to move with the company, although it is unclear how many will accept the offer.

The current product line is due to be phased out over the coming months, and American patients with existing implants will be provided with emergency care only.

8
NIGHT LIFE

When night hits Eden, the close-packed trailers light up with ratty old strings of paper lanterns, citronella candles, and the fleeting streaks of kids playing with flashlights.

I sit with Jim on his dimly lit deck, a crusty folding chair biting into my ass. The old man hands me a cold beer and we watch the nightlife of the park settle into the shadows. He doesn't speak and by now it doesn't surprise me.

Jim was right—battle lines are being drawn. Every third trailer or so lurks dark and empty. There are hardly any unmarked temples left in Eden—all the pure humans have packed up and moved on. In their place, harried families of amps have arrived from miles around. Renting the empties. Their gleaming new cars stud the parking lot. Newcomers are coagulating here at random, many of them with nothing in common except those little flecks of metal in their brains.

They're not here because Eden is safe or even welcoming. They're here because there's no other place to go. Nowhere else to rent or go to school or work. No more options. We're all running for our lives, in one way or another. Being left alone is the best we can ask for.

And we can't even get that.

I'm startled by how soon I get used to the spotlighters. The winking scrape of their lights over our trailers seems to live in my peripheral vision. Occasional gunfire and hooting laughter come from beyond the fence.

The local amps seem unimpressed. Across the way, a stained slab of concrete sits where some repossessed trailer used to live. A shirtless guy has got a clamp light hanging from a tree branch, the extension cord running to his trailer. It illuminates an old door supported by two sawhorses. Tools and empty beer bottles are scattered around the makeshift workbench. The guy is ignoring the field, busily fixing the knees of a plastic exoskeleton that's sprawled out like a corpse.

A fiery red dot sizzles across my vision. It's a teenager in a hoodie, jogging past. He's carrying a crummy old boom box that amplifies music from a portable player tucked in his pocket. The node on his temple throbs in time to the beat. A neon attachment the kid has made himself. I don't know if he's proud of being an amp or just oblivious to the stigma. Either way, the implant is impossible to miss.

All the ephemeral sounds of Eden—the low hum of campfire conversation, kids panting and laughing, the occasional shriek of an air tool, and even the distorted thump of bass lines—combine into a familiar babble. Human lives unfolding. It's comforting. Somehow, Eden is an honest-to-God functioning community. Pushed out here to the margins of society and huddling together for sanity but operating nonetheless.

Almost normal people living almost normal lives.

"I'm getting tired of the silent treatment, Jim. Why am I being hunted?" I ask. "What is the Zenith?"

Jim hushes me.

"Don't say that word so loud. Only a handful of people in the world know what it means. If you were smart, you'd wish you weren't one of them."

Jim looks around, suspicious. He continues, voice lowered.

"It's an implant like any other. Won't make you a superhero. Just helps your brain process the world."

"I need to know more than that, Jim. A lot more."

"I can't be responsible for you if you get hurt. I already done enough damage. Look at this place," says Jim. "And we thought we were helping these people."

Eden may feel calm right this instant, but tension crackles just beneath every movement. Every sound. It's a fragile picture of normalcy, wavering in the reflection of a soap bubble.

"My dad said you would explain. It was the last thing he said."

The old man sucks on his beer and sits quiet for a moment, thinking. Finally, he swallows a last mouthful of beer and starts talking.

"I only built the amp hardware—the army programmed them and your pop installed them. All thirteen. That was the whole run, but I don't have the whole picture. Before activation, it oughta be doing basic Neural Autofocus tasks. Pushing your mind in the right direction. But it also knows things. Military skill sets, probably. I don't know—I didn't program that part. All I do know is that when you turn it on, the amp takes over. You go faster. No time to think. If you're a good man, you'll do good things. If you're not, you won't."

"It controls you?"

"It's still you. Only the Zenith doesn't listen to you up here," says Jim, pointing at my forehead. "It listens to you down here." He taps my chest, over my heart. "It'll give you what you're really wishing for."

I consider that for a second. "How do I turn it on?" I ask.

"A trigger. Part of the programming. Could be some kind of action or series of words. Only Lyle could tell you for sure."

Jim pulls down the last draft from his beer, drops it, and pops open the next in a well-practiced motion. Doesn't say another thing.

Then something thuds into the boards under the deck. Jim pulls his mouth into a line and stomps his boot against the sagging wood. The blows reverberate like a marching drum.

"Get up here, Nicky!" he shouts. "You little prairie dog."

Covered in leaves and dirt, Nick crawls out from under the deck. He's grinning, stiff hair sticking up over his low ears. "I know'd it," he says. "I knew he was here to do something."

"Dammit, Nick," says Jim. "Where's your mother?"

"On her way. I'll tell her you're lookin' for her. See you later . . . Zenith."

Nick giggles and trots off into the darkness.

"Christ," says Jim.

"I'll talk to him about it," I say, but Jim's looking past me. Someone is coming. A woman walking slow and relaxed. She carries the kind of gravity that seems to pull light in around her.

At first, I can see only her pale lips as she emerges from the shadows. Then she pushes dirty blond hair from her face. Sets a pair of bright almond-shaped eyes on me. The glow of every dingy paper lantern hanging on the deck is reflected at me in her eyes, each reflection like a possibility.

Her temple is clean. She's not even an amp.

I set my beer down quick and open my mouth. Ready to spring into action. Ready for something. It's just that I can't think of what I meant to do. Or say.

"Howdy, Luce," says Jim. "Nick beat you here."

"He usually does," she says. "Brought you guys some supper."

She hands over a couple TV dinners, paper curled and brittle from the oven. Jim takes them and nods. His gruff version of a thank-you.

"This is Owen," he says. "Friend of mine's kid. Usual story. Was a schoolteacher, like you. Math or something."

"Hey," she says, extending her hand. "I'm Lucy."

I take Lucy's hand in mine. Force myself to let it go.

She's looking up the steps at me and I'm thinking about how pretty she is, and after a second I realize that I'm not saying anything. She grins, amused, I hope.

Her smile sticks with me for a long time. I guess I was memorizing it.

"Th-thanks," I say. "You didn't have to do that."

"It's the least I can do. Somebody has to make sure the old goat eats every now and then." She lowers her voice, leans in to Jim. "Are you making another run?"

"Leaving tomorrow morning," he says. "Be gone a week or so. Visiting with folks at Locust Grove, Lost City, Tenkiller."

"Where are you going?" I ask.

Lucy draws back and crosses her arms, eyebrows raised at Jim. "He doesn't know what you do?"

Jim takes another swig of his beer. Watches the park.

"He's our doctor," says Lucy. "Has been for ten years. The only real implant specialist in Eastern Oklahoma. Goes out to the smaller communities. Without him, a lot of people would be out of luck. Especially now."

"Why didn't you tell me?" I ask.

"Not that important," says Jim.

Lucy shakes her head. Her eyes settle on mine and I know. It's important.

Jim is out here paying his dues. Paying these people back for some sin, real or imagined. He built the Zeniths from scratch and let the military decide what they should do. It makes me wonder what might be inside the Zenith that was evil enough to make him uproot his life and sniff out the original Uplift site way out here in Sequoyah County.

A band of light scans across Lucy's face.

We all turn at once. See the car headlights. Hear distant sirens.

And the flow of everyday life splinters and falls apart just like that. People start heading inside, movements shaky with hidden panic. There's too much bad shit out in the darkness. It's not safe.

The crunch from the parking lot is loud enough to cause an echo. Reminds me of a sled bouncing over ice-encrusted snow. Tires shriek. A car is crashing. A dark shape that bounces and grinds to a stop on the edge of Eden.

A door thunks open. I don't hear it close.

Sirens scream in the distance, louder now.

"We oughta get inside," says Jim. He's already up, folded chair in one hand and the rest of the six-pack in the other, a few sweating cans of beer dangling from his fingers by the plastic rings.

I don't move. I'm watching the crowd. Parents are hurrying children inside trailers. But some of the grown-ups are staying put. Stone-faced, the men and women of Eden are standing tall and grim.

The sirens have arrived. Now they cut off. Red and blue lights flash in the parking lot.

"Get inside, Owen," says Jim. "Cops run your license and you're finished."

Lucy glances at me, puzzled.

Just then a kid bursts out between two trailers and stumbles into the central driveway. Huffing and puffing, he trips and falls in the dirt and catches himself with one outstretched palm. Keeps going. Head swiveling, he homes in on the nearest trailer.

Ours.

Jim moves to close the door. Too late.

"Thanks," breathes the kid, as he pushes past me and storms into the trailer. I notice a burnt-yellow splotch on his temple. Like everyone around here, he has a government-issued Neural Auto-focus. The "government cheese," as Nick called it. Makes an average kid a genius and a dumb kid average. Mostly, they gave them to the dumb kids.

"Dammit," says Jim.

The kid leaves behind the smell of sweat and grass and gasoline. He slams the trailer door shut behind him. Leaves Jim and me by ourselves on the deck, dumbfounded.

"See you next time," says Lucy. She's striding away, legs straining the cloth of her dress. "Welcome to Eden!" she calls to me, flashing that grin over her shoulder.

The quiet lasts for one fuzzy second. Men stand gaunt outside their trailers, chests rising and falling, like actors waiting for a cue. The shirtless guy has put on his grease-smudged exoskeleton. He's feeling it out, standing on one leg with his other foot pulled up behind him like a sprinter stretching.

I turn to Jim. "What do we do?"

"Nothing," replies Jim.

"Nothing?"

Jim squints out at the trailer park. Porch lights are blinking off. Eden is going dark.

"I've got to hide," I whisper.

"Sit tight," Jim says as he grabs the back of my shirt. "Run now and they'll give chase. You get caught with what's in your head and in five minutes Joe Vaughn will have the country convinced that weaponized amps are infiltrating our trailer parks."

I relax and Jim lets go of me.

A couple seconds later a cop claws his way between two trailers and into the clearing. He's big. Twice the size of the kid who came through. Dressed in black. Some kind of light body armor. His radio earpiece sprouts a dime-sized, green-glowing ocular sight that's mounted just below his left eye.

Jim whispers, keeping his face oriented toward the cop. "Keep your face out of the light and for Chrissake don't look at him."

The cop is ignoring us. Scans the ground. Sweeps his head back and forth like a predator, following the heat differential of recent footsteps. He pauses where the kid stumbled and nearly fell. Cranes his neck and follows the path that Lucy took. Spots her still walking away and then keeps moving along the kid's trajectory.

Closer and closer. Right up to our trailer. Our steps.

The cop stops and brushes his night sight to the side. Looks at me like I'm a piece of furniture. Maybe gauging how heavy I'd be to lift. He absentmindedly pats the radio handpiece that is velcroed to his Kevlar vest, up near his shoulder. Making sure it's still there.

"Move," he grunts, mechanically climbing the splintered wooden steps. I hear motors whining faintly and notice the cop wears an integrated lower-leg exoskeleton in his armor. Nothing fancy, just a stepper to lighten the load.

I'm not fast enough and the cop plows into me. The solid bulk of armor-layered muscle and compact battery weight sends me grasping for balance. I get hold of the rail just as the cop kicks open the door.

"You can't go inside there, sir," says Jim.

"I can do whatever I want," says the cop, and his tone is final. The cop disappears into the trailer.

He's right. Legally, we're living in limbo. I'm not sure there would be any way to prosecute this guy even if he decided to drag us into the street and shoot us all, one by one.

Jim and I stand on the deck, looking past each other, while the cop bangs around inside. Glass breaks. Muffled shouts penetrate thin walls. A minute later, the cop emerges. Not breathing heavy. Moving slow, without urgency, robotic. He's got the kid by the back of his shirt, dragging him out like a bag of trash.

With a swoop of his arm, the cop nonchalantly tosses his captive off the deck. The kid stutters down the steps, scrabbling on skinned and bloody knees. Trying and failing to catch his balance, he sprawls in the dirt. The cop follows, descending one whining electric footfall at a time.

Nobody in the trailer park has spoken. They just watch.

Showing surprising spunk, the kid pops up onto his feet. Tries to make a run for it, but the cop is right behind him and gets hold of his hair. Gives the kid a brutal yank, spinning him around with his bleeding hands out and flailing. And then the kid accidentally scratches the cop across the face.

A collective shudder goes through the people watching.

The cop pauses, sets his mouth, swallows a lump of anger. Likes the taste. "Mistake," he mutters. "That was a mistake."

The officer shoves the kid back down into the sandy dirt. Drops a stepper-enhanced foot between his shoulder blades. I hear a hoarse grunt as a lungful of air is expelled, raw and involuntary. The kid sputters, breath whistling through his throat. Trying to breathe, I guess.

"You're under arrest," says the cop to the wheezing kid.

A familiar anger sweeps through me and I take a step forward, but Jim touches my arm. Shakes his head. The old man nods at something in the darkness.

Seeing it, I get the sensation that I'm falling into space.

A swarm of neon fireflies stream toward us. It takes a second to realize that each radiant dot is attached to a temple. Blues and yellows and reds. Some color shifting and others sizzling in one hue. Swaggering young amps with glowing, hand-modified maintenance ports approach and surround the officer. It's a motley group. Some newcomers wear oversized hoodies and ball caps; others are in blue jeans and boots. Cowboy thugs. Scruffy beards and glassy eyes that reflect crisp speckles of neon light. These are the amped kids who hang around Lyle's knot of three or four trailers. His gang.

The police officer steps off the kid. His hand darts to the radio on his shoulder. He grabs it and speaks quietly, head turned. For his part, the kid lies on his side with his arms wrapped around his knees. Sucking air.

"King one oh three. Hold traffic. I'm at Eden, northwest cor-ner. Better start me some cars."

Static.

A flash of white as the cop's eyes widen. A gap has opened in the sea of bobbing stars. Lights parting for a spreading blackness. Someone is coming through—a man, maybe—someone whose presence is perceptible only by the lack of light.

"King one oh three. Do you copy?"

"What's happenin', fella?" asks a gravelly voice.

The identity of the black hole becomes clear. Lyle Crosby.

"Step away, sir," replies the cop, still grabbing at the radio handpiece. His thumb clicks the button compulsively. "All of you step away."

Lyle steps closer, smirks.

"Something wrong with your little radio there?"

The cop slaps the radio back onto his shoulder, but it falls, dangles to his hip by its coiled black umbilical wire. *Sssh,* it says.

"Sir, I am serious. I will shoot your ass. I will not hesitate." The officer reaches down and unbuttons his gun holster. Rests one palm on the butt of his gun. "I will not make another request. All of y'all need to back up."

A grimace flashes across Lyle's face. Something quiet, scary. Surging anger just below the surface. He opens his mouth to speak but stops as a pale hand closes around his upper arm. Lucy. The cowboy turns his head as she whispers something into his ear, gives his arm a little shake.

"Fine," says Lyle. "Fine, Lucy."

Lyle tugs his arm away, cocks his head, and closes his eyes. A dreamy smile flutters onto his face. He lifts his hands, palms out. The officer draws his gun, drags it from the leather holster with a squeak. Puts it on the high ready. Aimed at Lyle's chest.

"On your knees," he demands.

"Hush," says Lyle. "I'm listening."

The cop looks around at the neon temples. "What's the matter with this guy?"

"Static, Officer," says Lyle. "All I'm hearing is static."

Lyle takes another step. The cop holds his ground. Lyle leans into the gun. The barrel presses into Lyle's chest, dimples the fabric of his shirt, nosing into lean muscle.

"Got no backup coming," says Lyle, opening his eyes. "Your radio's all jammed up. Can't you hear it hissing like a rattlesnake?"

"Enough shit," says the cop. "Get on the ground! Now!"

The cop reaches for Lyle's shoulder, but the cowboy shrugs away like a shadow. His face is suddenly an inch from the officer's.

He is speaking to the cop fast and quiet. His voice rises and falls like water over stones. "Two hundred milliseconds. Takes that long just for your brain to tell your finger to pull the trigger, understand? Reaction time. Damn central tenet of mental chronometry. Trigger pull takes a hundred and ten milliseconds with a factory-set pull weight for that Glock of yours. Trigger releases the firing pin. Detonates the primer. Wait for the chemical reaction. Get your explosion and the bullet travels the length of the barrel, about four inches. Whole process takes a second and a half. Shit, man, might as well be an *eternity*."

The kid lies on the ground, watching this unfold from a worm's perspective. Breathing fast. Mouth open in wonder.

"You know why I know all that?" asks Lyle.

"You're some kind of goddamn freak," says the cop.

The crowd of neon thugs has moved closer. Almost imperceptibly. Lyle's gang is a wall of seething anger. Fast little movements as guys light e-cigarettes, flick empty nicotine cartridges to the ground.

"Careful talking like that. All by yourself. What with your legs not working."

The cop's eyes go wide. He grunts, trying to lift a leg. Nothing happens. The motors in his stepper are frozen. He slaps his thigh, punches it. Twists at the waist, too hard. Off-balance, he teeters on paralyzed legs, arms out. His gun glints darkly in his right hand as he paws the air.

Before the cop can fall, his legs come unfrozen. He catches himself. Red-faced, he glares at the crowd. Grabs his gun in both hands and clutches it against his chest.

"Let me ask you again," Lyle says. "You know why I know these things?"

The cop sputters. "I don't know, okay? Why? Why do you know all that shit?"

"Because I can dodge your bullets, Officer."

Lyle is not lying.

Abruptly, I wonder just what the hell is perched on my temple. And if Lyle is the only person who can tell me, I wonder if it's worth knowing. Maybe it's better to just let it lie dormant for the rest of my life.

The police officer looks at his own hands, wrapped moistly around the grip of his gun. "You're out of your fucking mind," he says.

The cowboy watches him, not blinking. "You can walk through us like we are ghosts, Officer. You got all the power in the world. But try and tell me power don't recognize power."

The cop isn't listening anymore. Taking those measured mechanical steps, somehow childlike now, we can all tell that he is trying not to run. He beats it out of Eden. Maybe he'll come back with more cops. Maybe he won't.

Just before I go inside, I notice the beaten-up kid. He's sitting in the dirt, staring at Lyle. He's got this odd look on his face, eyes shining. It's pretty obvious: the kid's got a hero now.

It takes a second to place the last time I saw that look. It was in the eyes of the audience watching Senator Joseph Vaughn give a speech outside his offices at the Cathedral of Learning in Pittsburgh. The day my world ended.

Lyle just turns and walks off. Ignores the kid and everybody else. Falls back into that sea of floating neon pixels. He still has a dreamy look on his face. I glance past him and notice Lucy. She's watching me watch Lyle, a concerned look on her face.

"Be careful around her," says Jim.

"Lucy? Why?" I ask. "She's the nicest person I've met so far. No offense."

Lucy seems like the most normal, well-adjusted person I've met in Eden. Bringing an old man his supper. Probably saved that cop's life. She's human.

"You see goodness in her because you're good."

"Are you saying she's not?"

"I don't know. But it's worth thinking on. Hell, your life might depend on it," says Jim. He pulls the half-finished six-pack out from behind his back and dangles a beer at me. "Her name's Lucy *Crosby*, son. Lyle's her twin brother."

TURN ANGER INTO ACTION
JOIN THE FREE BODY LIBERTY GROUP!

What We Do

The FBLG is a social justice organization devoted to defending the constitutional rights of implanted individuals and cultivating a national atmosphere of understanding and opportunity for all.

How We Do It

We are committed to expanding the grassroots power of the entire implantee community by training volunteer activists (both implanted and especially those without implants) to speak to the community, organize rallies, and gather supporters. In addition, we organize regional campaigns to advance pro-implantee legislation and defeat discriminatory policies. We do all of this while battling disinformation campaigns and exposing Americans to positive examples of implantation technology.

What You Can Do

People with mental and/or physical impairments caused by disease, birth defects, or injuries deserve to be cured without facing discrimination.

JOIN THE FBLG!
TELL YOUR STORY!
RECRUIT NEW ALLIES!
ATTEND RALLIES!

9

BEYOND THE FENCE

"So?" asks Nick. "Can you turn it on? The *Zenith*?"

The kid whispers that last word, clearly enjoying it.

I'm sitting on Jim's deck, holding a crummy old watch set to timer mode and keeping track while Nick manhandles his faded Rubik's cube. Solving it for the thousandth time, his fingers twisted around the toy like melted candle wax.

Apparently, the laughing cowboy kicked up his heels and disappeared after facing down that cop. It was the smart move. A group of sheriffs came back the next day, sunglasses and beards and biceps, huddled up shoulder to shoulder like ducks. They snatched the runner from the night before and served warrants on a few others. Dragged them all out of here with a look that dared anybody to say anything.

For the last week, a sort of local order has emerged in this new world of chaos. I get off work from the construction site at two o'clock. Put on a low ball cap and push my way through Pure Priders and sometimes counterprotesters from the Free Body Liberty Group. Walk two miles home and never show my face to the traffic. Drag ass back into Eden, quietly counting the new amp families that have arrived.

Nick picked up on my schedule pretty quick. Lately, I've found him waiting, crouched inside the rotten old hot tub sitting on Jim's porch. I can hear his giggles from the porch steps. Every day, he jumps out to surprise me—a demented jack-in-the-box.

And every day, I go ahead and act surprised.

"One thing is for sure," Nick is saying, studying his Rubik's cube and leaning back in a plastic chair, "we know you ain't supersmart."

"Thanks."

"Well, sorry. Autofocus'll make a smart person smarter, but it won't make a dummy a genius. Except sometimes people who *seemed* dumb just because they were distracted all the time can end up being pretty goddanged brilliant. Done."

He holds up the Rubik's cube, each face washed in solid neon colors.

"Twenty-two seconds," I say, resetting the watch. "Yeah, you're real smart."

"Shoot, it's just the government cheese."

Nick waves his hand at me in an aw-shucks movement, then tosses over the Rubik's cube. I mix up the colored squares, not paying particular attention. Nick watches my hands intently, probably memorizing the reverse series of movements to solve it—the little schemer.

He continues: "I'm guessing the soldier stuff works because the amp reacts automatically. Like when you prick your finger and your arm jumps back. I mean, you don't *tell* your arm to jump back. Some other part of your brain is in charge of that. The part that keeps you from getting hit by a bus and stuff. Your amp must be like that, except it can do more than just make you flinch or blink your eyes or whatever."

Nice, I think. An alien brain is coiled inside my head, able to make complex decisions without asking. Sounds wonderful.

"It can make you do soldier stuff like karate chops and shoot guns and—"

"Leap tall buildings in a single bound," I interrupt.

"It can make you dodge a bullet," says Nick matter-of-factly.

"Schoolteacher," I say, pointing at myself. "Remember?"

"Well, those Priders in the field don't care what you used to do."

I toss the cube back and start the clock, the tiny silver watch button digging painfully into my finger. Nick's hands are already moving when he catches the cube. So is his mouth.

"And we can't know what the Zenith does until we turn it on."

"No way, Nick," I reply.

The kid nearly falls off his chair, cube temporarily forgotten. "Aren't ya *curious*?" he nearly shouts.

Curious. A little. Afraid? Petrified.

"It's complicated," I say. "It's a *weapon*."

"Your dad gave it to you, right?"

I watch Nick carefully, my face flat.

"Yeah."

"He wouldn't do nothing to hurt his son. He loved you. He must have meant for you to use it."

"In an emergency only," I respond. What did my dad say to me back in the lab? *You have to give it permission.* Were those his last words to me? I can't even remember. Thoughts of that morning are shards of glass, too sharp to sift through.

Nick jumps up and spreads his small arms. "What the heck do you think *this* is?"

The kid slowly steps forward, beady eyes locked on mine, voice rising. "We're stuck here on this island. All alone and surrounded by bloodthirsty sharks. Running out of food and water. Getting desperate. Something's gotta give. I'm telling you, man. Our situation that we're in here is *dire*. Very dire, Owen."

He's been reading the dictionary.

"Plus," he says breathlessly, "every speed cuber knows that you got to think a bunch of moves ahead. Every move you make is part of a bigger series. Whether you know it or not. You got to *be ready*."

The kid is right. If and when an emergency comes, I won't have time to figure this out. *There's a lot you need to learn about yourself.*

I tilt my head at Nick. "What's your plan?"

Nick grows a little grin, hops off the porch. "Follow me," he says.

We walk down the dirt path toward the fields. On the way, I catch myself glancing into Lucy's backyard to see if she's out there, maybe hanging laundry on the clothesline.

Nick catches me looking. Makes the inference immediately.

"Are you gonna ask her out?" he asks.

I shrug. Nick starts chattering in his matter-of-fact way, leading me past his empty front yard. Lucy, he says, is perfect for a guy like me. She's pretty and smart. Has kind of a mean brother in Lyle. But Lucy herself, you got to remember, is really, really nice.

Nick says this word—"nice"—solemnly, as though it has deep meaning to him. I wonder how many nice people he knows.

"How did you end up living with her?" I ask.

Nick keeps walking as if I just asked him a regular question. The hollow timbre of his voice tells me it isn't. "My folks were reggies," he says. "They didn't like it here. Not sure they really liked me much either. Anyway, Lucy took me in once they were gone."

I slow down and follow the kid over to the fence. Give him some space for a minute. Finally, he turns and stands across from me like we're about to play catch.

"Getting back to the point. You got a brain implant," says Nick. "Switch must be in your head." He taps his temple. "Can you feel it in there? Can you concentrate on it?"

I frown at Nick. He shrugs and continues. "Because sometimes . . . I can feel the cheese, sort of, pushing me. Like standing in a creek with the water flowing against your legs, you know?"

Yeah, I do know what he means. I know exactly. I've spent most of my life ignoring this feeling. Trying not to notice that a foreign object in my head is affecting every minute of my life.

"Fine," I say. "I'll try."

Nick puts his arms up, quietly cheering.

I close my eyes. Send my thoughts out like tentacles to wrap around the chunk of plastic cocooned in my neurons. I can almost feel it there, shuddering with every heartbeat. *Fwish, fwish, fwish.*

Now, I hear the soft roar of the ocean in a seashell.

The white noise grows louder, collapses into patterns, waves of sound lapping at my consciousness. Words? The implant is trying to speak to me. Sounds coming together, growing louder, more distinct. One word: *Nick.*

I open my eyes.

Nick is smiling at me when the rock hits him in the face. It's a nasty little hunk of concrete. Smacks that crooked jack-o'-lantern grin right off his face. Leaves a ragged gash in Nick's forehead that wells up with blood, turns to a pendulous red stripe before it starts streaming down his face.

On the other side of the fallen-down fence, a blond kid hoots. There are maybe three or four of them, hiding out there in the tall brown grass. I can hear their harsh adolescent laughter.

Nick doesn't cry. Just puts one palm over his forehead. Squints at me sadly through the blood. A baby gargoyle. Clutches the Rubik's cube in chubby fingers, finally still.

Pure anger dumps into my veins and throbs through my body. My concentration breaks as all the rage ignites at once like jet fuel. Before I know what's happening, I'm striding toward the grass. Awkwardly pushing the wooden fence down, walking over it.

I climb the chain-link fence and hop it in one movement, limbs quaking from adrenaline. The field is mostly empty, save empty beer cans and trash. A ripped camping chair some spotlighter left behind. And three teenage boys.

"What's your fucking problem?" I hear myself shouting. "Hey!"

The teenagers don't run away like I half expect them to. Instead, they surround me quickly, naturally. Gathered around me, they take on a new form. Each of these kids might be okay on his own, but together they're a hydra: one monster, three heads.

"Why'd you throw that?" I ask. "What's the matter with you?"

"What's the matter with you?" mimics a towheaded kid in fal-setto. "What a retard."

More laughter.

"Amp retard."

I turn to see who said it, and a dirt clod catches me in the mouth, busts my lip, and explodes into dust. My eyes clench shut, trapping dirt behind my eyelids. I double over, blind and gasping in pain as tears cascade down my face.

"The fuck?" I sputter.

A burst of surprised laughter quickly turns raucous, takes on a vicious edge.

"Boom, baby!"

The first shove catches me in the lower back. I trip in the grass and fall to my knees. Another dirt clod catches me in the back of the head as I wipe my eyes.

My tears are turning the dirt to mud.

"Boys," bellows a deep voice. The laughter dries up instantly. The flying dirt clods stop long enough for me to clear one eye. Squinting, I make out a big guy with a ratty little beard. He's lumbering across the field with a can of beer in one hand and a shotgun in the other.

"Thanks," I call, climbing to my feet. "These kids are out of control."

"Shut the fuck up, amp," says the man.

The words are like a hard slap across the face. The kind you don't feel until later.

"Lucky I don't shoot your ass, out here fucking around with my kids," he adds, stomping toward me through the grass and getting in my face.

"Damn right, Gunnin'," calls the blond kid.

"Shut your mouth," orders the man.

"Sorry, Billy," says the kid.

I'm backing away. The alcohol-fueled hostility from "Gunnin' Billy" here is like a poisonous mist. Unlike the taunts from the kids, his words have a lethal momentum behind them. As I back away, he marches forward. Building up steam.

"These kids are citizens of the United States of America, amp. And you're not *shit*. You get that?"

Billy shoves me in the chest. My head snaps forward and I'm staring at a mark on the web of his right thumb. A tattoo of two tiny block letters. It's the *EM* symbol that I haven't seen since the Pure Pride rally in Pittsburgh.

I blink at it.

Then a kick connects with my side. Pushes me off-balance as I try to step backward through the grass. More kicks come in from all around. Laughter. Another dirt clod. I fall to my knees, trying to wipe my eyes and fend off the soft-soled tennis shoes jolting me from random directions.

"So keep your worthless amp ass inside your rat hole," says Billy.

I fall onto my stomach. I desperately try to clear my eyes while more dirt clods rain down. Climbing to my hands and knees, I hear sly laughter.

A wetness spreads over the back of my neck and I stagger to my feet in shock. With one arm shielding my eyes, I stumble back toward the trailers. More clods bounce off my back as I retreat.

"Don't come back!" shouts Billy.

They don't follow me past the other side of the fence.

Nick is gone. There's a spatter of blood where he stood. Tree branches swaying quietly overhead.

"Nick?" I call.

Just the seesaw buzz of cicadas in the trees.

I reach back and touch my neck where it's wet, smell my fingers. Piss. Those kids pissed on me while I was wallowing in the dirt like a helpless baby. Like an amp retard. That's what they called me. A worthless freak.

I wipe my hand on my pants and then freeze. Lucy has come around the corner of her trailer. Watching me. She's in blue jeans and in the morning sunlight I can see she's got a smattering of freckles beneath serious eyes. She's even more beautiful in the light.

"Nick is okay," she says. "I cleaned him up and gave him a Band-Aid. What about you? Do you need help?"

Me? Well, I've got a cold ball of shame wedged tight under my rib cage. Hot piss drying on the back of my neck.

Lucy steps toward me and I put on an unconvincing smile, try to speak—to tell her it was just a stupid thing that I'm laughing off. No big deal. But the words dig their heels into my throat and refuse to come out.

An aftershock of anger rolls through me, and I tuck my hands on my hips to hide their shaking. I want to smash skulls, gouge eyes, and—hell, I don't know—cry. Instead, I drop the trembling, not-fooling-anybody attempt at a smile and turn my back on Lucy.

"Owen," she calls, walking closer. "It's okay."

Pity is in her voice, twisting like a knife between my shoulder blades.

"I'm fine," I say.

She puts a hand on my shoulder and touches the warm urine, and now I know that I have got to get the fuck out of here immediately. I shrug my shoulder and she hangs on.

"Owen—" she's trying to say.

I wrench away from her. "Leave me the fuck alone!" I shout. "Damn."

"What is the matter with you?" she asks, plaintive, wiping her hand on her dress.

Oh my God. Anything. Anything to get away from this shame. I'm walking fast, away, away, away.

"Nothing," I call over my shoulder. "I don't need help. I'm not another stray for you to take in." Immediately, I flush scalp to spine with hot regret. I break into a trot until I can't hear her. Along the way, I yank my piss-soaked shirt over my head, ball it up, and hurl it lamely into the grass.

Back in Jim's trailer, I slam the flimsy broken door shut behind me. The sink piddles a weak stream of warm water and I let it pool in my dirt-caked fingers. Splash it on my face and let it carry away the snot and tears and dirt.

In the fart-smelling freezer, I find a plastic tray of shallow ice cubes. I twist the cracked tray and let the slivers of ice fall on the counter. Wrap them in a napkin and push the mass against my swollen lip.

Would things be easier if I were a reggie? Yeah, they damn well would be. I wouldn't stink like urine and humiliation. I could sit in my nice apartment and feel sorry for all those poor amps out there, instead of taking my own lashes here in this trailer park.

The reality of this new world is settling in. Spotlighters watching the fringes of town every night. Protesters outside the job site every day. Hiding here with nobody to talk to. "Head down, antennae up," as Jim says. And now, my ass handed to me by a bunch of teenagers. With poor Nicky there to watch.

And so much for Lucy Crosby. I guess I fucked that up pretty good.

I open the freezer again, more slowly this time. There's a bottle of cheap vodka wedged in the back, bearded in frost. Three-fourths full. I pull it out and set it down on the counter and let it sweat.

I slide open the silverware drawer. Pick up an ice pick with a worn wooden handle. Turn it back and forth in my hands.

Nick told me I was going to do something here in Eden. At this moment, nothing very good comes to mind. But if I'm here because of this goddamn thing in my head, then I think I'm ready to go face-to-face with it. Turn it on and find out what it is, one way or another.

I'm going to see what all the fuss is about.

FDA U.S. Food and Drug Administration

Neural Autofocus MK-4® Brain Implant National Recall
Recall Class: Class I (reasonable probability of adverse consequences)

At the bequest of the FDA and the United States Senate, General Biologics recently sent an urgent medical device recall letter to all documented customers. The recall notice explained the issue, identified the affected products, required distributors to cease further distribution and use of the product, and requested the return of unused product.

Intended Use: The Neural Autofocus® brain implant is intended to improve brain function in a variety of serious conditions, including forms of epilepsy, attention-deficit/hyperactivity disorder, post-traumatic stress disorder, and obsessive-compulsive disorder.

Reason for Recall: Complaints of behavioral side effects have been received. This type of failure may result in mood swings, depression, or manic episodes. These effects are poorly understood and unpredictable. In some cases, emergency surgery has been necessary to remove the implant. However, effects of the implant remain after removal due to the continuous training effect presented on neural pathways during use of the device.

Patients with implanted devices are advised to consult the list of government-approved clinicians included in Appendix A of this document. Unapproved physicians are not authorized to maintain the device.

General Biologics Corporation is advising customers to immediately discontinue use of any affected product and return all unused products.

10

COMING STORM

I've been flopping back and forth on the trailer's linoleum floor like a fish on a boat for most of the night, and now I'm trying to draw breath between clenched teeth and wondering if I've got myself a fresh traumatic brain injury or if I'm just going crazy.

In a daze, I can hear myself grunting and, well, kind of squealing with my mouth closed. My calls for help sound more like somebody left a dog tied up for too long. Only I'm the animal and I did this to myself.

The latest seizure is over. Meaning the next one is due any minute. I don't see any end to it. Jim is still gone doing his traveling-doctor thing and the only people I know in Eden must think I'm a pathetic coward. Last night, with alcohol-fueled bravery, I decided to try and turn on my Zenith. Tried to find myself. But what I found out was who I am with a broken implant. A spastic invalid.

On top of that, I'm hungover.

A nasty goose egg throbs on my shin in time with my heart. I got it when my leg slammed into the almost empty vodka bottle, shooting it across the room and under the couch. The pain in my shin joins the dull aching cramp in my jaw and neck and the rest of my skinned-up body. That bottle hurt me a lot more than I hurt it.

The plastic doorknob rattles.

For an instant I hallucinate a vision of Lucy. She's blond and lithe and gliding through the front door to check in on me. Only there is a soft darkness outside. Her face is indistinct, lost in black smoke. She can't get inside. Her thin fingers rake the doorframe. But she falls out into the darkness. Gone.

I try to call out, and a rope of drool drops sluglike from my lips. My stomach cramps and my cheek slides across the floor, smearing my face into the spit and old sticky footprints on the linoleum.

The trailer comes back in focus.

I roll my eyes back in my head and catch sight of the wood-paneled door shaking on its hinges. A gust of cool air hits my face as the recently repaired door is ripped open with a sound like masking tape coming off a new paint job.

A skinny guy pokes his head inside, blocking the raw sunlight. He's got a beat-up plastic bottle in one hand, sloshing with tobacco juice. He spits in it, eyes wide and searching.

"Howdy ho," he calls. "Jim? Ya here?"

It's Lyle Crosby. The laughing cowboy. The last person I want to see. But I'm in a bad spot right now and can't be too choosy about the company I keep.

Lyle's eyes travel to my spot on the living room floor. He surprises me and cracks a gap-toothed smile, then laughs out loud. Steps inside and closes the door behind him.

"Damn, buddy. You in here fooling with yourself? Don't be embarrassed. Half the amp teenagers end up like this at one time or another. A little bit of self-experimentation never hurt anybody, except when it did."

Lyle chuckles at his own joke. Then he saunters around the manufactured room, his shark-black eyes mechanically taking in the wood-paneled walls and mangy La-Z-Boy recliner and particleboard bookshelves half filled with dog-eared Westerns and thick, yellowed histories of World War II.

"I'm always telling Jim he needs a wife. Look at this place. No woman I know would put up with this crap."

Lyle grabs a *Reader's Digest* from the coffee table and riffles the pages with the ball of his thumb. He tosses the digest on a stack of other magazines. They collapse in a waterfall, brittle pages slapping the floor next to my face.

He snorts at the spitty snow angels I've been making.

"Okay. Where's your tools, buddy?" asks Lyle.

All I can do is breathe loudly through my teeth.

"Huh," says Lyle. He studies the area around me, thoughtfully adjusting the pod of tobacco wedged in his mouth. Eyeing me, he sucks in his bottom lip and carefully dribbles spit into the plastic bottle.

"Starting to worry me," he says.

With the toe of his boot, he nudges me over onto my back. My arms and face are scraped up and bruised, but Lyle doesn't seem to notice or care. Those obsidian flakes in his face are trained on what I'm still holding in my left hand.

Lyle gets very still. An unrecognizable emotion ripples across his sweat-slicked forehead. Concern. Or maybe anger. He spits again into his bottle, slow.

"That a fact?" he asks, staring pointedly at the streaks of dried blood on my temple. "Used a fuckin' ice pick? Damn, Jack. I guess you're not fooling around, huh? You trying to *kill* yourself?"

Not exactly.

I look up at him, focused on keeping my eyes wide open, round, and imploring. *Yeah*, my spit-smudged face says. *Yeah, I was shit-faced drunk and alone and I was angry. I thought if I turned on the Zenith I could walk outside and kick the living crap out of a guy named Billy. But it didn't work and I messed it up bad and I don't know what the fuck I'm doing. I take it back, okay?*

A hint of ozone sneaks into my next gulp of air. Shit. It's been years since my last one, but you never forget the feeling of a seizure coming on. In the seconds just before, it's easy to get fixated on little things. And this one feels like a real grand mal because I can't seem to tear my eyes away from the glint of that vodka bottle under the couch.

"I get it," says Lyle. "Couldn't take it no more?"

The trapped animal whimper comes out of me again and I can sense the storm gathering inside, feel the churning thunderclouds overhead sucking all the oxygen out of the air. I allow the panic into my eyes and wrench them up to meet Lyle's dark face. In the universal language of pain I'm chanting, *Please help me.* Please, please, please, oh please, don't let another one hit me.

"People been talking about you around the park. Kind of was looking forward to meeting you, actually. Course, I didn't think you were a coward at the time."

He spits tobacco, this time on the floor.

"Life *is* tough though, huh? And for an amp, life is even tougher. Maybe you just couldn't stand it no more. Working minimum wage. Got no lady. No respect. So I'll venture to guess, and this is just conjecture here, but from the evidence . . . I'm supposing you'd had yourself enough. It came on down to a logical conclusion: *Life as an amp ain't worth living.*"

Lyle stoops over and sets the bottle of spit and tobacco down next to my head. Then he casually grabs a handful of my hair in his left hand. He pulls my head off the floor, groaning theatrically like he's tired. Then he pulls harder, tugs my head up, painfully, so we're face-to-face.

"Know what, buddy?" he asks.

Lyle studies my half-lidded eyes. I can smell the tobacco on his breath mingling with the stinging flakes of metal that signal the coming storm. The creases of dirt in his tatted-up neck stand out like fault lines, pecked by tattooed crow beaks and clouded with feathers. I can just make out the silhouetted nub of the implant on the side of his head.

"I find that conclusion to be *personally offensive.*"

And he decks me. Just sends down a right cross and bats it out of the park. A knuckle catches me on the eye, and I can feel the socket filling with blood.

My head hits the ground like a dropped watermelon. A pathetic whining sound warbles out of my throat. When I push my eyes open, I can see the crumbs and dirt on the floor mixing with my slobber. A spattering of fat bright droplets of my blood sit on the floor, mutely reflecting a square of window light from some place up high that I can't turn my head to see.

Jim was right. Lyle is crazy. But being punched in the face is nothing compared to the electrical frenzy that's about to slam into my brain like a Martian cyclone.

"You wanna die?" Lyle asks me, real soft.

I can't tell whether it's a question or an offer.

Lyle looks at the door. At first I think he's going to leave me here, but then he spins back around, and the hardened leather tip of a cowboy boot connects in the pit of my stomach. My body bounces in the air like so much rubber. *No, no, no.* I'm wailing with my eyes, but who can see? The first tremors of the seizure jitter through my limbs like aftershocks.

"No problem," mutters Lyle. And the boot comes again, harder this time.

"Unless maybe you *do* want to live?" asks Lyle. He circles around, methodically kicking: legs, arms, back. He avoids my head.

"Do you wanna live?"

Air hisses from between my lips. I'm empty except for the pain. Lighter than nothing. Never felt this way before. I fold myself up into my head and swim with the air down the black river of my throat. Up and out and over the teeth and tongue. With all the mental will I can muster, I reach down and tug on the dead meat of my tongue. I grab my molars and bend my jaw closed, and slowly but surely my voice comes. It's almost inaudible but somehow Lyle hears.

"*Yes.*"

Lyle stops kicking. I listen to his heavy breathing and the sick trickle of tobacco juice and spit oozing into the plastic bottle.

Then something lands next to my face with a *thwap*. Through a blur of tears I see a scabby brown satchel the size of a wallet.

"That's all you had to say, brother," says Lyle. "That's all you had to say."

I barely hear him. The storm is here. Thunderclouds burst and I feel ice-cold pinpricks of rain erupt all over my body. My limbs curl and I scream through clenched teeth. I'm lashed to a tree in a vicious storm that's shredding me from the inside out.

Lyle's dirty boots creak faintly as he squats next to me. But that's part of another world now. He can kick me to death and I'll never feel it, because he could never hurt me as bad as I'm hurting myself.

Somewhere far away, the laughing cowboy speaks to me. But my brain is broken. The sounds swell and ebb through my head like ripples on a pond, meaningless. And then, nothing.

The storm dissipates. My tree wafts gently in the wind. And then my tree is gone and I'm back on the linoleum, smelling the ripe manure on Lyle's boots. Above my head, his skinny arms move in precise jerks, tattoos flashing, a blurred confusion of flying, fighting crows. One of them has a flaming torch grasped in its claws.

Lyle's brown satchel is open and glistening with rows of delicate instruments. Beat-up implant maintenance tools. Familiar but filthy. I've only seen the sterilized, surgical steel versions in my father's office.

Lyle turns his head and smiles at me sort of crooked. He leans over and takes a closer look at my port. Some glint of recognition is in his eyes. Did he see the Zenith? Recognize it?

With quick flicks of his wrist, he turns my implant back on. As he works, he speaks in a quick whisper: "Maybe I had you wrong, brother. It ain't easy to trust the machine. Knowing it's inside you. Been called the classic anxiety attack of the new century. Panic brewing way down in the reptile part of your brain, three hundred million years old. Older than language. The alien inside. Fear in you like claustrophobia. Leaves you clawing at the roof of your coffin. Except you don't want out of it—you want *it* out of *you*."

A shiver pulses from my temple and spreads through my body. Lyle's hands are moving in efficient bursts in my peripheral vision. I think of Nick and his cube as Lyle keeps talking.

"Gotta understand the machine's a part of you. Lose the amp, you lose your mind. Brain is the sum of its parts. Hindbrain's got your instinct for survival. Limbic is where love and hate live. Neocortex has got your imagination in it. And your amp is another part. What it does is up to you."

A final twist of his hand.

"Friggin' ice pick," he says, shaking his head. "Every amp should have his own tools. Doctors are illegal. Now, how's that feel?"

His words come into focus before my eyes do.

"Better," I whisper.

Lyle's hands go under my armpits like steel clamps. He drags me over to the recliner, rests my back up against it. He disappears for a second, then comes back and hands me a glass of water in a mason jar and some ice cubes wrapped in a fast-food napkin. I sip the water and press the ice to my face.

I look up to thank Lyle and then stop flat. His face is serious, carved out of wood.

"You got a Zenith, like me," he says. "I can tell just by looking at the port. How the fuck did that happen?"

Of course he would recognize it. It was wide open. I say nothing.

"Fine, me first," he says. "I was too smart for the army. Went to Special Forces. Volunteered to join a new operational detachment. Echo Squad. Watched a hundred other soldiers wash out. They were teaching us meditation, breathing techniques, visualization.

Weird shit for the service. Twelve of us made it into the Zenith ODA. And when they told us we were going under the knife we said *sir, yes, sir.*"

Lyle laughs and he sounds more genuine, less insane. I get the feeling he isn't seeing me, just his memories. Old friends and comrades.

"Me and the other boys showed up soldiers and they made us into a new breed," he says, face darkening. "Twelve of us. Brothers. Only four of us left that I know of. Rest have been hunted down and killed." He pauses. "So, let me ask you again. Where'd you get that Zenith?"

Moving slowly, I set the mason jar on the floor. Biting my lip from the pain flaring in my ribs, I manage to shrug my shoulders. "Dad's an implant doctor," I say. "I got hurt bad when I was a teenager. He did what he had to do—to fix me."

I take a couple breaths, then continue. "I tried to turn it on."

Lyle tilts his head, thinking. "Turn it on?" he says. "Can't use a friggin' ice pick to turn it on. What's the matter with you?"

The realization settles on his face. "Wait one goddamn second. Nobody ever taught you to *use it?* You got a cherry turbocharged hot rod in your head and you never even started the engine?"

I shake my head. Lyle stifles his excitement.

"Well, goddamn. You are just shit out of luck, buddy. Did you hear me? Somebody is *killing* Zeniths. Somebody in the government. Murdering us one by one. Did you know that?"

I nod.

"Jim told you, huh?" asks Lyle. "Well, he may have built the hardware, but he don't know jack about it. Not like I do. I'll show you some shit that will curl your toes, son. I am going to *wake you up.*"

I sip my water and jam the ice against my eye. Lyle is standing and pacing with excitement. Now, he stops and looks at me again, remembers what just happened.

"Listen. That Zenith makes you live your life *harder* than regular people. Walk around with your eyes open wider. You see more, hear more, understand more."

Lyle grabs my shoulders, leans in.

"There's one thing that regulars know deep down and it scares the shit out of 'em. Being an amp don't make you any less human, brother. Being an amp makes you *more human*."

He leans back on his haunches and I can see the gears spinning in his head as he scours my face for some evidence that I heard his message.

"More human," he repeats. "Don't forget it."

"Thanks," I manage to say.

Lyle nods. He stands up and stuffs his tool satchel back into the waistband of his jeans. Grabs his plastic bottle.

"No big deal. You just owe me your life is all."

Lyle stands in the doorway while an awkward second ticks by, like he's making up his mind.

"Get yourself cleaned up," he says. "I'm going to show you what amps can do."

The Wall Street Journal

Protecting the Endangered Human

By JOSEPH VAUGHN

Regardless of your ethical system, it is clear that neural implantation of this sort is a crime against humanity. I mean this statement in both the most general and most specific interpretation.

Specifically, implantation beyond natural abilities (that is, the creation of those entities known as *amps*) constitutes a crime against humanity as defined by the Rome Statute of the International Criminal Court, in that it is "part of a government policy" that "constitutes a serious attack on human dignity or grave humiliation or a degradation of one or more human beings."

These implantation techniques demolish the essence of what it means to *be* human. It is worse than assault, worse than rape, worse than torture—all odious acts that are committed against human beings and yet *leave behind* human beings. Implantation is an act against human beings that leaves behind an *amp*. It not only demolishes human dignity but precludes the victim from having the ability to *experience* human dignity.

And this creates a dilemma for the rest of society. Membership in the human species is a prerequisite for the application and enforcement of human rights. By definition, an amp is an entity not deserving of human rights. It is an entity who operates outside known ethical limits and thus threatens to topple the moral foundation that our civilization is built upon.

11

BEASTS AND GODS

"Oh, look at this sonofabitch," says Lyle, gesturing with a program rolled tight in his fist. "This guy is priceless. He's why we're not sitting in the front row."

We're just up the road from Eden in a crowded warehouse turned stadium. We sit on cramped folding chairs that surround a boxing ring wrapped in a chain-link fence. Below, the man thing Lyle is talking about strides toward the ring, bullish, strafed by glimmering spotlights. It moves with a kind of slow-motion massiveness, muscles rippling with each plodding step, meaty back gleaming wetly through the haze of cigarette smoke. Its head is lowered and eyes leveled on its adversary—the monster ignores the hundreds of mere mortals who are here to watch with wide eyes, to scream without hearing, and bet stolen money on a battle between, well, what?

Something more than men. Not gods, surely. But titans.

Lyle's got three friends with us. The ones called Stilman and Daley sit together. They glance at me when they think I'm not looking. The third man, Valentine, doesn't speak. Just watches warily. Freckles dot his face like a handful of thrown confetti. All three of these guys are as dense and muscular as Lyle is rangy. Sitting stock-still in the middle of this chaos, calm as monks.

I can't tell if they're his buddies or his bodyguards or both.

Around me, the crowd is mostly made up of pure humans, but every now and again I see an amp's temple nub, sometimes along with the gleam of an artificial limb. Everybody here seems equally guilty. I get the feeling this event isn't strictly legal.

"Is this safe?" I ask Lyle, thinking of my close call on the drive out to Eden.

The cowboy chuckles, glances at the other three men. "Relax," he says. "I'd feel sorry for any cop who tries to stop us."

Over fuzzy speakers mounted somewhere up high, the announcer dramatically bellows a name. Sounds like "Brain." In the ring, the titan opens its mouth and bellows. I can feel the roar in my chest. Lyle's friends watch the man below without blinking, their eyes doing silent arithmetic.

"What happened to that guy?" I ask, yelling over the guttural chanting of the crowd.

Lyle cups a hand to my ear and shouts back, "The Brain? He's a first-generation diagnostic amp. Totally experimental. Got it to maximize his training. Banned from the NFL for body monitoring. Guy can see his blood pressure, heart rate, perspiration. Control it. He can *turn off his pain*."

Lyle taps the nub on his own temple and mouths the words "Smart mother."

I have my doubts about that, based on what is crouched and waiting across the ring from the Brain. It's a science-lab nightmare that would make Dr. Frankenstein piss his lab coat. The other fighter is long and lean and he moves constantly, bouncing and bobbing. I have to pay close attention just to get a good look at him.

There is no mistaking it when they announce his name.

The Blade. The body amp stands maybe seven feet tall, graceful, his skin covered in geometric tattoos. He is planted solidly on custom-fabricated carbon fiber legs with painful-looking backward knee joints. His slender arms are riddled with lumpy biomechanical implants visible through his skin, snaking into his muscles and joints. When he punches the air, his gleaming bladed fists disappear into a blur.

Stilman whispers something to Daley and he nods thoughtfully. Valentine glances at them, suspicious, seemingly out of whatever loop they're in.

I wonder what kind of doctor would do this to a man. Ninety-nine percent of amps are regular people who happen to have a dot on their temple. They are mothers and fathers and children. *This* is something I've never seen or even fathomed—a harbinger of a new world, populated by new people who I can hardly recognize as human.

A bell clangs and the two monsters advance on each other. The Brain is focused, brow furrowed, like this is a life-sized chess match. He lunges and the Blade leaps away with incredible dexterity. I don't know how this big pink bull is ever going to get a hold on that bouncing, flying bundle of razor wire.

The impending carnage is too much and I look away.

People are fascinated by what they fear most. For their own reasons, both the amps and humans in the crowd seem terrified by what they see. Terrified . . . and thrilled. What's happening in the ring sounds nauseating. I hear whistling, whiplike punches and wet, blunt smacks. The Blade is silent, but the Brain emits an almost constant, subterranean groan.

I look up just in time to see it.

Like a trap springing, the Blade sends his right foot blade streaking upward. It slices through the flesh of the Brain's pectoral muscle with just a little tug. The Blade continues up and over into a back flip, a sheet of bright blood arcing away into the crowd. As the audience collectively groans, the Brain charges forward, his nearly severed pectoral muscle flopping sickeningly.

In the corner of my eye, I see Valentine nudge Lyle. Stilman and Daley shoot concerned looks at the cowboy. Lyle holds up a finger as if to say, *Wait*.

The Brain doesn't even notice his wound. His huge pink palms are outstretched and groping. He nimbly catches the Blade as he steadies himself from that devastating kick.

A torrent of blood courses down the sculpted column of the Brain's torso. Then, just as suddenly as it gushed out, the flow stops. Now the Brain has got hold of the Blade with one hand under his thigh and the other over his shin. The Blade struggles wildly, but his body is held completely off the floor.

The Brain's pink mouth opens wide and a landslide of muscle pulses up from his arms and neck; his face darkens from the titanic effort.

Prap!

The Blade's mechanical knee joint shatters with a sound like a piston being thrown from under the hood of a hot rod. Slivers of carbon fiber shrapnel perforate the immediate audience. Screams of surprised pain from the crowd up front mingle with the faceless roars of approval from behind.

Lyle nudges me in the ribs, taps his temple. Stilman and Daley have gone still again, unblinking. Valentine looks queasy. But Lyle is enjoying this, watching these fighters kill each other. These guys who aren't so different from us. I want to, but I also can't look away from the shining arena.

The poor guy who calls himself the Blade is convulsing now pretty severely. That amputated piece of technology was hard-wired to his implant; and even though it was a prosthesis, his central nervous system is convinced that his leg has just been torn off. He twists his face my way, sending a spray of sweat dancing against the lights. His lips are curled over gritted teeth, and his chest contracts reflexively as he emits short grunting shrieks.

His amp won't let him lose consciousness.

The Brain just looks interested, head cocked like a smart dog, as he systematically pops the next joint. Again, he ignores the inflamed, howling crowd as though they aren't there. Abruptly, I realize that they probably aren't. If Lyle is right, the Brain can turn down his sensitivity, dial out the screams and waving arms and flying beer bottles. The Brain is alone out there, facing down his nightmare opponent in an empty, smoky room.

It's getting hard for me to breathe. The gruesome spectacle is winding down, but the audience around me has transformed. Joined together by the blood and shrapnel, we have become a many-headed creature, leering from the darkness, shrieking and slavering and breathing smoke.

The white noise of the crowd rises to a jet turbine roar. The Brain is about to make his finishing move. As he lifts the Blade's quivering body to the sky, I turn my eyes upward to the blinding-white spotlights. For a single moment, Lyle and I stand like brothers, arms around each other's shoulders, balanced on our chairs in the haze of cigarette smoke and tangy smell of blood and burned electronics. The afterimages of the spotlights dance in my eyes and my ears ring with the screams of the spectators and fighters. And, yes, my own screams, too.

Somewhere far below I think I hear a spine snap.

Then, without warning, I slip off my chair and onto my knees and puke my dinner onto the filthy concrete.

I flinch when Lyle kicks open the side exit with one shit-stained cowboy boot. I can feel the heat and noise pulsing out from the warehouse behind him like the blast of a furnace. It's a slaughter-house in there.

Lyle steps out onto the cold concrete slab and looks me up and down. He's got a toothpick wedged in the corner of his mouth and a questioning grin. His three friends emerge quietly behind him, stepping slowly like cats. They insinuate themselves around Lyle. Swivel their eyes past me, out into the darkness.

I'm standing, leaning against a corrugated metal shed across a narrow alley, arms wrapped around my sides, shivering and trying not to show it.

"Hoo boy," chuckles Lyle. He waits for a few seconds, but I don't have anything to say. Or I don't know how to say it.

"If it makes you feel better," says Lyle, "you ain't the only one in there lost his lunch."

I wipe my mouth with my arm and spit.

"Saw an old lady barf up her nachos. All over the back of a reggie's head. Grossest thing ever."

Against my will, a grin drops into the corner of my mouth. "Is the other guy, uh, alive?"

"Sure, the Brain broke him is all. Just earning a paycheck. The big man's not a mindless piece of meat. He's got a brain like a dolphin."

I raise my eyebrows.

"One part sleeps while the other part's awake. It's why dolphins don't drown at night. Old boy can turn some parts on, other parts off. Course, that kind of diagnostic shit is first-level function for a Zenith. Baby stuff. He's smart but not smart like *us*."

Lyle puts two fingers together and twirls them, gesturing to his friends.

"You're all Zeniths," I say.

The fact drops into place, suddenly so obvious. Valentine. Stilman. Daley. In all the carnage, I didn't recognize the names right away. More Echo Squad soldiers from the police broadcast. All wanted for "questioning" in relation to terrorist activities. Like Lyle. And me.

"Stilman has the Chicago area," says Lyle. "Daley takes care of Houston. Val runs Detroit."

The men glance at me, go back to scanning the darkness. I wonder what they're looking for out there. Who or what do they think might be stalking the weedy twilight?

"Runs what?" I ask.

Lyle raises his eyebrows at me, moonlight glinting from a spray of beer on his cowboy hat.

"The amp resistance, man. Astra. We're the only legit group protecting amps nationwide."

Stilman digs an electronic cigarette out of his shirt pocket. Bites off the activator and spits it on the ground and speaks. "I got around thirty thousand amped civilians in my district. Four times that if you count their families. Maybe a thousand amp soldiers. A hundred solid ones. Out of all Chicago."

Stilman looks disgusted.

"The original Uplift program mostly hit little kids and vets," adds Lyle. "Some of the kids are old enough to fight now, but most aren't. People only want to fight if there's no other way out. So we're always looking for more soldiers."

Stilman nods, takes a drag.

Daley speaks without looking at me. "Sixty thousand in my area of Texas. Rural, like here. Spread out in clusters of a few hundred to a few thousand. Hard to protect. Keeps my soldiers on the road."

Valentine, a little taller and skinnier than the others, speaks quietly. "I've got a hundred thousand people. Probably forty thousand amps. All in the abandoned outskirts of Detroit and forgotten. Easy to protect them. Toughest job is to keep them from killing each other."

These men are generals. Now I understand what they see out there in the darkness—a war. And here I've been standing in the middle of it, oblivious, like a turtle crossing a highway.

"What about you, Lyle?" I ask.

"I got the Oklahoma City area but I'm here and there," he says cryptically. "There are four areas, including ours. Earlier this year, we lost a fifth area out east, near DC. Together we account for nearly three hundred thousand amps, most of them pretty geographically concentrated. Another couple hundred thousand are outside our areas. But there's a leader for every region. A Zenith."

"Does Lucy know?"

Lyle cocks his head at me. "Now, why would you go and ask that?"

I shrug.

"You got a thing for my sister, Gray?" he asks me, starting to grin. When I don't say anything, he keeps going. "Lucy is a good girl. Hell, she adopted that kid after his reggie parents took off and she don't even get paid for that. But she don't know much about this. And we don't tell her. Bad people are looking for us. Knowing isn't good for her safety, you understand?"

"That's why you're always traveling," I say.

Lyle shrugs.

"Gotta keep 'em guessing. And I got my tricks. Remember that cop with the frozen legs?" Lyle flashes a piece of flat black plastic tucked into the waist of his jeans, dimpling his skin. "Modified stutter gun. Low-power electromagnetic pulse generator. Neural Autofocus is built on ruggedized circuits, so it can deal with chickenshit EMP. But those cop steppers are cheap. Fucks their radios, too. Of course, sometimes it don't matter how rugged a circuit is. If a nuke drops, for instance, we'll all be brain fried before the sky gets pretty."

At this, Daley chuckles. Stilman takes a drag from his e-cigarette. Steam rolls silently out of his nostrils and gets lost in the curls of his beard. Val just blinks.

"The real question," says Lyle carefully, "is why *you're* here."

All four men have their eyes on me now. A blistering, familiar intelligence is behind each of their gazes. And a sudden glint of malice. This is a test. A pop quiz and I can feel the lies evaporating in my head, gone before they can reach my lips. So I find the truth.

"When things got bad, my dad told me to come here. Said Jim was a man I could trust. But the real reason I'm here is that a student of mine, an amp, stepped off a building. Killed herself in front of me. She was fifteen years old. Her name was Samantha. She was a genius and they said I pushed her."

Lyle picks his teeth with the toothpick. Stilman casually rests one knuckle on his hip, just above the oblong denim imprint of a pocketknife.

"But Samantha told me something just before she died. She said there was no place for us in this world. That amps don't belong. I don't believe that."

The three generals stare through me, crossed arms rising and falling on even breathing. They're waiting on Lyle.

I take a half step back without thinking about it.

Stilman nods at Lyle almost imperceptibly. Daley shakes his head, tosses the e-cig. Thumbs-up, thumbs-down.

Eyes wide, I turn to Valentine. He's watching me like a chess player, working out all the moves in his head. Finally, he bobs his head once, quick, then goes back to watching the empty lot.

"Good enough," says Lyle, and all the men relax

I suspect that Valentine has just saved my life. I exhale.

The cowboy leans against the warehouse and puts a knee up. He takes off his hat and wipes a forearm over his sweat-soaked forehead. Pushes his hat hair up out of his face. The generals relax slightly.

"That girl was smart," he says. "And she was right. The world we knew ended and nobody told us. The world we belong to doesn't exist yet because we haven't *created* it. Thirteen Zeniths were made, including you, Gray, but only the five of us are left now because the government is afraid of the new world that's coming. But what they don't know is that they can't stop us. We're already so close to the end."

"Who is hunting Zeniths?" I ask.

Nobody says anything. For all their measured cool, these former soldiers don't have any idea. They're clueless.

With the toe of my shoe, I scratch a symbol on the dirty pavement. It's the icon I saw on the page of Joe Vaughn's speech. The one tattooed on Billy.

EM.

"Elysium," I say.

Stilman and Daley glance at the dirt, recognition in their eyes.

"Do you know what this means?" I ask.

"Where did you see that?" asks Valentine.

"Everywhere," I say.

The men glance at Lyle. Some silent inscrutable communication is taking place.

"We think it's some kind of elite Pure Pride group," says Daley. "Close associates of Senator Joseph Vaughn. We've found members all over the nation. Most are law enforcement or security."

"Soldiers," I say. "The ones hunting Zeniths?"

"Maybe," says Valentine. "We don't know for sure."

I feel the night pressing in. The warm breeze rustles the grass out there in the darkness and every half-glimpsed movement makes me want to bolt.

"Tell me how to activate my Zenith," I say.

Lyle grins at his friends. An I-told-you-so grin.

"Here we go, then."

He holds up three fingers on his right hand, thumb and pinky touching. "Default configuration. Think of the device," he says. "Feel that tickle in your head. Concentrate on that, while you do this." Then he counts down quickly, dropping his fingers to rest on the back of his thumb. *Three, two, one.* He tucks his fingers underneath, making a tight fist.

"Simple as that," he says. "Think of the Zenith and count down with your right hand. You don't picture the Zenith, it won't activate. And if your hand ain't working, just *think* about moving your fingers. It'll be enough."

"What? In case someone cuts off my arm?" I joke.

"Right," he says. "There are five levels. You got to consent to each one. After you drop a level, that's how deep you go from then on. Every time."

Lyle looks me up and down. "You never been in the military."

"No," I say.

"Don't matter. The Zenith knows stuff. It can tell your body what to do. How to stay alive in bad situations. How to escape. And how to kill, if you let it."

The word orbits there for a few seconds: *kill.*

"How do I turn it off?" I ask.

"That's the hard part, ain't it?" Lyle says. "What goes down don't necessarily come back up. You got to focus. Concentrate on yourself, on your actions. Force the amp to give back control. It ain't always easy. But you'll figure it out."

Lyle extends his hand, palm open.

After a second, I shake it gamely. He pulls me in and claps me on the shoulder. "You never activated that Zenith, so you got no clue what you're capable of. But you'll find out, Gray. And we'll see what kind of man you are pretty damn fast."

"And what kind are you?" I ask. Valentine bites off a chuckle.

"Me?" asks Lyle. "I'm a mystery man. Full of surprises. For one, you really think I brought you here just to watch these meatheads tear each other up?" Lyle looks up at the sky, finds the moon, and squints at it. "Come on," he says. "Should be about time."

Around the side of the shed, a rectangle of light splays out onto the brushed concrete. Lyle's teeth shine in the moonlight. He puts a finger to his lips and we creep.

Just outside the door, Lyle straightens his shirt and cocks his hat back on his head. Stilman, Daley, and Valentine form up outside the door, turn their backs to it. Lyle plucks the toothpick out of his mouth, looks at it, then crams it back in. He walks into the light.

I start to follow him but freeze up when I see what's inside the toolshed.

Shirtless and massive, the Brain sits on a rolling stool. Steam rises from his wet skin. He stares expressionless at the rusted tools hanging from the wall while a skinny doctor in a dirt-stained lab coat methodically sews up his torn pectoral muscle. The hunk of meat flaps from the Brain's chest as the doctor works, but the man might as well be a statue. A big, meaty statue.

The Brain's deep-set green eyes flicker over to us as Lyle swaggers inside.

"Hey there," says Lyle. "You don't know me but—"

"I don't want any," says the Brain. His voice has the low hollow strain of a big mammal. A bull or an elephant.

"That's good, because I'm not here to sell you nothing," says Lyle.

"I'm not for sale, either," says the Brain.

"Settle down, now," says Lyle, hands out.

With a menacing scowl, the Brain starts to rise. The doctor steps back, impatient for Lyle to get beaten down so he can get back to work. Lyle watches the mountain of a man carefully, his boots scratching lightly on the concrete as he backs out of reach. For an elastic second Lyle actually seems scared, and then something locks into place behind his eyes.

"Ho there, partner. Just came to talk. I was a Son of Silence like yourself," says Lyle.

The Brain stops rising. "What chapter?"

"Northside Dirty White Boys," says Lyle.

"Mad Dog set?" says the Brain.

Lyle pauses, thrown. Then he takes the toothpick out of his mouth and points it at the Brain. "Dragon set, you redneck fuck," he says.

The Brain eases back down. The doctor goes back to stitching him up in precise lunges with a spool of black thread that looks more like clothesline rope.

"Right," says the Brain. "What do you want?"

"Street ain't the place for men like us. Running drugs, it's for peons. And look at you. Cops see you coming a mile away. You and me were meant for something bigger. What I want is to invite you to be part of another brotherhood. A group of people that you can *relate* to."

Lyle takes off his hat and pushes a lank piece of hair away from his forehead, revealing the nub of plastic on his temple. The Brain's small eyes flick between Lyle's nub and my own. I can almost hear his thoughts: Does this really make us brothers? Is there finally someone I can trust?

The cowboy is here to recruit muscle—the sort of muscle that doesn't even exist outside of amp circles. And for some reason, he also wanted me to see *this*. The outer limits of human amplification.

"You ought to come out and see us at Eden," Lyle urges. "Hang out. Be yourself for a little while. Nobody there to judge, you know it?"

Unconsciously, the Brain reaches up to his own bald head and touches the nub there. As his great arm rises, I catch a glimpse of something on the back of it—a peach-colored slick of mottled scar tissue. Burned skin. It's a removed tattoo.

Faint, very faint, I catch sight of an outline that could be a dragon head. Some kind of gang insignia that's been burned off the back of the Brain's arm.

Clever cowboy.

The relic of the tattoo disappears into a fold of muscle as the

Brain sends his massive arm out like a crane, hand extended. Lyle pops his hat back on and bounces forward to shake it, his nimble fingers disappearing into that massive paw.

The Brain's fist closes tight and he yanks Lyle forward. The Brain frowns, small eyes trained on Lyle's forearm. A phrase is tattooed there. Tight black capital letters: *AD ASTRA CRUENTUS*.

"What's it mean?" asks the Brain.

Lyle flashes a grin, impenetrable as ever. "It means we're going to the stars together, stained in the blood of our enemies."

ARMY RESEARCH LABORATORY (ARL)

White Sands Missile Range, NM 88002-5513

Impact of Experimental Zenith-Class Neural Autofocus on Battlefield Situational Awareness

ARL—TR—6445

Reaction Time (Excerpt)

Decreasing the time course of mental operations in the human nervous system confers wide-ranging advantages, particularly for amplifying situational awareness. Previous research gauges average human reaction time to visual stimulus at approximately 60 milliseconds. This is widely recognized as a hard limit.

Brain implants, however, allow us to drastically increase the speed of reaction time for complex behavior involving multiple brain systems (sensory, cognitive, and motor). Completely bypassing input from higher brain regions, implants may autonomously intercept and monitor sensory information and direct action at the speed of reflex.

High-level behaviors such as situational awareness, evasion, and even combat maneuvers can be turned over to the implant. In the following study, we demonstrate that implanted test subjects become capable of acting in complex real-world situations with hard limit spinal reaction times—approximately twice as fast as nonimplanted control subjects.

12
DARK PLACES

As I finish shaving the next morning, I see myself in the mirror and I can't help but marvel at how *normal* I look. Last night, I saw what implants can do to a person. Saw what people can become when they let the technology inside.

And for the first time, I understand why Priders are scared: we've gone and become our tools.

In the distance, I hear the puttering of Jim's pickup truck. Like most people around here, he's got an old manual drive. Can't afford the safety of an autonomous car. It makes a hell of a racket as he pulls up outside.

I can't help thinking that the men in those freak fights are a type of person that has never existed before. Clawing each other to pieces in a ring lit up like an operating theater, they looked like newborn creatures exposed under the spotlights, blind and mewling, skin glistening. New breeds of men that have Joseph Vaughn and his Priders scared crazy, foaming at the mouth.

The unblinking generals—Valentine, Daley, and Stilman—went home to their own cities last night. Of all the new breeds, I think the Priders should fear them first. Zeniths, like me.

And yet a normal-looking former teacher is staring back at me in the mirror.

Knock, knock, knock.

The flimsy bathroom wall shudders.

"What happened to the front door?" asks Jim, voice muffled.

I step into the dim hallway with a towel around my waist, squeezing the ratty carpet between my toes. Jim waits for me, a serious expression hiding in the wrinkles of his face. It looks like he hasn't slept since he left.

"I met Lyle Crosby," I say. "I'm in. If I want to be."

"He know about your Zenith?" asks Jim.

"He knows. It's why he's interested," I say. "He's building an army."

Jim rubs his eyes with the balls of his thumbs. "Yeah."

"Claims he's the only thing protecting amps," I say.

Jim stands in the hallway, breathing steadily and slowly. "Hell, he may be right, but it's already gone too far. He's going to give the reggies a reason to start a war. Make all Vaughn's crazy predictions come true."

Someone bangs on the front door. We both ignore it. I push past Jim into my bedroom. Throw on some clothes. Jim stands in the doorway, face shadowed.

"Watch him, Owen. Learn what you can. But for God's sake, be careful," he says. "The rest of the world is waiting to come down on us like a tidal wave. Not just Eden. All the amps. Half a million innocent people."

The banging isn't stopping. Light, repetitive taps that shake the screen door. Again and again.

"Lyle wants me to turn it on, Jim," I say.

"Then you need to know everything," says Jim, sighing. "After activation, you'll enter a consent mode. Yes or no. You might hear a voice or see it in your mind's eye."

Bang, bang, bang.

"What does it *do*?" I ask.

"Autonomic delegation," says Jim. "Your body acts and reacts faster than you can think. Action without thought. Your true self making the calls. The deeper you go, the harder it is to turn it off. And once you go down a level, you'll always go that deep. No coming back. It can take you to dark places."

The banging stops.

"It'll turn me into a weapon," I say, my voice suddenly loud.

"All you got to do is curl your hands into fists and you turn into a weapon," says Jim. "Your body is just another tool. This technology changes nothing; it only amplifies. You decide how to use your tools. Whether to do good or evil."

There's a scratch on my bedroom window as someone hoists his face to the crack. "Owen," says a familiar high-pitched voice. "It's Nick. Lyle sent me. C'mon, you gotta come see this!"

Nick leads the way, stubby arms swinging. He's so little to be in the middle of this. Just a baby on the railroad tracks. Once we're out of earshot of the trailer, I put a hand on his shoulder. Slow him down so we can talk.

"Nick," I ask, "has Lucy said anything . . ."

"About you yelling at her?" he asks.

I blink, surprised. I didn't know it was that loud.

"Nope," he says. "But you should apologize."

"I am sorry for that. And I will. But I meant . . . about Lyle," I say. "Is something going to happen around here? Something big?"

Nick shrugs. "Who knows? He's always telling her to buy a gun. But the guy is weird. You can ask him yourself here in a second."

As we approach Lyle's trailers, I see a crowd of about a dozen of his followers loitering around. They're peeking in the dusty windows of a rotten, spray-painted trailer. I recognize some, but they give me a lot of space. I've got Lyle's aura on me now—it demands respect, and fear.

"This is messed up, man," says Nick, breathless.

"Go home," I say. "I'll tell you about it later. Go on."

Noncommittal, Nick backs away into the crowd of legs. The others step away from me, forming a ragged patch of space. I knock on the waterlogged front door. Instantly, the hinges squeal and the door parts. In a stripe of light, an eye appears.

"Get your ass in here, brainy smurf," whispers Lyle. Turning sideways, I squeeze in through the door. Lyle shoves it closed behind me.

My stomach sinks when I see what's going on.

In the dim, damp interior of the trailer, I see two teenage boys. Strapped to plastic lawn chairs with lots of duct tape. Not struggling. And they don't look like they have implants. They look like those kids from the field, probably sixteen or seventeen.

God only knows what Lyle is doing here.

"Thanks for coming, doctor," says Lyle. "These boys are just about ready for their implants."

My mouth pops open audibly.

Lyle puts an arm around my shoulder. "Don't worry about your tools, doc. Your nurse is bringing them. Should be here any second."

The two strapped-in teenagers are watching me, a strange mix of fear and anticipation on their faces. I know I should hate these little bastards for what they did to me, but they look so young and stupid sitting there. A couple of dumb kids who just fell into a shark tank and don't even know it.

"What?" is all I can get out.

"Besides," continues Lyle, "before you get started operating, we've got to make sure and get permission from these young men. Ain't that right, boys?"

"Y-yes, sir," they both say.

"Now, where do y'all live?"

The bigger one speaks up. "Just across the field there, sir."

"And why exactly are you here?"

"To see about getting an implant, sir."

"We wanna get amped," says the other one.

Lyle looks over at me, smiling. Keeps on questioning the kids, watching my reaction to their words. "And why is that? Why do y'all wanna get amped?"

"Cause we heard you could do stuff. Fighting type of stuff."

"Like it makes you faster and smarter and stuff," chimes in the sidekick.

"And stuff," repeats Lyle. "Your parents know you're here?"

The kids glance at each other. Try to have a conversation with their eyes. Fail at it. The big blond one rolls his eyes as the smaller one admits, "No, sir."

"That's fine. We don't care about that. Y'all two are young men. You can make your own decisions. If you want to get an implant put in your noggin so that you can get smarter and stronger *and stuff* . . . why, that's your call."

The kids smile hesitantly at each other as Lyle continues. "*Men* fight. Think about the Zulu War. Africa. 1879. A few hundred British troops used Gatling guns to mow down a horde of over two thousand enemy soldiers. Not a single British casualty. There were gods on the battlefield that day. When we're done with you, you'll be the same as them."

"The British?" asks the small kid.

Lyle throws his head back and cackles. It reminds me of the first day I saw him, shirtless in the street and hurting people. A manic energy is building inside him as he speaks. "No, you little dumbass. The *Gatling guns*. A new standard. Human beings, perfected by our own technology. Only to be wielded by the chosen few. Not by the sheep but by those who are *better*. Those who are willing to make it to the stars through blood."

"Oh," says the kid.

The teenagers are glancing at each other now. Panic starting to build. Lyle keeps going. My teacher instincts are kicking in, and now I'm thinking about how to get the two of them out of here.

"I won't lie and say the procedure isn't painful, because it is. Gonna be a lot of bleeding. Lot of drilling and sawing. When it's over, y'all gonna have a big old mark right here."

Lyle taps the dot on his temple.

"Everybody is going to know exactly what you are. Only they won't know what you're capable of. Not at first."

The smaller kid is starting to squirm under his duct tape. His breath is coming in quick shallow gasps. It's pathetic and I don't want to see Lyle torture them anymore.

"So you see, guys," I interrupt, "you don't want to do this. Why don't you just go back home and forget about it?"

Shaking my head at Lyle, I kneel next to the blond kid's chair. Start ripping off the duct tape.

"C'mon, what's the matter?" asks Lyle, throwing his arms out.

"Well," squeaks the small one. "Can we get it so that . . . I mean, we can't have anybody know."

"Whatcha talking about? Spit it out, kid," says Lyle.

The big one blurts, "Can you do it without the maintenance nub? On the temple? Otherwise our folks'll find out. We'll get in trouble. You understand, right? I mean, we don't wanna be *amps*."

That word "amp" just seems to lie there like a dog turd on the carpet. I urge my fingers to move faster on the duct tape. These kids are brainless and Lyle is unpredictable and the whole combination is going to explode any second.

Lyle chuckles harshly. "Amps, huh. We sure wouldn't want that. Talk about wanting your cake and eating it, too. Ain't that right, doctor?"

"Meaning no disrespect, sir," says the blond one.

"No can do, little amigo," says Lyle. "No nub means no fixing the implant. Have to cut your head open every time we need to adjust the contacts. Besides, you gotta coat that thing with bio-gel. Otherwise the inside of your brain scabs up until the whole thing shuts down. Lights out."

A knock comes from the flimsy door, hard enough to shift the walls of the whole moldy trailer. I hear the wet wood splintering.

"That must be our nurse," says Lyle.

He dances across the room and yanks the door completely open. At first, I think it's dark outside. Then I realize the Brain is standing in the doorway, huge and slump shouldered. Both the kids blink in fear, trying to grasp the size of this human being.

I finish freeing up the blond kid. Move on to the smaller kid. Curious faces are gathering in the clouded window.

The Brain steps inside, plywood floor groaning under his weight. He says nothing. Leans forward to avoid brushing his bald head against the mold blooming on the ceiling. In this enclosed space, the sound of his breathing is epic. It's like being locked up in a room with a prehistoric animal.

The kid in front of me starts squirming harder.

Lyle shakes his head at me. "Wanna do good cop, bad cop, huh?" He holds up three fingers on his right hand, preparing to activate his Zenith. *Three.* Smiles at me, lowers a finger. "All right then."

Two.

"No, Lyle," I say. "Why?"

One.

"We're sorry," sputters the younger one, wriggling to get his hands free. "It was his idea. He dared me to come."

Zero.

Lyle's eyes go hard and mechanical. Like somebody blew out the candle in a jack-o'-lantern. Face gone slack, he spits out his words in a torrent. "Did you little reggies think you could just show up here and we'd welcome you in? Make you one of us?"

And then Lyle's face is inches from the blond kid. I blinked and while my eyelids met, Lyle *moved*. I keep tearing at the duct tape, frantic now.

"You *can't* be one of us," says Lyle. "You haven't got the grit. Your hearts are full of fear. You dumb fuckers belong in that field, holding on to a spotlight like it was your dick. Afraid of the dark and for good reason. You *better* keep that spotlight burning bright. Because there's something out there in the dark. Something dangerous. Not fully human."

Lyle smiles and his canines flash. There's that dullness again in his eyes, like he's acting or watching this unfold on television.

I'm done. The kids are both free.

The smaller one looks over my shoulder at the window. I follow his gaze and see Nick's face. He's got the Rubik's cube in one hand and the windowsill in the other. A moist Band-Aid still clings to his forehead. No emotion on his face. I can't tell if he's happy to see these bullies punished.

"Enough," I say. "C'mon, Lyle."

I reach for Lyle's shoulder, but he isn't there. Now he's standing in the middle of the room. The way he moves is sickening, fast.

The little kid's lips are shaking. "I'm sorry about Gunnin' Billy," he says to me. "He told us to watch the field."

The bigger kid shoves him, and the little guy shuts up.

Only now do I realize my opportunity.

"Billy?" I ask. "His tattoo. What does it mean?"

No response.

"Answer me," I say, "and I'll make him stop."

Blurry faces crowd the window. Lyle doesn't look, but I know he sees them. He's putting on a show for those gathered outside.

Lyle breathes in hard through his nose, savoring the fear. "It's me out there in the dark, boys. Me and mine. And we're not human. Not like you. We're better than human. Better than you." Lyle taps his temple. "Scared little rabbits. I can feel your hearts all aflutter. I can make them freeze up just by thinking about it."

The blond kid has started shaking. The trailer is warm and moist as the inside of a fresh-cooked biscuit, but he's got his sun-burned arms wrapped around his torso and his elbows are bouncing around like he's riding in the back of a pickup truck.

Lyle curls two fingers back and makes his right hand into the shape of a gun. He steps back, extends his arm all the way, and lowers it. Points directly at the middle of the blond kid's heaving chest.

"What's the symbol mean, kid?" I ask. "Elysium? The *EM*? What?"

I'm a ghost to Lyle, invisible. Not part of whatever show is playing in his mind.

"Ready to die, kid?" he asks. "The United States Army gave me this power. They did this to me. Took away my life and made me good for one thing: killing."

The little one has started crying. Eyes closed, hands unbound but down at his sides anyway. Helpless in the shadow of the Brain. "It's a secret club," he blubbers. "They call it Elysium. Billy and them have special meetings and stuff. Only the ones with the tattoo get in. I don't know nothing else."

"Shut up!" shouts the big kid.

Eyes half lidded, Lyle presses his fingers into the big blond kid's chest. "You are going to die today," he says.

The blond kid whimpers, shaking uncontrollably now. "Please," he's trying to say in a strained whisper, "please, no."

"Who's in charge of Elysium?" I ask.

"Vaughn," whispers the blond kid. "Billy knows him. He's the boss. The spotlighters are out there because he said so. Please."

Lyle lifts his hand. Then he abruptly drops it, presses his fingers into the kid's chest. The kid takes a deep breath and holds it.

"Boom!" shouts Lyle, and bursts into a hyena cackle.

The blond kid shrieks. Keeps shrieking. Goes rigid and slides off the chair onto the soggy floor. Scrabbling and screaming. Eyes open but blind. His little friend slumps, sobbing in his chair.

All of it against the backdrop of Lyle's wild laughter. And under the gaze of the Brain. The giant man stands motionless save his breathing, a placid boulder.

I try to pull the blond kid up off the ground, but he's lost his mind. Grunts and shrieks. Lyle leans over and slaps the kid across the face. He keeps screaming, so Lyle tries to slap him again.

I grab Lyle's bicep, pull him back. It takes all my strength. "Brain," I say, putting Lyle into a full-on bear hug. "Dump them in the field. Don't hurt 'em."

The Brain says nothing, glances at Lyle. I'm not a general like the other Zeniths: Stilman, Daley, Valentine. But the cowboy has gone vacant, so the Brain obeys me. Grabs both the kids by the back of their shirts, one in each hand, and drags them out the front door. Two sacks of squirming meat wrapped in T-shirts.

I let go of Lyle and he drops to the floor. Scoots back to lean against the wall. He rests a tattoo-stained arm across one knee. His forehead wrinkles as he tries to come out of it. His limbs quiver and he grimaces, shakes his head. I start to breathe normally again. I could puke, but damned if I'm going to lose it in front of Lyle. Not ever again.

"What the hell was that?" I ask him.

Lyle wipes his face with his sleeve. He stands up and peeks out the window. Grins, daylight flashing from his shark eyes.

"If you're gonna be useful, I needed you to see," he says. "You got to know how bad they want what we got."

Thousands Attend Pure Pride Counterprotest

PHOENIX—Doctors, libertarians, technology workers, and pro-choice advocates attended a huge statehouse rally Thursday, saying that leaders nationwide had gone too far in pushing an agenda opponents consider an attack on the American citizen's right to control his or her own body.

State police said more than 8,000 people gathered outside the capitol building at the rally's peak, making it the largest at the Arizona capitol in years. Hundreds of supporters for the Pure Human Citizen's Council also attended, separated by a strip of parking lot but with both sides trading insults. An atmosphere of hostility permeated the event. Local police monitored both groups, intent on preventing violence.

Jared Cohen, head of the Free Body Liberty Group, delivered a stirring speech under heavy security, telling a cheering crowd of thousands that "America is built on a foundation of freedom, and that includes the freedom to choose what technology we put into our bodies."

Senator Joseph Vaughn, president of the Pure Human Citizen's Council, claimed the FBLG had gone too far and that, if left unchecked, implantable technology could destroy the fabric of society. "They are calling for a war on humanity. And this is a battle that we must win, if not for ourselves, then for our children and our children's children."

13
NO LIMITS

Jim leans forward in his squeaky La-Z-Boy recliner, the fabric on its arms shined to a high gloss by his knobby elbows. The chair looks like a stray dog covered in burn wounds, but Jim is oblivious, blue eyes bright.

"I told ya, kid," he says. "It's not too late."

It's right there on the tube, on the evening news. The Free Body Liberty Group out of Arizona. The FBLG is protesting at the Arizona State Capitol. Behind a chattering newscaster, I can see the angel of justice perched on the roof of the capitol building, her sword raised. The crowd there is loud and proud and standing up for an American's right to decide just exactly what to do with his or her own damn body.

Maybe Samantha was wrong.

Jim is cracking a smile at me from across the living room, gray stubble collapsing into mirthful wrinkles. He sits at attention like an exclamation point in the wood-paneled living room. A dust-coated deer head stares down at us from its mount on the wall. Head lowered and horns poised, challenging infinity with black eyes.

"There's still goodness in people," muses Jim, watching the television. "Take that, Vaughn, you *dickhead*."

I'm grinning back at Jim. Trying to enjoy this moment—the first time we've seen an organized group of people holding up the amp end of the dialogue.

"This is how it has to happen," says Jim. "The regular folks have to fix things. We can't force them into it."

These are vanilla humans standing up for their family and friends. Most of the temples on the television are bare. A minority but finally vocal. I can't help thinking that if those were amps standing on the capitol steps, well, it would be a different scene.

Somehow, Jim hears it coming first. Moaning floats through the window, too shocked to be crying anymore. Without a word, Jim pries himself out of his La-Z-Boy and hauls ass into his bedroom.

I'm half out of my seat when the front door bursts open. Lucy staggers inside, carrying Nick in both arms. The kid falls onto the couch.

There's a rivulet of blood coming from his temple.

"What happened?" I gasp.

"Spotlighters," says Lucy. "Must have got him crossing the field."

Nick moans again, but I can't make out the words. Something is different about him. Something I can't quite place . . .

His maintenance port is gone.

That little nub stripped right off his face. The skin around it is raw and puffy and bleeding.

I can't believe he is still conscious.

Lucy looks over, and I turn to see Jim framed in the weak hallway light. He's got his worn old doctor's bag pinned under a skinny bicep.

"Get a wet rag from the kitchen, Owen," Jim says.

The old man is all business, squatting by the couch next to Nick. He glances up to Lucy and starts to say something, stops, lower lip quivering. Sets his jaw and starts again.

"Can he still see?" Jim asks Lucy.

It's a simple, short question. But after he asks it, the old man swallows a lump of emotion. Forces it down past his Adam's apple and into his paunchy stomach. Down there, the despair can chew him up slow instead of consuming him all at once.

"I don't know," says Lucy. "He found his way home. But they tore it out."

"Christ," he says. "I'm not sure what we can do without the port."

I drop a wet dishrag into Jim's hand and he dabs at Nick's temple. Scrubs the dirt away, leaving pink, inflamed skin. The rag comes away filthy and dark with blood. But the boy starts to stir. His eyes open and rotate back and forth.

"Nick," says Jim, waving at his face, "what do you see?"

Nick turns and squints up at his adoptive mother. Doesn't say anything. His thin lips press together in a white line, and he closes his eyes again and a new wave of tears streams down his face.

"Baby, you're gonna be fine. You'll be okay," says Lucy, stroking his cheek with one hand and methodically wiping tears from her eyes with the other.

"You're doing great, Nick," I say.

Jim strokes Nick's head, pushes wet strands of hair out of his confused face. A goose egg is growing on his forehead, cratered by a small red gash. Turning dark fast.

Lucy and Jim look at each other. A question is in the set of her lips, in the concerned wrinkle of her forehead. She leaves it unspoken.

"Best case it's just a concussion," Jim says. "I'm going to need to get a look at what's left of the maintenance nub to find out. Seems okay for now. The implant itself is still in there. Port could have come out clean at the connector. But you know, worst case, if it came out rough . . ."

Lucy says what Jim can't.

"Brain damage."

On the television across the room, a fat sweaty guy with a sign is yelling. Face turning red. Other Free Body protesters surround him, screaming mouths on flushed faces. The yeller's voice has gone hoarse and he barks the same two words again and again like a piece of broken machinery.

"No limits!" he is shouting. "No limits!"

"Turn that shit off," snarls Jim, "and get me some light."

I snap the television off. The front door is still open, a yawning mouth leading to a warm dark throat outside. The stars didn't come out tonight and the crickets are singing about it in the shadowed grass.

On the couch, Nick's small eyes are wide open and scared and sad.

Jim yells for light again. I trot to the kitchen table and grab a cheap desk lamp off a stack of old newspapers. Pens from forgotten companies and keys to long-junked cars spatter to the floor. I plug the lamp in next to the couch and hold it as high as the short electric cord lets me.

Jim's got a thumb hooked under Nick's eyelid, pulling down the skin. The lamp light shines down weakly and Nick's pupil retreats, collapsing to a black decimal point. The outline of the retinal implant floats there, rudely visible. The shape of it is square and angular and so clearly man-made compared to the natural mottled brown of his eyes.

"What's your name, son?" Jim asks.

Nick's eyes slowly snap to attention, focusing on Jim's face. The old man gently cradles the boy's head. Nick blinks up at him. Moves his lips into the shape to make words.

"Nick," he says, voice slurring. The boy turns and sees Lucy. "Momma?" he asks.

"I'm here, honey. Where did they hurt you?" asks Lucy.

Nick raises one fist and taps the side of his head. His wrist is bent, fingers curled up in a way that's not good. Jim winces, tries to hide his reaction.

"Nowhere else?"

Nick shakes his head. Drops his fist.

"Who did this?"

Nick just looks up at Lucy. Eyes wide and brown. No response. The boy's lips start to move, quivering. Again, nothing comes out. The boy squeezes his eyes closed and shakes his head, tears slithering onto the couch cushions. He reaches up and wipes his eyes with one hand that's still curled into a fist.

Like a baby.

Jim slumps onto his haunches. Lucy puts the back of her hand against her mouth. I lose concentration and the lamp doglegs. I feel Lucy's gentle fingers on my spine and I reach behind me and take her hand. We don't look at each other, just feel the warmth of each other's hands.

I don't know if Nick has got brain damage, but this isn't good and he's so *young*. I can't even imagine it. Some reggie tried to tear the fucking amp right out of his head.

Maybe I should have let Lyle beat the shit out of those reggie kids.

Jim stops poking around and looks up, works the hunch out of his shoulders. There is relief on his face. "Looks like the maintenance nub came off clean. Implant is fine in there. I think he'll be okay. But he's gonna have to rest until we can find a replacement port," says Jim. "Home is fine. Hospital won't work on this anyway."

"Whoever did this is outside right now," I say, "laughing about it."

"Nothing to be done," says Jim.

The way the words catch in his throat makes me feel suddenly small. I have a vision of our trailer from high above. A tiny cube of warmth, jaundiced light spilling out the windows onto dead grass. Trailer sitting here like a rotten shipwreck, alone and long forgotten on the abyssal plain of the ocean floor.

Nick puts his fist on his chest. I reach over and take his fingers in mine. Our eyes connect, and he opens his hand. As his fingers uncurl, something small and yellowish and electronic falls onto his chest.

His missing maintenance nub.

"Good job, Nick," I whisper. "Smart boy."

Jim eagerly pulls out a pair of surgical tweezers. Plucks the device off Nick's gently rising chest. The old man holds it up to the light and inspects it, squinting.

"Can you put it back in?" I ask.

"Need to sterilize it. But not yet. Drag that old TV over here," Jim says, grunting as he stands up.

"Why?"

Jim holds up the implant. "Because if Nick can't tell us what happened, why, we'll just have to watch for ourselves."

In a ditch, not far from here, little Nick is dragging himself up on bloody knees. Running as fast as he can. In a streaking flash he glances over his shoulder. A group of men are giving chase. They wear grins like Halloween masks. Mouths soundlessly coned into hooting O shapes. Lips peeling back and eyes glittering from flashlights, apelike and predatory.

We sit in the living room and watch the world through Nick's eyes. The retinal chip floating in Nick's eyeball never stopped recording. It sent images to his implant where the information was cached on a tiny hard drive. It only kept about twenty minutes, up until the moment it was disconnected. Now that the nub is plugged into the right receiver, we bear witness.

No sounds. Just a vision of violence.

Nick falls again, lands in the rough caress of his own shadow. Digs his torn fingernails through dead bristles, clawing forward. A spotlight is aimed at his back. Before him, his lunging silhouette slithers through spiny stalks of brown grass.

The spotlighters caught Nick coming into the field after dark. We're free to come and go during the day—nobody has tried to set up roadblocks, yet. But it's different at night. Some of the other trailer park kids must have thrown Nick's Rubik's cube over the fence. He was cautious, searching for it. He saw the spotlighters, watched them from a distance. But he got too close. The field was too dangerous after sunset.

Full of sharks. Sharks in lawn chairs. Cheap hollow-tubed aluminum chairs sitting cockeyed in the field. Shotguns leaning against them. Empty silver beer cans littering the grass like dead fish. A scene bathed from above in Rapturously bright light, inky shadows rooting through the dirt and stalks of grass. Like a little fake moon landing being staged every night here in our field.

The electric generator for the spotlights is on two wheels with a muddy trailer hitch jutting out. Looks like it used to be that trademark John Deere green color, but now it's rusted and caked with sooty exhaust from spending long nights keeping an eye on us. It supports a leaning aluminum tower about twelve feet tall, sprouting four glowing spotlights like metal flowers.

To his credit, Nick tried to stick to the shadows. Stepped carefully. Kept an eye on the pool of light and scanned the grass for that familiar cube shape. He stayed in the darkness, but it wasn't enough.

A handheld spotlight hits him and he freezes. Puts his palm out against the light and squints. All he can see is that acid burn of brightness from the dark. Looks like somebody says something to him, because he turns and starts to move away fast. Toward home and safety.

He doesn't make it far.

Flashlights strafe back and forth across the grass. Nick is running now. His sneakers slash through shadow and light. The last thing I can make out clearly is Nick looking toward Eden. One small trailer with warm light spilling out. Home. He twists violently as someone grabs him from behind. A hairy forearm closes over his chest and then confusion. The image is blurred by hair and dirt and flashlight streaks, and then finally, tears.

Our world here is getting smaller every day.

I can feel the vise closing in. Those men in the fields. And an army of them beyond the field. A nation of reggies locked arm in arm and taking one step closer to us every night. Closing ranks around us and all the other Uplift sites, compressing our crowded neighborhoods into ghettos.

Lucy squeezes my hand tight but never turns away from the screen. Her teeth are clenched but she doesn't look scared. She just looks sad.

"Animals," she says, "a bunch of animals."

"We've got to do something," I say. "Go out there."

"What then?" asks Jim. "Start shooting? Nothing to be done except sit tight. The kid will be okay. Things will go back to normal."

"How can you believe that?" I ask.

"Because most people are good," says Jim. "But not when they're afraid."

I glare out the open front door toward the field. The spotlighters are still out there. Getting drunk. Hooting and hollering. Raking their lights over our trailers. I'd love to go out there and seek retribution. I know how to activate my Zenith. But I have no idea what I'm capable of.

"The assholes who did this don't seem afraid," I say.

"They're terrified. Waiting for an excuse to start shooting. If we set one angry foot in that field, it won't end out there. It will end here, in Eden. We have to swallow this. Nick is safe. It's a small price to pay."

"It's a price we shouldn't have to pay."

Jim kicks the coffee table, shouts. "We're *lucky* to pay it! Because Joseph Vaughn will take *any excuse*. Any excuse, Owen.

His Priders would love to come in here tonight and shoot us down like dogs. We are sitting on gasoline-drenched kindling from sea to shining sea. You want to be the match that lights the fire?"

I blink at Jim, surprised. His sudden rush of anger has sapped the venom from my veins.

"Owen," says Lucy, softly, "we have a bigger problem."

A wiry hand clamps onto my shoulder from behind. Gently, I'm shoved out of the doorway. A skinny cowboy walks past me and into the trailer, boots clomping on the linoleum. He smells like gasoline and beer.

"My nephew all right?" asks Lyle, impassive.

"He'll be fine," says Jim, moving to block Lyle's sight of Nick's temple. He's too late.

"Spotlighters did that?"

Jim says nothing. None of us do.

"You with me, Gray?"

"We can't go into that field. Not tonight."

"Okay then," he says and turns on his heel. He strides out the door and into the warm night. Just the ghost smell of gasoline left behind. Gone so fast it's like he wasn't even here.

Except we all know where he's going.

Police Use Tear Gas on Pro-Amp Protesters

Are you there? Share your photos and videos.

Last Updated 7:48 p.m. Riot police in downtown Phoenix have fired canisters of tear gas at protesters, dispersing the crowd of thousands after it refused to move off the steps of the state capitol building.

Phoenix police explained their use of tear gas in a statement:

> "Our police officers deployed a limited amount of tear gas according to established protocol to clear a small area of protesters who had turned violent. The protesters were throwing objects at police officers, including rocks, firecrackers, paint, glass bottles, and paving stones. In addition, protesters were destroying public property on the capitol grounds."

Last Updated 10:43 p.m. In a similar show of force, hundreds of officers in Chicago have coordinated an operation to clear out a group of about 1,000 demonstrators who refused to vacate Lincoln Park. At least 200 people connected to the Free Body Liberty Group were arrested, and small amounts of tear gas were used before the camps were dismantled, The Chicago Tribune reported.

"The city is committed to protecting free speech rights, but our duty to protect the safety of our officers and the public welfare of our citizens must always come first," Chicago police said in a statement.

14
SPOTLIGHTER

Thirty seconds later I'm trotting down the empty main street of Eden, listening to my own whistling breath, and I can't help but picture it: the end of Lyle's sad, furious life. Inescapable as the sunset.

The skinny cowboy strides into that dry field, talking about war and new worlds and retribution. Takes a shotgun spray to the belly. Goes down cackling and firing his pistol, guts in the grass. Nails one or two of those beer-soaked morons and they go down like sacks of mud. Then, spotlighters flood into Eden on a rampage.

The scene plays out in my mind so clearly, it's got the familiar feel of a memory. I jog faster down the dirt path, past dark trailers and buzzing streetlights.

The shouts are already starting from beyond the fence. Rising on the breeze, thin and shrill. Lyle must have marched straight into the field. He's pure anger and military trained, but he's alone and the spotlighters have firepower.

Five Zeniths left and it looks to be four real soon.

Coming around Lucy's trailer I have to push past gawkers. People stand in clumps, keeping away from the porch lights. Some of their faces are familiar in the twilight, but many more are new-comers. The stream of cars packed with blankets and groceries hasn't let up. Every day it's another family, another car parked in the lot, another dog leashed to a tree. And now just about all of them are watching the field, worried.

I see why pretty quick: it's just Lyle out there.

From behind the fence, I make out a semicircle of maybe two dozen spotlighters standing two or three deep around Lyle.

Thankfully, none of Lyle's soldiers in Astra have figured out what's happening. Otherwise this wouldn't be a fight. It would be a war.

Guns and beer bottles and clenched fists. The mounted spotlights blaze down on Lyle's thin frame and a flurry of handheld spotlights hit him from odd angles. In a wifebeater and dusty jeans, he's a prizefighter slouched in the ring, outmatched. There's nothing to the guy, just that thin silhouette burned in crisp detail. A dozen narrow shadows splaying out behind him like knife blades.

The fighting hasn't started yet, but I can see in the angle of Lyle's shoulders that it's close.

A twinkle of light flutters past Lyle's head and he doesn't flinch. An empty whisky bottle bounces into the grass, thunks into the fence a few yards from me.

"You ready to fuckin' die, Frankenstein?" calls somebody.

I clamber over the fallen wooden fence, scale the new shiny chain-link, and jog into the field. My breathing isn't coming easy. Moving toward Lyle, I'm having to concentrate on pushing my breaths out. Each pant squeezes out of my mouth as a strained, grunting curse.

Fuck me. Fuck me. Fuck this.

As I cross the field, a few lights swing my way and shove my shadow out behind me. Light-kissed moths flutter overhead. For one absurd second, it feels like Little League baseball. Like I'm trotting onto the field for a night game. Must've left my glove on the bench.

Then someone fires a shotgun into the air, and a cold tickle of fear crests my scalp and cascades down the back of my neck.

"Here comes your girlfriend, cowboy," calls a voice from behind the lights.

Laughter.

I get close to him, but Lyle doesn't turn around. He's swaying in place. I can hear him humming a tuneless song. I grab his shoulder and turn him around. Thank God he doesn't have a weapon in his hands.

"This isn't happening," I hiss.

Now that I see Lyle up close, I get the feeling he isn't seeing me back. His eyes are black and dead, half lidded, like they were in that rotten trailer. Just a pair of lifeless doll eyes anchoring an idiot grin to his face.

Lyle has gone inside his own mind. Letting the machine step in and do the work. Now I know we're in real fucking trouble.

"Where are you, Lyle?" I whisper. "Come back."

The circle of spotlighters is closing in. Catcalls coming louder. Another bottle flies past.

Lyle's eyes finally flicker to life, speckled with lights. With an effort, he focuses on my face. A ghost of a smile surfaces. His eyes are shining with tears.

"We're gonna change the world," he whispers.

"Don't do this, Lyle," I say.

"I'm whole hog, man," he replies. "Level five. It's fuckin' beautiful."

One hand clamped to Lyle's shoulder, I turn and face the circle. Try to smile while I pull him away. "We don't want any trouble," I say.

Lyle starts humming again, like a slack-jawed escapee from a mental ward. He's taking deep breaths, savoring the breeze. For just this one second, it's nearly silent in the field. Only the far-off puttering of the generator and thousands of pounds of cool night air sighing, dropping down onto our shoulders out of the infinite black sky.

The circle of men around us is complete, closing in like wild dogs. Reflexive group movements unfolding according to an ancient script. Everybody knows his part. These guys have probably all been practicing since grade school.

"He's just drunk and wandered off," I say. Lyle smiles at them, still humming. "We're going."

A flannel-shirted guy steps out, and my legs go numb with adrenaline. This is him. The guy who watched, laughing, while those teenagers worked me over with dirt clods. The one with the tattoo. Gunnin' Billy.

"Hey, buddy," he says, "we're *all* drunk. That ain't getting you nowhere."

He's flashing a strained smile through a week's growth of stubble. He holds a black pump-action shotgun with the butt propped on his hip, casual. The weapon's not tucked under his armpit with the muzzle down, like a hunter, but arrogantly aimed at the sky. More like a bank robber.

Watching me, Billy digs a cherry-red shotgun shell out of his jeans pocket. Shoves it into his shotgun, then rams it forward with the ball of his thumb. Digs out another shell. And another.

Snick. Snick. Snick.

"Told you not to come back, didn't I? Already gave you the score and here you are again. You ain't just getting beat down this time, amp," he says.

Somehow, the oxygen has rushed out of the field. The main spotlight is behind Billy and his face is in shadow. Except for his teeth. Straight and long and yellow. His teeth glint as he talks quietly.

"Y'all got to know your place. We're here for the safety of the town. We men are the only thing standing between you animals and our wives and families. Our kids."

I can't hold back. "You nearly killed a helpless kid tonight."

Those yellow teeth wink at me from the beard. "He ain't a kid," says Billy. "He's an amp. There's a difference. Besides, we was trying to help him out. Did a little surgery. Tried to make him into a human being. It was a goddamn favor."

"Little shit's lucky we let him keep his robot eye," says a man and nudges the guy next to him. They snicker.

"Yeah, he is lucky," I retort. "His retinal recorded everything. We've got video. All your faces. And it's going straight to the police or the FBI or whoever will listen."

A wave of chuckles erupts around me.

"Oh, that's precious. I'm the *sheriff*, numbnuts. Billy Hardaway at your service. And any evidence you want to share, well, I'd suggest you stick it straight up your ass."

The group breaks into guffaws.

Lyle joins the laughter, chest heaving. Expressionless and standing straight-backed, he barks out a repetitive cackle. The sound is mechanical and grating, and it goes on for a long time.

The circle of men seems to shrink away from us like shadows from a campfire.

"I know this amp," says Billy, pointing at Lyle. "I know you."

Lyle keeps on barking, and I notice his hands are closed into fists now.

"No," I say. "Don't you fucking do it. Let's run."

Billy steps forward, closer to Lyle. I tighten my grip on the cowboy's shoulder. But I can feel the black hole forming, the light sucked into it, too deep and old to stop.

"You're the one who ran off my deputy the other night. Where's all your little buddies now, huh? Not so tough with just your girlfriend here."

"Respect," mutters Lyle.

"What the fuck you say?" asks Billy. His eyes gleam, boring into Lyle's face. He steps back and pulls the shotgun up across his chest. A hand curled under the forestock and a finger on the trigger. Its barrel-mounted flashlight stabs a ray of light into outer space.

"Respect," says Lyle, clearly this time. And when he moves it is inhuman. The cowboy shrugs out from under my hand and just goes. I hardly see any movement from him yet he's already flying forward. A prairie king snake gliding through the grass, disappearing in plain sight.

Lyle's worn boot heel catches Billy dead square in the sternum like a lightning bolt. Snaps his collarbone audibly. His shotgun goes off and a tubby guy standing a few feet away loses his hat in a spray of buckshot.

"Ah *fuck*," shouts somebody in an oddly high-pitched voice.

Billy carps his mouth, stunned. Drops heavily onto his ass. Next to him, the fat guy who used to own a hat pulls a finger out of his own ear. It's bloody.

"Goddamn, Billy," he whines.

But Lyle has not stopped. His fists are slashing and those tattooed crows are in a frenzy as he leaps to the next man in the line. And then the next. I can hear him breathing hard, making little grunts with the effort of each tight swing. Moving quicker than an electrical current. Punches coming in flurries, three- or four-strike combinations, the dull smack of calcified knuckles on soft body tissue. Throats, eye sockets, temples.

Whole hog.

Three men drop before I notice Billy has got his bearings and has the black eye of his shotgun staring me in the face. We make eye contact and I see the way Billy's jaw tenses. His upper lip curls into a snarling murder look and I dive to the ground. The shotgun booms, and I feel the shock wave wash over my neck. Speeding shrapnel rips through the air over my head.

I'm on my hands and knees now, and there's no hope. I've already heard the *schlick-schlock* of Billy's shotgun cocking and its flashlight is throwing my shadow out in front of me. Three guys have got hold of Lyle, and from the yelling and cussing it sounds like the cowboy is already down to biting people. It won't be long before I feel that lead shot burrowing under my skin. Even so, I keep crawling as fast as the loose dirt will let me.

Spotlighters in front of me are scrambling the hell out of the way, and I feel the hot presence of that shotgun on my back.

"You're fucking dead," Billy says, and I don't doubt it.

I dive forward just as the shotgun goes off, and it's like somebody shot out the lights. The field goes dark. A spray of dirt tattoos my neck, the sandpaper grind of tiny rocks. My body hits the ground with a rubbery thud. For an instant I'm wondering if this is death. Then there's a high-pitched ringing in my ears. The tail end of a breath caught on the back of my tongue. I'm alive.

Somebody killed the generator is all.

A half-dozen flashlights flicker toward the silent machine. Across the black field, I see a pale face peeking over the rusted generator. Eyes shining, Lucy looks like a possum caught in car headlights.

"Get that bitch!" someone shouts.

Shotguns start to belch flame. Pounds of lead buckshot hit the generator in a hellish symphony. Lucy's face drops out of sight between flashes.

Lucy.

I don't remember deciding to stand.

I'm stalking, head down, toward the nearest spotlighter. My right hand is out, three fingers splayed and my eyes are half closed. I'm picturing the Zenith in my mind huge, the way a floating gray zeppelin is enormous in the sky, trailing tethers in the wind. It's time to see what I'm capable of.

Three. Two. One. Zero.

And the amp speaks to me.

It's a startling, synthesized voice in my head: *Level one.*

Diagnostic access. Battlefield situational awareness. Mission essential fitness. Mobility and survivability. Do you consent? Do you consent?

The amp is inside me and speaking directly to me for the first time after lying dormant for all these years. This piece of plastic is alive in a terrifying new way, yet the voice I hear is as natural as my own thoughts. Just a part of me, after all.

My eyes are closed now and somehow so are my ears and my skin and nostrils. I'm completely inside. The darkness of my own mind. And in this still womb, there is nothing except for the question. So I answer.

Yes, I say. *Oh, yes.* And I can feel again. I open my eyes.

Exhilaration. Air surges into my nostrils, and I swear I can feel my blood being oxygenated, the liquid fuel coursing into my limbs and making them strong. My skin embraces the breeze, sweat evaporating into the atmosphere. The threshold between my body and the world evaporates with it.

The field is singing.

Strange flashes of light streak over my vision. Nonsense lines and pinwheels. I blink them away. Things go black and then erupt into almost unbearably intense flashes of white. The shotgun blasts.

Between flashes, my fists fall gracefully through space in a way that feels inevitable, guided by fate. A gurgling choke as the palm of my right hand smacks into a random man's bearded throat. As he falls, I grab the shotgun out of his hands and hurl it out into the darkness. It tumbles end over end far into the night, like a UFO.

"Where's the cowboy?" shouts Billy. "Keep shooting!"

I can see only faint outlines of the grass, clouds twisting overhead, and frantic shapes of men around me. Infinite fingers of white light sweep the field.

I snatch another shotgun and toss it away.

A dark blur lurches past. Lyle is dragging a mob of four men. One of his arms breaks free and it cuts the air like a scalpel. More screaming.

Another shotgun coughs into the night. One of the spotlighters shouts in alarm. "Did I get ya?" asks another. "Shit, buddy."

A couple of dark shapes are running away. Hustling and limping toward the row of houses on the other side of the field. "Fuck this," mutters somebody.

"Come on, y'all!" shouts Billy. He's wheeling around, strafing the scattered men with the light mounted on his shotgun. "Get your asses back here."

Then Lyle strides past me, knifing straight for Billy. Slides right up behind him and pauses. Before I can stop it, he sinks a bony fist into Billy's kidney. And I mean he really sets his feet and follows through.

Billy's knees go slack and he drops into the grass, writhing and trying to breathe. His shotgun drops, its attached flashlight illuminating a small round patch of grass in exquisite detail.

Lyle stands over him, a slump-shouldered shadow, black on black.

"Come down with me, Owen," whispers Lyle, gesturing at the stumbling shapes fleeing into the night. "Come down in the dark and let's go hunting. Whole hog, buddy."

Down, down, down. I want to go. This Zenith feels stupendous. The tingling awareness of the world flooding through my eyes and nose and dancing over my skin. I can see my eyes seeing. Happiness. Madness. I'm falling into myself. And as my thoughts drop back to the Zenith, I see her silhouette stumbling my way.

Lucy.

"No," she is saying. "Come back."

I'm swimming up to her from deep water. Bursting through the surface.

"Lucy," I breathe. I stumble and she catches me. Hugs me desperately and in the dim light I run my hands lightly over her face. She's fine, she's okay. Crying a little. She shoves me away and turns to Lyle.

Dropping to his knees on the other side of Billy, the laughing cowboy looks up at us. His black eyes catch the light from the fallen shotgun. Reflect it. I don't know where he is right now. Some piece of efficient machinery is intercepting his experience of the world, making his decisions with stern, unblinking precision.

Billy coughs, rolls over. His elbows dig into the dirt and he cocks his head up. One hand over his collarbone, he is snarling at us, his canines peeking over wormy lips. "You're going to pay," he says. "You fuckers are going to pay for this. We know what you're planning. Your little army."

Lyle watches Billy with vacant curiosity.

"Think we sit out here for fun?" Billy coughs. "It's my *job*. We know you. Pure Pride knows you. Ask your little friend in Detroit. What's his name. Valentine."

That gets Lyle's attention. His eyebrows drop.

I grab a fistful of Lyle's shirt and pull him away from Billy. Dazed, the cowboy stumbles. He's still coming up from whatever deep place he's been. Blinking away the cobwebs. His hands are open, knuckles crusted with dark bloody cuts.

"Valentine?" Lyle asks. "What about Valentine?"

Frantic sirens howl in the distance.

"We got eyes on your boy and he's a talker." Billy laughs. "Whole file on him. About the smartest amp we ever saw, but we can take him anytime we want. Any goddamn time, amp. Bet on it."

Lucy is next to me. I push Lyle toward her.

"Get him home," I say. "Away from here. Okay?"

She takes one of Lyle's limp hands and pulls him away. As she moves into the darkness, I reach out and touch her shoulder.

"Thank you," I say.

She blinks at me, sad. Wipes her nose on the back of her forearm. "Don't thank me," she says. "I came here for my brother. You were supposed to keep him out of this. You were supposed to be different."

"Lucy—" I'm trying to say.

But she turns. Recedes into the darkness with Lyle. Leaves me here in the torn-up field, my face throbbing with blood.

"You got woman trouble," Billy says with a laugh, still lying in the dirt.

I squat down next to him.

"No, what I've got is a question," I say. "How do you know Joseph Vaughn?"

Billy grins at me through his beard, breathing hard. Shakes his head.

I pick up his right hand, force it toward his face. Work my fingers between his knuckles so that Billy whimpers and spreads his hand. And there's that tattoo, buried in the web of his thumb.

EM.

"What's Elysium?" I ask him. "You and Vaughn have a little club?"

At first he doesn't say anything. Together we listen to far-off sirens getting closer. I dig in my fingers until my forearm is flexed solid, long tendons tugging my skin into hills and valleys. He takes the grinding pain for a few seconds, then lets out a burst of breath and finally speaks. Tells me one last thing before I have to run.

"My family," says Billy. "That's a family crest. And real soon, amp, my family is gonna eat yours up."

The New York Times

U.S. Officials Release Warning of Imminent Terrorist Threat

WASHINGTON—The Department of Homeland Security has issued a nationwide alert, warning of an increased potential for a terrorist threat to major metropolitan areas in the United States.

A spokeswoman for the department said the alert was a precautionary action after operatives had received credible information of an imminent threat of terrorist attacks. She would not comment on the nature of the threat or how long it is expected to last, saying that local law enforcement agencies had been contacted with further details and told to review their security precautions.

"We just want citizens to be vigilant," said the spokeswoman.

A police official, speaking on condition of anonymity, said in a telephone interview that a confidential bureau memorandum had been distributed. The memorandum describes the threat as being from implanted extremists belonging to the Astra terrorist organization. Specifically, officers were ordered to "exercise heightened vigilance and to immediately detain any implanted individual exhibiting suspicious behavior."

15

TRIAL BY FIRE

The old man is on the trailer roof again, right over my bedroom ceiling. I can hear him up there. His exoskeleton motors sigh in time to the creaking over my head.

I figure I'll give him five more minutes and then I'll climb up and say good-bye.

My duffel bag is on the bed, half open, a ragged cornucopia spilling balled-up T-shirts and blue jeans. I packed it a few minutes ago in a kind of hazy panic. It's the middle of the night, but the law will be coming for us after what just happened in the field.

So much for keeping my head down.

Stepping outside, I watch a group of three or four neon-modded temples float past my window, streaming toward Lyle's cluster of trailers. More have already congregated. Something is up.

I climb the wooden ladder tipped against the end of the trailer. Jim is barefoot and bare chested up here, wearing his exoskeleton. The old man slowly lunges through the motions of one of his tai chi routines. His skin gleams in the light from antique sodium arc lamps. I watch him practice the martial art for a few seconds, somehow soothed by each deliberate movement, every slow-motion strike and block executed with centimeter-level precision. Whatever form he is doing, I imagine that with the help of the exoskeleton he's executing it more perfectly than any ancient master ever did.

"How's Nick?" I ask.

Jim nods. "Got the port cleaned and attached to the implant. Slathered it in the last of my bio-gel. He'll recover."

"Good," I say. "I'm headed out. Going with Lyle."

Leaning forward, palms out, Jim slowly straightens and turns. "Where?"

"Detroit. A Zenith there needs help."

My family is going to eat yours up.

Jim nods at me, sweat beaded on his upper lip.

"We should have gone slower," he says. "Introduced the Autofocus to fewer people. It was too much too fast."

Jim's not thinking about what happened tonight. He's thinking about a thing that happened years ago. Something he's only paying for tonight.

"You did good, Jim," I say. "You cured people. Same as my dad."

Jim slows and stares at his hands. It doesn't look like he believes me.

"Can you control it?" he asks.

"I think so," I say.

"Mind and body," he says. "You know what you get when the mind and body act as one?" he asks. Jim resumes moving, sinking toward me. His hands scoop the air, rise with animal grace. "You get harmony," he answers. "Remember that. There is no *you*. There is no *it*. Mind and body need a single purpose."

"Why are you saying this?"

"You're walking a dangerous road. The choices you make from here on could save us or damn us. Lyle and them are soldiers. All they understand is force. I hope you can show them a new perspective. Provide some balance."

"I'll try. Look after Nick and Lucy for me."

"Always," he says.

"I probably just killed my chances with her."

Jim doesn't respond. Might have ducked his head a little.

"I won't be gone long," I say.

"I'll be here," he says, "breaking rocks."

As I climb down, I hear his motors whirring again. Watch the silhouette of his face slip out of view over the lip of the roof.

Around me, more of Lyle's gang are walking toward his boxes. They mostly look past me or through me, but I catch a hint of something on some of their faces: pity for me, maybe, or fear.

A shifting blue glow comes from inside Lucy's trailer. I stand on her porch for five minutes, shivering, before I finally get up the nerve to knock quietly.

The sun will be up in another hour. But there is something I have to do before I leave. Something I should have done days ago.

Lucy pulls the door open and lets me step inside. I can't read her face. Nick is sleeping on the living room couch, a warm lump under a pile of covers. The muted television dribbles a soft idiot light into the room. It dances in Lucy's eyelashes. She's the best thing I've found in my short time in Eden. She treated me like family. Saved my life in the field. And I've given her nothing in return.

I'm starting small.

"I'm sorry," I say, eyes lowered. "I'm not in control, Lucy. I've never been in control. I tried to stop Lyle and I couldn't. I couldn't protect Nick. I yelled at you because I was beaten up and embarrassed and I felt like an idiot. You don't have to forgive me—"

And that's when I notice it.

My shirt. Hanging over the arm of the couch. It's the same one that I was wearing the day those boys beat me up and pissed on me. I threw it stinking into the weeds and forgot about it. Now here it is—washed and dried and folded neatly.

Lucy follows my eyes.

"I wasn't sure how to give it back," says Lucy.

A warm breeze sighs in the window. It smells mostly like grass and a little like motor oil. Lucy is standing a foot away from me, delicate and freckled in the dim, stuttering light of the television. Her lips turn down at the corners, but the skin beside her eyes is creased with years of laughter.

I'm smiling now and none of today's madness can stop me.

There's nothing I would love more than to kiss Lucy Crosby. And with this realization, I'm ten years old and standing on the end of the high dive. Shivering, inches from the abyss. Jump already, kid.

"I'm doing the best I can," I say.

"I know."

It's probably the wrong moment. But I step forward and slide my arms around Lucy and I kiss her anyway. She kisses me back. We stand together in the still living room, bodies pressed against each other and finally, blissfully not thinking.

When I take a step back, I notice that her eyes are wet.

"Lyle is back at his trailer," she says, running a finger across the strap of the duffel bag hanging over my shoulder. "Should be ready to go."

I lean in for another kiss and she puts a hand on my chest.

"The cops will be here soon," she says.

"Okay," I respond.

"So be careful," she says.

"Can I ask you something?"

"What?"

"Will you go on a date with me? When I get back?"

"You know I have a son."

"I kind of like him."

"I live in a trailer park with a bunch of social outcasts."

"And you're the prettiest one. By far."

"I'll think about it," says Lucy.

And she smiles and gives me that last kiss.

. . .

I'm headed for the trailers on the edge of Eden, trailed by the last of Lyle's soldiers. This crowd must have come in from all over the county tonight. Wondering about it makes my mouth go dry.

The sun's almost up. Time to go.

The halo of bravery I felt a couple minutes ago fades the closer I get to Lyle's boxes. The half-dozen trailers are scattered haphazardly around a campfire, shoved to one corner of Eden. Fossilized tire tracks gash lewd grins in the hard-packed dirt.

Dark people shapes surround the campfire, backlit by the flames, each accompanied by a pinprick of neon light. Someone has dragged out a couple of rotten old couches. Amps swarm the cushions like ticks, listening to tinny music that jangles from a chipped boom box on an extension cord.

Something big moves, like a skyscraper swaying in the wind. It's the Brain. Sitting on a tree stump, he's got a forty in one hand. Makes the beer look the size of a sippy cup.

Standing here on the periphery of the firelight, second thoughts start creeping in. These people are younger than me, tougher than me. Unpredictable and feral. I get the feeling that I've fallen into a cage at the zoo.

This is Astra and I'm scared of it.

I never see Lyle coming. He slaps me on the back, hard. It staggers me and the loud clap gets everyone's attention. People turn to look at us. Lyle wraps an arm over my shoulders and roots me to the spot.

"Gray," announces Lyle. "I've been waiting for you."

Half of Lyle's face is lit up red by the fire. His implant is a dark blemish on his temple, like mine.

"Need you to formally meet some of the boys," says Lyle. As he says each name, Lyle squints one eye and points at the person with his index and middle fingers pushed together, like a gun. Finally, he gets to the looming shape on the tree stump.

"And I believe you've met the Brain."

Lyle puts a hand beside his mouth, whispers loudly at the side of my face. "Try and keep your lunch down this time."

People chuckle. I wonder how much they know about me.

"Let's go," I whisper, ducking my head so the others can't hear. "Cops are going to tear Eden apart looking for us. We've got to warn Valentine. Did you call him yet?"

"Won't matter," says Lyle. "They got him under surveillance. If he makes a move, they'll take him."

"They'll kill him. We have to get him out of there."

"Don't you think I know that?" asks Lyle, putting his back to me. He is a thin dark shape blocking the flames—an absence of light. "But before we go, you got to join Astra."

"Okay."

"Okay what? You got to say it."

"I want in, Lyle. I want to join Astra."

Lyle puts an arm back around my shoulders. Addresses our audience. "This is Gray, y'all. I vouch for him."

Lyle turns to me.

"But there's only one way in or out of Astra. We welcome you tonight with our fists. If you're strong enough, we'll have you. Otherwise . . ."

Dry chuckles seep in from all around me.

I take a step back. But Lyle's wiry fingers clamp harder onto my shoulder. Dark shapes are rising behind him. Looming up to form an ominous wall. A shifting, bobbing sea of neon-colored stars. Lyle pulls me toward him, whispers into my ear. "You know the part of you that's listening right now? The part making decisions? The little man at the steering wheel right between your eyes?"

Lyle pushes his index finger between my eyes.

"Yeah," I say, shaky.

"That's your executive function. Does all your planning. Abstract thinking. Picks your actions. All the rest of your body is on automatic. Digesting your food. Sweating, bleeding, balancing. Recognizing the faces of your brothers."

"Okay."

"You got executive and you got automatic. With me?"

"Yes."

"Execute your trigger action. When you're inside, take that executive—that little guy who is you—and send him on down to automatic. Step on his shoulders and stand up. Drop down through those levels and you'll be fine. Can you do that, Gray?"

"Yeah."

"You kicked some ass in the field tonight. But now you go deeper. Whatever you got, you better use it."

"Why?" I ask.

"Because we're about to do our best to beat you to death."

"What?" I gasp.

"Ad astra cruentus," says Lyle, and the people around the camp-fire mutter in unison: "To the stars. Stained in blood."

He means it. My right hand instinctively goes to a three count. Pushing my focus to the Zenith, on the verge of the trigger, tickles something. Like pressing a hidden button.

Three, two, one, zero. Fist.

It's as though I've fallen through a trapdoor and into my own brain. Thoughts are written on the inside of my forehead. I can see them scrolling there. White text on black background. Speeding past at the speed of thought.

Level two. Close-quarter combatives. Fluid shock striking technique. Vital points. Nerve motor points. Defensive stances. Do you consent? Do you consent?

In a distracted way, I notice Lyle's first punch land on my diaphragm. I stop breathing. A red haze settles over my vision.

Yes, yes, yes.

I see the words. Then, the words are replaced by my own thoughts. The little man at the steering wheel of my mind. I read my own impressions as they appear and in a secondhand way, I am alarmed.

The words say that beyond this room in my head, there is a campfire surrounded by five trailers. A lanky cowboy covered in crow tattoos means me harm. Strangers are amassing with evil on their collective mind. My body is in danger. And here on the inside, hands on the controls of myself, I wait for the raw external world to attack again.

And it does.

Lyle leans into a lazy swing, going for my face this time. It's a tight right hook, accelerating fast to vicious, a wicked elbow up and out to catch me on the chin if the punch misses. But the fist and elbow whiff past my face. The breeze of minutely displaced air feels cool on my upper lip.

I count the tendons rippling across Lyle's forearm. Watching them, I find I can predict which muscles will flex. Where his tattooed arms will go. Those white-knuckled fists floating in darkness.

The next few punches come in flurries, quick combinations. But I am a tree, swaying in the wind and avoiding contact. From my perch inside, I watch this ballet unfold.

After a fruitless thirty seconds of attack, Lyle stops. Puts his hands on his knees. Sweaty hair hangs in his face. He spits on the ground, panting.

"You're a quick learner, Gray. Shit."

I am faintly aware that my body is balanced on the balls of its feet, arms raised slightly for balance. Fists uncurled, fingers relaxed. Breathing steadily and evenly, blank faced.

I mentally kick toward the surface, searching for the cradle of my body.

"Not yet," whispers Lyle. "Not yet."

He pushes his hair out of his face, turns to the crowd of people now standing and watching. Backlit by the fire, it is hard to see their faces. But in shifting neon glints, I catch a few traces of awe—and many more of grim anticipation.

"All right, y'all. Let's welcome our brother with our fists, as we were once welcomed," says Lyle. "If he lives, he can fight along-side us."

The hellish shapes come for me, but I am safe inside. I dance with the shadows of the campfire, untouched as dark fists push the night air around my body.

Local Scrap Causes National Outrage

NOWATA, Okla.—Twenty-two people were injured, seven of them seriously, in an apparent gang fight Tuesday in a field outside the Eden Trailer Park on Cottonwood Avenue near Spiro.

One of the victims, Sheriff Billy Hardaway, reported that a group of implanted youths approached the field armed with baseball bats, knives, and sticks. Unprovoked, the youths attacked a group of local men who had convened in the field to form a candlelight vigil in support of pure human rights.

"After hearing reports of unrest from inside Eden, some local citizens were gathered in the field to ensure that any violence coming from the trailer park did not affect the rest of the nearby community," said Sheriff Hardaway, who added that he himself required a visit to the hospital after the attack.

Sequoyah County police, aided by state troopers, are still looking for suspects in the late-night ambush. News of the skirmish has been picked up on national talk radio and televised news reports.

Senator Joseph Vaughn, the head of the Pure Human Citizen's Council, urged the U.S. government to "crack down on these amped delinquents before the violence can spread beyond their crime-infested ghettos."

16
WOUNDED SUPERMEN

"You never ate Mister Chicken? Damn, how do you *live*?" Lyle asks me.

We're outside a fast-food shack, a few hours outside Eden, sitting on molded plastic chairs that have faded to the color of dirty cotton candy. The building is perched on the side of a hill, hugging a winding road. A motley collection of trailer houses are roosted along the steep route, bleached and broken, like flotsam left behind after a flood.

"How have *you* lived this long, driving that shit heap?"

Lyle's blue pickup truck is sitting ten feet away, engine still ticking. The sun-blanched dashboard is buckled with tectonic cracks, and coiled springs root through the foam seats, only occasionally, painfully, breaching. The rattling monster gives me bad memories of high school. And Lyle starts it with a screwdriver. No kidding.

The cowboy points at his car with a nugget of fry bread that trails gossamer tentacles of honey. "Sometimes you gotta go backward before you can go forward. That heap may be shitty, but she's never been touched by the government." Lyle takes a bite, talks with his mouth full. "Lucky for us, Oklahoma never bought into safety inspections."

I poke fingers through the red plastic ribs of my chicken basket. The food is greasy, hot, and astonishingly good.

"Did you call Valentine?" I ask.

"Yeah," says Lyle. He activates an e-cigarette and lounges back in the chair. "Couldn't say much with him under surveillance. Told him enough to put him and his boys on lockdown."

"Let's hope we get there before Vaughn's Priders," I say.

Lyle nods lazily, pushes steam out of his nostrils. The hypnotically wailing cicadas and restless grasshoppers fill in the conversation for a few minutes. It's peaceful out here. The sporadic rush of cars going past is like a fall wind.

"What do you really want out of this? Astra?" I ask Lyle.

He tosses an empty e-cigarette cartridge onto the ground, where it joins a hundred others in various states of decomposition. Activates another.

"Change, man," he says. "You ever hear of the *scala naturae*?"

"Aristotle. The great chain of being. A medieval categorization of living things. Before there was a difference between science and religion."

Lyle shakes his head at me, lips curling up at the corners, takes a drag.

"Teacher," I say, shrugging.

"Then you know the order," says Lyle. "Plants, animals, men, angels, then God. Difference between men and angels is that men are stuck in a body. They feel pain, hunger, thirst. But me and you, we don't have to feel them things. Body diagnostics come on level one. Easy. We can turn off the human condition. So maybe we're closer to angels, you know? Creatures of the mind. A higher morality."

I push my food to the side. "The machine doesn't make us into something new, Lyle. It only amplifies our abilities. More of the same."

Lyle stands up, paces.

"But when you're whole hog, the decisions come from so far down . . . *goddamn*. The machine takes us deeper into our souls.

That far inside, we're capable of anything. Way beyond right or wrong."

"A friend of mine once said that if you're good, you'll do good things. If you're not, you won't."

"Don't let Jim fool you, Owen. We've all got a killer inside us."

I watch the cowboy pace for a moment, trying to judge how serious he is. "We're men, Lyle, not angels. The Zenith can't take the blame. If anything, it makes us more responsible. We can do more."

Lyle smokes and watches the road. I ignore the fluttering grasshoppers and winding cars, pulse pounding in my peripheral vision. If Lyle really believes that he is beyond right and wrong, then I have a serious problem.

Finally, Lyle turns and claps me on the shoulder. "Maybe you're right," he says, walking around the side of the shack. "Because I got to piss like a racehorse and I never seen an angel do that."

Lyle and I drive maybe a couple hundred miles northeast before the cowboy wordlessly pulls off the main highway. Thirty minutes later, we've reached a dust-choked road lined with rusty barbed-wire fences. We follow it until we come upon a tractor trailer beached by the side of the road.

Lyle slams on the brakes, spraying rocks and gravel. Our rooster tail of dirt catches up to us on the breeze as we get out of the car. I sneeze as the haze swallows the tractor trailer. Leaves it looming there like a Jurassic dinosaur.

"Pit stop," said Lyle.

We're somewhere in Missouri, I'm guessing. Not to St. Louis yet. Maybe a quarter of the way to Detroit. "We don't have time," I say.

There are only four generals left in charge of protecting amps nationwide and one of them is on the verge of being ambushed.

"It's worth it," says Lyle, getting out of the truck. Reluctantly, I follow.

The rear half of the abandoned tractor trailer sits cockeyed, sunk hubcaps deep into the reddish dirt. It looks like it's been here through a few prairie-swept rainstorms, leaning into a sagging barbed-wire fence like a bull scratching himself. Waves of brown grass lie down and stand up at the whim of a hot breeze. It's been a long day driving.

Pretty soon the sun is going to go down and the rattlesnakes can all go home.

We walk closer and I see a beat-up generator sputtering around the side. Next to it, about a half dozen of Lyle's soldiers sit in the shade of the trailer. A few of them pass an electronic cigarette between them, the LED tip of it glowing in time to their puffs. They nod to Lyle like soldiers.

Lyle's got one blood-crusted hand on the clasp that will let those double doors swing wide. He flashes a wry smile my way and gives her a yank.

I'm hit by a sudden blast of refrigerated air from the back of the trailer. It carries a sharp antiseptic smell that reminds me of my dad. I blink a few times, trying to understand what I'm seeing.

Some kind of mobile surgery station.

A surgeon stands in the very back of the trailer, glaring at us with his eyes over his surgical mask. Several layers of clear hanging plastic separate us, but he's outlined by bright circular spotlights that are mounted from the ceiling, hovering like alien spaceships. A patient sits facedown on a paper-covered massage chair, not moving.

The surgeon waves his latex-gloved hands at us, urging us to hurry up and get the fuck inside already.

Lyle nudges me in the small of my back, and I scramble inside, getting a lift from the trailer hitch. He follows me up and we stand in the leaning doorway.

"Shut the door," says the surgeon, voice muffled behind his mask.

Lyle hauls the doors closed. The surgeon drops a magnifying monocle over his right eye and gets back to work.

"This looks like a bad idea," I say, breath frosting.

"You need this," says Lyle.

"I'm not going under the knife."

Lyle sighs. "A lot of amps are depending on us. In Eden and all over."

I remember that anatomy poster on my dad's office wall. Frontal lobe. Temporal lobe. Motor cortex. Sensory cortex.

"What are we talking here?" I ask.

"A simple sensory suite. Retinal and cochlear. Eyes and ears. Outpatient shit. Takes fifteen minutes. It links up with your Zenith and I'm offering it to you for free. And it ain't even close to free—right, Norman?"

In reply, the surgeon waves a small shiny tool at Lyle. Then he jams it into his patient's temple, bracing the guy's head with his other hand. I hear a pneumatic click, and shudder.

"Why?"

"You'll see better in the dark. Hear better than a field mouse. All that shit. But the real advantage is in the *connections*. Zenith will use the extra information. Retinal talks. Cochlear talks. Zenith takes you to another level. Full sensory network."

"And why do you think I'd want that?"

"Why, to protect Eden," he says.

He's right. Thinking of those spotlighters, of Nick sad and bleeding, makes me want to claw through those plastic sheets and leap into the chair.

"All my generals have it," says Lyle, eyebrows up. "Get it. Learn to use it and you won't bother to hide your face no more. You'll be the baddest motherfucker on the block. You'll be Astra."

A general? I've only been down to level two. Am I ready to lead an army?

Ducking under a leaf of plastic, I take a closer look and my breath catches. The reality of those surgical instruments drops onto me. Gleaming silver, razor edges, and hypodermic tips.

"Relax, man," says Lyle. "Even little Nick has one of these. They're so simple to install that this guy can do it in a goddamn trailer in the middle of nowhere."

"I—I need to think about this—" I stutter.

"You think Vaughn's gonna let us just walk in and warn Valentine?" asks Lyle. "You're gonna need every advantage you can get. We don't have time to fuck around."

Lyle gestures at the patient. He's a Hispanic guy curled on his side, eyes wide as the surgeon works on his temple. "Look at us. Amps. We're morons smarter than Lucifer. Cripples stronger than gravity. A bunch of broke-ass motherfuckers, stinking rich with potential. This is our *army*. Our people. Strong and hurt. We're the wounded supermen of tomorrow, Gray. It's time you got yourself healed. New world ain't gonna build itself. And the old world don't wanna go without a fight."

"Where's yours?" I ask.

In response, Lyle leans forward and pulls down his lower eyelid with a greasy fingertip. Faintly, I make out a rectangular square floating over the white of his eye. A trace of gray, it's nearly invisible.

"Came with Echo Squad. Part of the package," he says.

"You never seemed like the military type."

Lyle snorts. "Military was my family for a long time. But all that ended once they put the Zenith in me. Saw things clearer then. Realized I had a whole new family—one that needed me."

"So you got lucky that the names of your unit were leaked and the army kicked you out?"

"Yeah. Lucky," says Lyle, smirking. Something in the tilt of his smile is off. Some memory, half suppressed. "And you're lucky, too. This kind of hardware only goes to my closest. Folks with potential. You handled your initiation like a man. I know you can handle these upgrades and a lot more. I'm proud of you, buddy."

Lyle's smile goes genuine.

Something bumps into me, and I see it's the patient. He's stumbling out of the operating room on wobbling legs. Lyle reaches up and grabs the guy's shoulders, steadying him. Cups the guy's cheeks in his dirty hands, orients his face toward me.

"Check out his retinal," he says.

I peer into the guy's eyes. They look the same, except the right one. It has a small rectangle sort of floating on it. Like a circuit diagram or a microscopic tattoo. Hardly noticeable, like the one Nick has.

"Thank you, Mr. Crosby," says the guy.

"*Ad astra,*" says Lyle.

"To the stars."

Jim told me to trust myself. Absorb the technology into my body and hope like hell that I'm a good man. We'll see if he was right.

"If I do this," I say, "we find who is hunting Zeniths. It's not enough just to help Valentine. Whether it's Priders or the government or the military—I don't care. We've got to find out who it is and put an end to it."

"You'll find out," says Lyle. "I promise."

I push through the last plastic sheet and into the operating room. Lyle fades to a blurry figure on the other side. "Your vision is about to get a whole lot clearer, Gray," he calls. "You'll be seeing shit you can't imagine."

I take a deep breath and sit down on the padded chair. Nod at the doctor. Then I call back to Lyle. "How can you pay for this?"

"It's covered," he replies.

"By who?"

Lyle stops for a second, thinking about how to respond. Finally, he pushes his blurry face against the plastic and looks me dead in the eye.

"By the boss. Who do you think?"

My mind and body are still out of tune.
I hope they run into each other real soon.

—JIM MORRISON

Attacks Deplored, Inquiries Pushed

OKLAHOMA CITY—Against a background of violence and uncertainty, a special federal grand jury was convened today to investigate the outbreaks of violence between implanted and nonimplanted citizens that continue to plague the nation.

Assistant US Attorney Clarence Albad, in his charge to the grand jury, emphasized the savage beating of Pure Pride demonstrators in Eastern Oklahoma last week that injured two dozen people. Similar incidents have been reported in major metropolitan areas across the nation, including the burning of a house in Houston that was used for Pure Human Citizen's Council meetings.

From his offices in Pittsburgh, Senator Joseph Vaughn has announced that a round of new Pure Pride protests have been scheduled to occur around the country. Sequoyah County, near where the beating incident occurred, has become a symbolic destination for protesters. The governor of Oklahoma announced that 300 Oklahoma state troopers and 500 National Guardsmen have been put on alert statewide, ready to back up local police if violence erupts.

17

HERE TO HELP

I'm staring up at a four-story row house made of moldering red brick. Shaggy yellow moss coats the seams between bricks like tooth decay. The roof is partly caved in, and swollen slats of plywood cover all the windows but one. Someone has spray-painted a hand-sized image of a bloody star on the porch, and vines have eaten all but the star's points.

This building was beautiful once. That was a long time ago.

Blinking, I feel the rasp of my new retinal implant under my eyelid. My eye is a little tender, but otherwise I feel the same. Lyle says it takes a while for the Zenith to acclimate to the new information being collected by retinal and cochlear. My new eyes and ears.

"Valentine is in charge of the whole Detroit area?" I ask Lyle. "And he lives in one of *these*?"

Lyle makes his way carefully down the sidewalk toward me. Puts a finger to his lips. Points to the house.

I stare up into that lone dark window and a wave of white light suddenly bleeds across the surface of the building. The blackness behind the window fades up to gray and I glimpse something inside. I wince and the dazzling light fades. The retinal implant has some kind of autoexposure and it's always on. I squeeze my eyes shut to block out the overexposed building and to block out something else.

A glimpse of something gnarled and man-shaped, standing behind that window.

"Valentine *is* in charge," Lyle says quietly, cracking his knuckles and sizing up the boards that cover the front door. "This neighborhood is Beverly Hills compared to the others. There's ghettos like this over southwest Detroit. Amps got no other place to go."

These few blocks of row houses are huddled together in the middle of an abandoned industrial park, falling against one another in a decomposing heap. The carbon lick of extinguished flame rises from some of the gutted windows. At least most of the debris on the street has been stacked or burned. Twisted piles of plastic, broken glass, and scrap metal are scattered like modern art.

I follow Lyle farther down the block. The front stoop of the house next door leans at a vertiginous angle, permanently italicized by rot and the elements.

"Let me check this one," he says.

"Are you sure he knows we're coming?" I ask.

"Told you I sent word. But there's only five Zeniths left out of twelve. He ain't likely to answer the door to anybody. Even a good friend like me."

"Where are Stilman and Daley?" I ask. The other generals haven't been back to Eden since their little vote. Off protecting the amps of America, I suppose.

"They're around. Checking a couple other spots."

Lyle smiles with nicotine-stained teeth. I have no time to wonder why we're sneaking around, because he's already on the move. He climbs the broken stone steps with wary grace. As he leans forward to peer in a cracked window, Lyle's jacket hitches and I catch a glint of black metal. A pistol tucked into the crook of his back. A numbness creeps in around my shoulders—this feels wrong.

This whole place feels wrong.

Around us, the grass and trees are twisted and dead. With each breath I feel the metallic sting of air pollution on the back of my throat. A rust-colored grime coats everything: the streets, sidewalks, and abandoned cars and trailers along the side of the empty roads. Under this overcast sky, with the sun a glowing haze on the horizon, the street has an otherworldly, Martian feel to it.

And I can sense the eyes on us.

Families haunt the broken porches up and down the block. They sit on old couches and faded lawn chairs. More people are inside their homes, looking out through cracked panes of glass. A kid on a bike makes lazy loops in the street, somberly watching us, tires scratching over the grit. Unseen dogs bark from the shared backyards behind the row houses.

Different place, same story. Families like the ones in Eden. Regular people who happen to have technology under their skin and no other place to go. Over the months, they must have filtered out of the suburbs and the country to this place and hundreds of others like it. Shuttled along by friendly reggies, but hustled away just the same. Amps with no jobs or family to turn to.

Lyle speaks to me quietly, cupping his eyes against a dusty window. "He could be in one of these. I don't know which. Haven't been here in a year. But we need to hurry. Priders could be here already."

In the distance, a crumbling factory glares at me with a thousand broken eyes. It would be the simplest thing in the world for Vaughn's men to camp out in there with a pair of binoculars. Or maybe a rifle. I scan the street again.

My retinal picks out vivid details. Seamlessly lays the extra information into my vision. The device works all the time, slipping more visual data into my head.

I point to the house next door, the one with the collapsed roof. It seems abandoned, with a front door that is barricaded with rotten two-by-fours.

"He's in there," I say.

"How you know that?" asks Lyle.

I shrug and nod at the bleeding star that has been spray-painted on the front porch. The symbol is hidden by weeds and the dirt that coats everything, but it's unmistakable.

"Ad astra," I say.

"Damn right," says Lyle. "No use messing with that front door. Follow me."

Lyle climbs back onto the fallen porch next door, quick and silent. Scales the rotten spine of the fallen porch roof, testing each footstep on bloated wood before going higher. I follow him up, stepping gingerly without my amp activated.

I'm only human, for now.

At the top, we both jump from the splintered porch to the roof of the porch next door. This porch is more sturdy, buttressed by a tar-covered layer of galvanized steel that is warped into black waves. That empty window breaks the cold brick face of the house. Its frame sprouts fanglike shards of glass.

The cowboy considers the window. Pulls a piece of chalk from his pocket and marks a white *X* on the brick beside it. Drops the chalk and peeks inside.

"So our friends know where to meet us," he says.

"Careful. Something's in there."

Lyle cocks an eyebrow at me. "You mean some*body*, right?"

Before I can answer, he ducks under the glass slivers and into the window's dark throat. For a moment, I'm alone on the sagging porch. The window, just a hole in the bricks, has the treacherous feel of a spider's nest.

Turns out, that's not far from the truth.

I hear somebody's shout from inside, cut off. Hurrying, I crouch and manage to drop inside the window without cutting myself. For a split second, it's too goddamn dark and I can't see anything. A body hits the brick wall next to me with a slap. In the reddish slant of window light, an unconscious man falls into view. I step out of the light and press my back against the sweating bricks while my retinal amplification kicks in.

Lyle's boots crunch off down the hallway. Now I can make out the guy at my feet. A young amp in an army jacket, lying still on a bed of stiff, moldy carpet and rain-bleached trash. I watch him until I see his chest rise and fall.

More strangled shouting comes from deeper inside the house. A crunch of plaster and a shriek. Lyle is long gone. This room is weather-beaten and empty. A dim rectangle of light leads to a claustrophobic hallway, choked with swathes of paint hanging from the ceiling like moss.

Eyes squinted, I take one step toward the hall before I see it coming for me.

The man-sized thing is black on black and galloping toward me in fast, insectile lurches. A spurt of childish bogeyman fear shoots into my veins. I step back and put out three fingers without thinking. *Three.* The thing falls sideways and bounces off a wall, keeps coming. *Two.* I can hear its breath hissing in and out. *One.* A nightmare bursts through the doorway and into the room.

Zero.

Level three. Tactical maneuvers. Evasion. Room clearing. Flanking. Improvised weaponry. Combat medicine. Do you consent? Do you consent?

Yes, oh fuck, yes, yes.

This thing looks like a twisted rag doll come to life—a scarecrow escaped from an abandoned field. It leaps for me and I'm instantly on my back, elbows crunching through broken glass and water-stained trash. Shrunken black fingers claw for my throat. I can see in flashes, my retinal feeding this thing's movements to my Zenith. I grapple with impossibly thin and strong arms. Wrestle for position against spidery legs. Scrabbling through debris, I feel a shard of glass dimple the skin of my right palm, penetrate, and lodge itself warmly between flexing tendons.

It should hurt, but it doesn't.

In a detached way, I notice that I am fighting something less than a man. And somehow more. There isn't much but a torso and head with a four-limb prosthetic replacement. Each wire-thin prosthetic leg and arm has been wrapped in black plastic trash bags held in place with twine and rubber bands. As the wire man manipulates his prosthetic limbs, muscles in his chest and stomach flex like bugs crawling under his skin. He's strong as rebar and quicker than me.

But he's light. I manage to heave him up and off. Leaning back on the bricks, I scratch and grope my way to my feet. I make a mental note that my right hand is pretty fucked up. A piece of smoky glass shark fins out the side of my palm, stuck there.

I run for the hallway. About halfway across the room I hear him coming and I turn. The wire man sways toward me, alarmingly fast on his knotty stick legs.

His prosthetics are too strong. They swing at me like baseball bats, bruising my forearms each time I deflect them with the uncanny speed-boost of my Zenith. And his basic physics are off. The wire man's arms are longer than his torso indicates they should be. The discrepancy seems to fool the built-in mechanics of my Zenith. He feints and one arm dips, hooks under my neck. A brutal metallic knee crushes into my diaphragm, pinning me to the wall.

While I gasp for air, two gnarled arms wreathe my torso and squeeze. I'm impaled on the blunt knee, breath rushing from my lungs. I wrap my fingers around the plastic-encased metal arms, pushing with every fiber of muscle I have. Even with all my strength, I can't breathe.

The thing leans its face in close to mine. When it speaks, I can see that inside those shrunken cheeks are nothing but purple gums and a wormlike tongue. "Valentine won't go easy, Zenith," it hisses.

I have no breath in me to tell this thing that I'm a friend.

At level three, I am deep inside. The glass shard embedded in the butt of my right palm throbs, but the pain is informational. I force myself to let go of the wire man's arms. His knee plunges even harder into my diaphragm and my vision erupts with pin-pricks of capering light. I've got enough oxygen for another second or two of consciousness.

So I better make it count.

In one deliberate jab, I drag the side of my right palm across the wire man's forehead, just over his eyes. The shard peels his scalp open even as it bites deeper into my hand. The wire man shrieks in pain as warm blood gushes out over his eyes.

That anvil lifts from my chest and I fall to my knees, coughing and gagging. The wire man writhes on the ground, spewing spittle and curses from wrinkled lips. I'm able to scramble to the hallway, shove the water-warped door closed behind me on broken hinges.

I put my back against it.

Looking at my hand, medical information telegraphs into my head. I bite the fabric of my shirt sleeve and rip a piece off with my good left hand. Fabric dangling from my teeth, I yank out the blood-coated sliver of glass and drop it on mildewed carpet. I wrap my hand tightly and tie it off.

There is no pain, no urgency. There is only the Zenith.

Through the floor, I feel the tremor of fighting in another room. The Zenith tells me where Lyle is, like an intuition. I dart through the broken hallways and stairwells lit only by the grayish amplified light of my retinal. A couple of times, I see motionless people shapes lying on the floor as I pass by.

Finally, I see a blade of light on the moldering floor. Wrench-ing open the door, I find Lyle standing with his back to me in a wide-open room, a patch of dusky sky visible overhead. Several interior walls have been torn down and part of the ceiling opens up to the evening air. The wood floors are bleached gray and the weather has washed the trash into congealed clumps along the walls. A couple of trees are growing in here, reaching awkwardly for the ragged hole of light above.

Gaunt and tall and breathing hard, Valentine leans against the far wall, his long fingers splayed out behind him. His green eyes are wide and unblinking, collecting information. He hunches forward slightly, collarbone pushing through his olive green T-shirt. His army jacket hangs loose.

"You okay?" Lyle asks me, without looking.

"Fine," I say. "This is not going according to plan."

"What makes you say that?" he asks, advancing toward the cornered amp.

"Hey, number thirteen," Valentine calls to me. He tries to grin, but a thrill of panic chases the curl out of his lip. His eyes dart back to Lyle. "How much does he know?"

"The right amount," says Lyle, taking a step forward.

"We're here to help you," I say. "Stop running."

Valentine laughs once gutturally. "You don't know enough, kid," he says.

"I know that Elysium has a whole dossier on you. You've been compromised. We're here to warn you," I say, walking deeper into the room.

"Check out the desk, thirteen," says Valentine, "then get back to me."

He lowers his forehead and trains his eyes on Lyle. His fingers have stopped drumming the wall. I look back and forth between the two soldiers. It strikes me how still they both are, like gunslingers, two sweaty palms hovering over gun butts.

"Lyle—" I begin to ask.

Quick as a mousetrap, Valentine has pulled his arms away

from the wall. He wraps his thumb around his pinky and leaves the three remaining fingers splayed like knives. In the greenish light, his spotted forearms are the mottled color of a shallow ocean floor. His face looks like he's about to cry.

"No," says Lyle.

Valentine lets his fingers collapse into a fist: three, two, one, zero. His body shudders once, jerks as though he's just completed an electrical circuit. Lyle is already diving forward as Valentine's lips twitch.

I know from experience what he is saying: *Three, two, one. Yes, yes, yes.*

Lyle lunges and hits the wall, collapsing rotten plaster with his elbow. But Valentine is gone, already pivoted on his foot and stepped perfectly out of the way. His red hair hangs sweaty over his forehead, and underneath it I can see that his eyes have gone slack and empty in a familiar way. Breathing harshly through a snarl, he lifts one leg and blindly kicks out the window behind him.

"Shit," mutters Lyle, as Valentine hunches like a crab and spins in place. He disappears through the window without a sound, without touching the jagged remaining glass or so much as tickling the frame. Here and gone like a vampire.

Lyle pauses, looks at the desk, then the window. Makes a decision and follows Val outside, moving just as naturally, with eyes just as dead. I can hear the iron fire escape outside clattering against the building as Lyle gives chase.

On Val's rust-eaten metal desk, a spray of papers and folders lie open. My retinal is picking out the words in the dim light before I can even think of reading them. *Mission Analysis and Planning.* Familiar names pop out of the dense text: Stilman, Daley, Valentine, and Lyle Crosby. My name. And the names of places: Houston, Chicago, Detroit.

. . . *necessary to execute synchronous combat operations on key political targets to continue decreasing regional stability* . . .

The words describe a battle plan.

. . . escalate operations to precipitate "crisis moment" that spur regional factions to engage local forces independently, triggering widespread chaos . . .

Civil war.

. . . as a Zenith you have a destiny, Valentine. Failure to respond to this proposal will be recognized as a tacit rejection of your duty to your squad, your people, and to Astra. It will be met with lethal response . . .

And the signature at the bottom: Lyle Crosby.

The laughing cowboy doesn't want to warn Valentine; Lyle is here to kill a rogue Zenith.

My world realigns, shifts into new focus. On the roof, Lyle is doing his best to murder an innocent man who refused to join him in a new war.

Cradling my hurt hand, I duck through the window and onto the rattling fire escape. I climb the rungs, one-handed, my cloth-wrapped palm stained with dirt. The sun has just slunk over the horizon, leaving the clouds bloody.

A gunshot punches into the twilight as I reach the top of the ladder. Pigeon wings flap in my ears like an echo. I peek over the edge.

The rotten sloping roof is empty. Dirty-pink insulation peeks through collapsed holes like diseased flesh. At the far edge, two silhouettes embrace. Lyle holds the gun in his right hand. His left arm is wrapped around Valentine's shoulder. He lowers Val to the rooftop.

"Sorry," I hear him murmur. "I'm sorry, Val."

Valentine lies on his side. He tucks his right hand under his left armpit, forearm over the wound to his chest, shoulders arched in pain. His breath is coming in shudders and his shirt is dark and heavy with spreading blood. Lyle crouches next to the fallen soldier, head bowed, his back to me.

Val's green eyes open and he spots me. His mouth spreads into a red smile, teeth washed in blood. "Thirteen," he chokes. "Good luck."

Lyle stands up and faces me. I watch him, motionless. Only my head is visible over the lip of the roof.

"You saw the pages," says Lyle, with a tone of finality. "Valentine was talking to the Priders. He was going to warn them. I can't have a rogue Zenith on my hands, Gray."

I hear movement in the room downstairs.

"I'm not the bad guy, understand," continues Lyle. "And that girl who killed herself . . . Samantha. She was right, Gray. Made the coward's choice, but she was right. This world is never going to accept us. There's no place for us in it. We've got to fight to make a new one. Especially if you're a Zenith."

On the ground behind Lyle, Valentine's chest stops rising and falling.

"Think of it," says Lyle. "Coordinated strikes on reggie targets, timed to create maximum confusion. Guerrilla warfare, house-to-house. Not just us soldiers but all the amps against all the reggies. Forging a new country out of plastic and titanium and silicone. It's happening tomorrow, Gray, on a scale you can't imagine."

"Why are you doing this?" I ask.

"Change, man," he says. "Carving out what's mine. Every living thing will fight to survive. And if the people don't want to fight, we'll make them. You don't pick your revolution. It picks you."

My eyes flick to the open window a story below me. I catch sight of Stilman and Daley inside. The two Zeniths are moving quickly and efficiently around the room. Stilman is carrying a dented gasoline can.

"Four of us left," says Lyle. "What's your choice?"

He raises the gun and trains it on my face, steadies his hand.

"Fight or die," calls Lyle. "Stilman joined. Daley. The rest died. Are you my general or not?"

Valentine's eyes are open and glassy, reflecting the gory clouds in the darkening sky. Sweat still evaporates from his forehead. The wind caresses his red hair.

Lyle pulls the hammer back. "Nobody is surprised when an oppressed people fight back. We are not the aggressors, Gray. We're freedom fighters, joining the tradition of our ancestors who fought for their humanity. They won't give us rights? We'll take them. We'll take everything we want."

In my peripheral I can see the hood of Lyle's truck just up the street. I know that the screwdriver that starts it is lying loose in the floorboard. Slowly, I lean my body away from the railing. Feel the wind breathing on the back of my neck.

"Okay," I say.

"You'll fight?" Lyle asks, warily lowering the gun.

"Yeah," I say. "I'll fight."

And I let go of the railing.

Chicago Tribune

AMPS ATTACK

By JANET MARINO

Hundreds dead as detonations rock Chicago, Houston, Detroit
Amp Extremists claim responsibility for horrific carnage

The Associated Press
CHICAGO

A simultaneous series of detonations crippled the downtown metropolitan areas of three American cities late last night in what witnesses described as a highly coordinated terrorist attack conducted by trained teams of amp extremists.

. . .

18
VERTIGO

Ten hours on the road, and my eyes feel rough as cracked porcelain. Not even Lyle could run fast enough to catch me when I bolted. Got this truck started and peeled out before he could even get off a shot.

I've been hightailing it back to Eden ever since. Got to find Jim.

Traffic started bogging down a few blocks away from Jim's work site. I saw a lot of people gathered and it was a bad sign, so I skirted around on a side street. Crunched Lyle's old pickup to a halt in a weedy ditch.

The rattling truck is finally stopped, but my body still tingles with phantom vibrations. My hands don't want to relax their grip on the plastic steering wheel. I put my forearm across it and rest my sweaty forehead, feeling my injured palm throb in time to my heartbeat.

Try to think.

The reports on the radio are chaotic. I don't know what to believe. Timed detonations in cities around the country. Buildings falling. Hundreds dead, maybe thousands. Astra claiming responsibility for the start of a new war. Lyle must have thousands of amps ready to fight. A whole rank structure. Training and upgrades. He's building a new world and I was too late to stop him.

It is chaos in the parking lot out in front of the site. Full to overflowing with screaming demonstrators. More than just the guys who lost their jobs. Priders are here from everywhere. I wonder what Lyle is planning to do to them.

The double-wide chain-link gate is closed and locked today. Just inside, I spot a familiar hulking figure. The Brain, unmistakable, flanked by dozens more of Lyle's gang from Eden. They stand behind the flimsy metal links, staring out. Taunting the demonstrators with smiles and crossed arms.

Lyle wasn't fucking around.

I haul myself out of the truck. Scale the back fence and hop over, keeping a lot of room between me and the Brain. The work site is about half as full as normal. Mostly just the old men, heads down. Still doing their jobs while the angry crowd outside builds and builds.

I scour the site for Jim until a worker points upward.

Four stories up, I exit the wooden scaffolding to find the old man unloading bundles of rebar off the crane and stowing them in long lines for the rod busters to drop into concrete. Jim is working relentlessly, drops of sweat hanging off his chin, the putter of his exoskeleton motor cutting through the quiet air up here. The way he is moving is thoughtful and automatic at the same time. Calm compared to the madness unfolding downstairs.

"Hey," I call out.

Jim turns to me, looks me up and down without saying anything. His eyes settle on the weeping improvised bandage wrapped around my hand. With a sigh, he sets down a piece of shivery rebar.

"Let me look at that hand," he says.

The first-aid box is at the base of the building. Jim signals the crane operator that the load is finished. Then he leads me down the creaking scaffolding to the ground floor. The subbasement for the parking garage isn't complete yet, and the three-story drop still tickles the pit of my stomach. In the cool cement interior of the half-completed structure, Jim pops open the rusty first-aid box and sets out the antiseptic, cotton balls, antibiotics, gauze.

In here, the rumble of the people outside sounds like distant traffic, punctuated by an occasional angry shriek. Other old men are standing outside the building, smoking and trying to look calm.

"You save that Zenith?" asks Jim.

"I . . . no," I say.

"Jim—" I start to speak and then stop. I can't think of the right way to say this because there isn't one. Sometimes you've just got to blurt it out. "Lyle is the one killing Zeniths. Astra isn't defending us. It never was. Lyle's trying to start a chain reaction . . ."

I trail off when I see the look on Jim's face.

"I'm too late," I say.

Jim pauses from wiping dirt off my hand with a cotton ball.

"Shit's hit the fan. After the tri-city attacks, Priders are rioting and looting amp neighborhoods all over the country. They got Joe Vaughn himself rallying up the road," says Jim, turning my hand and examining the wound. "He's outside the old post office, a mile from here, whipping these people into a goddamn frenzy.

"I don't know how we're gonna—" he is saying, wrapping my hand in gauze, but his voice is swallowed as the dull roar of the demonstrators rises an octave. The front fence starts ringing like a bell. Sounds like it's being tossed around by a tornado.

"Priders are coming in," I say, looking around and seeing no easy way out of the site. "We can make it out if we run now."

"I didn't want this to happen. But that doesn't mean I can skip it."

"What do we do?" I ask.

Jim gives me back my hand. Surveys the work site—taking in the worried faces of his elderly coworkers. His face is grim when he turns back to me. A saw blade slides out from under the forearm of his exoskeleton.

"We fight," he says.

. . .

In the winking shadows of the half-finished building, the old men stand side by side, dirty jeans and flannel work shirts wrapped in titanium exoskeletons. Scowls on wrinkled faces. Their blades and saws are out, whirring like cicadas under the biting heat.

Jim and I join them as a wave of Priders pushes down the rest of the fence. They're trampling into the site, grabbing improvised weapons off the ground. Pipes, boards, and pocketknives. Lyle's people are fighting back. Not the erratic, robotically efficient fighting of a Zenith but old-school brawling. Sharpened reflexes fueled by real anger.

The police officers who were patrolling outside are coming in, too. Stepper-wearing riot cops, pushing forward in a line with plastic shields up. Batons out and guns holstered, for now. Obsidian statues crashing into a line of amps, just a bunch of kids with heads full of government cheese. The kids aren't trained as well as soldiers, but they strike fast and bounce out of harm's way quicker than fleas.

The Priders are surging in around the cops, pushing one another forward in a faceless crush of human limbs. It's a tidal wave that pushes the line of old men back. Makes fighting nearly impossible.

Jim shrugs off a tubby guy with a tough-guy mustache, arms swinging. Another guy gets hold of me, and Jim accidentally runs his blurring saw blade over the man's forearm. The guy gapes at the red slash and it gapes right back at him. The crowd eats him up and he stumbles away clutching his arm.

The horizon rushes in until it's a wall of stinking sweat and body heat and shouting faces. Jim and I retreat slowly, side by side, shoving violent demonstrators away from us. Punching only when we have to. Jim's saw blade spews bluish smoke as he waves it at Priders dumb enough to get close.

Then rocks and chunks of gravel start falling in on us. Priders out beyond the fence are throwing them from a safe distance. The stone rain adds to the confusion, hitting amps and Priders alike. A jagged hunk of concrete cartwheels past Jim's leg, a tangle of wire barely missing his calf.

We keep backing away until we can't.

At the scaffolding alongside the base of the building, we run out of ground. Behind us, stripes of warning tape crisscrossing a three-story drop to the subbasement. In front, a boiling wall of anger advances. Regular people gone insane, buttressed by stepper-wearing cops in body armor.

The sharp shoulder of Jim's exoskeleton digs into my arm. The world is closing in around us. Not even a Zenith could save me now.

"I'm sorry, Jim," I say. "I guess I was never meant to protect Eden."

"All a man can do is fight," says Jim. "You fought."

A flash.

It's so bright and vicious that at first I think it came from inside my own head. My ears ring and my skull thrums with it, vibrating like fine crystal. I mash my palms against a concrete wall and brace myself against sudden vertigo.

I gag, then vomit.

Screams. I think I can hear screams through the ringing in my ears. Shoulder muscles knotted, I drag my face away from the wall. Lift a numb forearm and wipe drool from my mouth.

"Jim?" I ask, leaning against the wall, letting the gritty surface anchor me to reality. I can barely hear my own voice. The atmosphere seems leaden, too thick to transmit sound. I smell fire.

Blinking away dust, I'm able to focus on the ground.

A Rorschach blob of yellowish vomit stains a piece of dirty plywood at my feet. I watch a glistening drop of blood heave itself from my face, dropping toward the center of the earth. A tacky wetness creeps down my cheek, a slug trail from temple to jawline.

"Jim?"

I turn to Jim and there is no Jim. The warning tape is gone.

The reality of what this means settles coldly over my shoulders. My head bobs idiotically as a surge of grief claws its way out of my chest. "No," I say, and I can't hear the word, only feel the fluttering vibration of it in my throat.

On my knees, I clamber to the edge and look into the subbasement. Another drop of my blood leaves my temple and escapes into the world, pulled away in a shining arc. I see only dust falling down the shaft in a silent waterfall. Down, down, down. My retinal brightens the image. There's Jim at the bottom of the shaft, lying on his side in fetal position. One arm is outstretched, still reaching for balance. His body is coated in chalky dust from head to toe, a bas-relief.

There is no blood. It looks like he fell asleep down there.

For some reason I think about his trailer. Two miles away. Sitting empty and still, hot water heater ticking to itself in the closet. Sunlight groping through the blinds, doggedly starching the pages of old magazines on the coffee table. Cards still laid out in an unfinished game of solitaire. Empty now, empty forever.

I stand up and swallow a cough and look out on the site.

At the front gate, a plume of smoke swirls madly upward. The crane's latest bundle of rebar oscillates over my head, buoyed by the upswell of dusty wind. In the haze, elderly men lie sprawled like fallen mannequins, exoskeletons frozen in whatever position they were in at the moment of detonation. Inside each exoskeleton, an old man struggles. Mice caught in particularly complicated traps. The machines have stopped working, frozen, but the men inside are alive.

Some of the Priders are crouched for cover. Others are getting in kicks and punches while they have the chance. Amps are holding their heads, moving sluggishly. Even the cops are struggling to get out of their steppers.

A bomb. The Priders must have let off a bomb, the kind that

makes an electromagnetic pulse. The EMP passed through us all like the ghost of an explosion. But where the pulse finds electronics, it generates a surge of current that can freeze a motor or make an implant so hot it burns your skin.

I smear blood and dust across my face trying to wipe it clean. My hands won't stop trembling, but I'm still alive. Whatever they set off wasn't strong enough. But I imagine the next time this happens, they'll do the job right.

Only one person stands.

Lyle Crosby moves across the parking lot like a ghost, side-stepping fallen bodies and swinging Priders. That plume of dirty smoke sprouts behind him as he strides toward me. The laughing cowboy is shielding his eyes with one hand and advancing fast and confident. In his right hand, he has a pistol out and swinging. The explosion must have gotten his attention.

He spots me through the dust.

I throw myself forward, staggering, running for the fence. But somehow my feet are tangled together and my palms are out and skinned as I fall headfirst. Sliding through the dirt, I'm already climbing onto my knees.

"Jim fell," I say. "Jim's hurt—"

Crouched, I turn and see Lyle standing over me.

Three, two—

Lyle's knife-handed strike catches me in the side of the neck before my trigger can go off. I land on my stomach in the dirt, diaphragm muscles seizing, head buzzing with pain. He casually walks past me, leans over the gap, and peers into the subbasement.

"Damn," he says.

Hands on his hips, Lyle surveys the work site.

"EMP, huh? Them Priders are crafty. But it didn't have to be this way," he says. "I did everything I could. Coddled you like a goddamn baby. You wouldn't fight to save your own life. And now look at you. Look at Jim. Eden was never going to last, Gray."

I choke out the word. "Lucy."

"Jesus Christ. I *sent* Lucy your way. How blind are you? I saw that dopey look on your face the night I kicked that deputy out of Eden. Wanted to know more and she told me all about you. Thought I could get you on my side, fangs out. But Daley was right, you ain't got any fangs."

Flashes of memory. Lucy dropping by to talk with Jim, staying to talk with me. Squeezing my hand in Jim's trailer. My piss-stained shirt, cleaned and pressed and waiting for me on the arm of her couch. Our kiss.

"What?" I ask.

Lyle is pacing. Manic. He wheels on me then stalks away, again, speaking all the time. "Wuh-wuh-what? Why you think she came over to your place? So friendly? How do you think I found out you were a Zenith? You think I showed up at your trailer that day and saved you by *accident*? You got a head full of rocks. And that's sad, too, because, man, you had some serious fucking potential."

He taps his temple with a finger, presses it in hard enough to make his fingertip go white.

"Did you know I qualified for Echo Squad out of two thousand two hundred and twelve Army Rangers from all three goddamn battalions? And I'm Zenith class, but, Jesus Christ, the shit you got ain't even military grade. It's *better* than military grade. They don't make 'em like that anymore because they *never* made 'em like that. I don't know what your daddy was smoking, or whether he saw the end of the world coming or what, but that man was *not* fucking around the day he put that shit in your head."

I gave you something extra, is how my father put it.

I'm a means to an end. A soldier in Lyle's make-believe army. My breath is back now, passing ragged through a bruised larynx. I'm leaning against a piece of plywood. Watching Lyle pace.

"You used me."

"Correction. I *tried* to use you."

I lean forward, grunting to get up. He raises a lanky leg and drops a boot onto my chest, crushing the air out of me.

"Sit down, hero," he says. "I don't have time for this shit. These people think they're fighting now, but I haven't even got started yet. I've got a goddamn ace up my sleeve that's been waiting there for ten years. Since the birth of Pure Pride. Wait until I show them what I got, Gray. Then they'll know war."

That gun glints darkly in his hand. Curses and shouting come in a steady torrent from the front gate. Lyle glances over his shoulder and licks his lips. His chest is rising and falling like he just ran a marathon.

Pinned, I struggle to wriggle out from under the boot. I don't want to die here, groveling in the dirt.

Lyle lifts his foot, looks at me like I'm a carpet stain. "I'm not gonna kill you, Gray. There's something better planned for you."

He saunters ten feet away, then turns.

"When you get arrested, don't resist," he says. "Try to have some dignity when the feds lock you up for the rest of your life. After all, *you're* the leader of Astra."

Violence Plagues Nation in Wake of Attack

HOUSTON—Anger over the tri-city amp attacks on Chicago, Houston, and Detroit has quickly erupted into escalating acts of violence nationwide.

The Federal Bureau of Investigation estimates that over 120 incidents of violence against implanted individuals have occurred since the attacks were perpetrated.

Reports of harassment and assault are pouring in from all over the country but are concentrated in the cities directly affected by the attacks.

Instances continue to pile up: In Chicago, a man on an anti-implantee rampage fatally shot an implanted panhandler at a gas station. In Detroit, a Molotov cocktail was thrown Tuesday at a community center run by the Free Body Liberty Group. Three were injured and the downtown building was severely damaged. Possibly the worst incident occurred in Houston, where a mob of 500 people surrounded the home of a local implantee. The man was beaten severely and left in critical condition and his home partially burned before the group was dispersed by police.

So far, the government has been unable to quell the violence. FBI Director Greg Wright has repeatedly told the press that "vigilante attacks and threats against implantees or their loved ones will not be tolerated."

19

DIRTY MOVE

Lyle stalks away, head lowered. His right hand is out, fingers extended. Three, then two. One. He makes a tight fist.

The laughing cowboy trots and then breaks into a run. Skips across the dust-smeared work site too fast, movements bird-like and stomach-turning. Ducking between Priders and amps alike. The Zenith is clearly whispering in his ear.

Got a new world to build, he said and I know immediately where he is going.

A mile from here, the Pure Human Citizen's Council is staging a rally that's brimming with good, upstanding reggie citizens. Joseph Vaughn has got politicians and speakers and reformed doctors on a stage raised to the eyes of the world. The cowboy is going to continue his fight.

Lyle laughs hoarsely as he dodges through the crowd of dazed Priders. He calls out commands to the other amps. The plume of smoke still rises over broken exoskeletons and police-issued steppers. A half dozen of Lyle's gang jump up to follow him, grinning and panting. I hear his boots slapping the empty street erratically, skipping in unnaturally long strides. Then he's around the corner, out of sight, gone with his trained seals into the industrial neighborhood that wraps around the construction site.

I wrench myself up and stagger after him. My legs are swinging heavy and stiff in bloodstained jeans. But the grime on my face is dried up and whatever electrical surge happened to my amp is over now.

On my own I'm too slow to catch Lyle.

Taking a deep breath, I try to hold out my fingers. Still wrapped, my hand will barely obey. So instead, I visualize my hand. Curl my imaginary pinky and slide the ball of my thumb over it. As I perform the mental countdown, I take a perverse pleasure in it. Try to think good thoughts as I oh so carefully engage the Zenith. Gentle, like you'd tap a hot water faucet in a crummy shower. Level three and that's it, Jack. I'm not going any deeper than I have to.

Three, two, one, zero. And when my eyes open, the Zenith shows me more.

For one, I see that I've got a bigger problem now. About seven feet and three hundred and fifty pounds of problem, looming with its hands out, breathing like a bull. Blocking the open fence and my way out.

The Brain.

The titan stands watching, as alien to me as a Cro-Magnon must have been to a Neanderthal. I know he's human. But he used that diagnostic amp to sharpen his training, to push his body within millimeters of the breaking point, day after day. He used sheer willpower and pinpoint mental control to become the template for a new species.

I consider this as the Brain puts out his meaty arms. He shakes his great head at me slowly, tendons in his neck the size of my biceps. *He's only human,* I remind myself. *And he's not a Zenith.*

The body, no matter how bizarre, is just an extension of the mind. And my mind is bigger than his.

"Let me through, Brain. You know what I can do."

His face splits into a pink smile. "And I know what you won't do," he says.

The dreamy look on his face reminds me of his fight with the Blade. The Brain was alone in his own mind then, according to Lyle, fighting in a smoky room. Focusing on his face, I dial out the writhing old men around us. Let the grayness seep in around the edges and absorb all distraction. I even banish the sadness and shock I feel for Jim, sensing it laced through my thoughts like venom.

My view of the world is purified.

I feint to the left and try to scramble around the Brain. My lunge doesn't fool him. With a mauling grip he catches the back of my shirt, twists me up into the air. My shirt collar gags me and then rips, and I slip out of his grasp, hitting the concrete hard on all fours.

A black motorcycle boot lifts out of my vision and I roll, knowing that the boot is coming back down like a pneumatic hammer. I almost make it. The heel mashes the fingertips of my left hand. Grinding pain corkscrews into me and I gasp, remembering the time I caught my fingers in the hinge of a car door and wondering how this could be so much worse. Then I tune it out. Yank my hand from under his boot, leaving bloody finger paint on the street.

Grabbing the Brain's trunk of a leg, I yank myself upright and keep going, climbing up his back. It's like mounting an angry elephant, the smell of sweat and heat coming off his neck in waves. Muscles slither under his skin as he swings his arms at me.

The first blow sledgehammers into my shoulder blades, and I squeeze my arms tighter around his chest and suck wind. His fists are dense as a sack of ball bearings. I reach up and wrap a hand around his forehead where he can't bite me. The next fist thuds into me and the light starts doing funny things in my eyes.

"I'm sorry," I whisper. With one hand I grip his forehead tight, and with the other I dig my thumb directly into his port. A dirty move. Dirty as sewage. Twisting, I cram my thumbnail into the puffy flesh of his temple. His head twists violently and that arm rises again, and I tense for impact. But something gives. The tip of my thumb sinks in a quarter inch. The arm wavers and then drops, hesitant. I let up.

The Brain coughs a couple times, the choke of an old car that won't turn over on a cold morning. He stumbles, arms out for balance. Finally he collapses to his knees like a dynamited building.

I slide off the Brain's back and quickly check his face. Even kneeling, he's as tall as I am, staring vacantly ahead. He sneezes once, expelling a cannonball of air from his lungs.

"Brain?" I ask. "You okay?"

He takes a halfhearted swipe at me, eyes still unfocused. I take that as a yes and leave him, hurry across the empty street. Just after I cross, four police cars whiz by in a line behind me. Doppler-shifted sirens pushing and then pulling me along.

Toward the mayhem.

Running hard, I leap over cracked pavement, charge past roll-top doors and beige commercial warehouses. The thrum of several thousand people rolls toward me from somewhere up ahead, but the streets are oddly empty. Plastic bottles and discarded flyers stalk each other in the breeze. Locked doors and closed garages. Hazy clouds and the faint smell of smoke.

A half-fallen wooden roadblock slants across the street ahead.

I hear the shouts before I see anything. Sporadic gunshots and the edge of naked panic, unrestrained anger in the cries. Two women and a man appear and hobble past me. One of the women is holding a blood-soaked shirt against the man's face. She shrinks away when she spots my temple.

Rounding the corner, I stumble into a full-blown melee.

I'm too late. Way too goddamn late. Every one of Lyle's amps is here and they are attacking Pure Priders with anything on hand: rebar from the construction site, two-by-fours, rocks, and fists. Some have guns and some carry scavenged riot shields. The amps are charging in from the side streets, trapping reggies in the intersection. Other reggies are making a run for it. It's a slaughter.

In seconds, I see an overweight amp smash another man's cheekbone with one fist and keep on running, catching another guy in a sternum-crushing bear hug. A group of four reggies have got another amp by the arms, his shirt ripped mostly off; he slithers out of their grasp and sets about taking them apart with his fists and elbows.

Other people are lying facedown, not moving.

A burning car throws smoke over a cluster of reggies in front of the stage, back-to-back against the onslaught. These people are bloody, scared to death. Their signs are forgotten on the ground, trampled underfoot along with those who are hurt. Homemade T-shirts with angry slogans have been ripped into strips, turned to bandages.

Black uniforms intermingle with the group. Police separated from one another. On their own, defending the demonstrators and themselves with nightsticks and Tasers and sidearms.

And then there's Lyle.

For just an instant, I spot the cowboy standing on the stage itself, above the scrum. He takes in the havoc with his knuckles resting on his hips, fingers curled up like feathers. Scans the crowd, eyes flickering past me without settling, and turns. Speaks to someone behind him, neck tensing with a shout.

Lyle leaps off the back end of the stage.

I fall forward into the fray, and the Zenith guides me as I shove and dodge my way toward the cowboy. The fighters batter my body back and forth. Rolling off sweaty backs and ducking fists, I skirt the defensive line of reggies and mount the stage two steps at a time.

Craning, I spot Lyle sprinting down a backstreet, away from the fight.

I cross the stage and leap down, follow Lyle as fast as I can.

Flatten my palms and let my knees pump like pistons. Behind me, the concussion of multiple gunshots boomerangs around the intersection. I press onward, accelerating even as my lungs ignite with pain. The cowboy is so goddamn fast and everything is on the line and I can't help sliding backward, going deeper into myself.

Level three just isn't cutting it anymore.

Level four. Man-portable weapon systems. Small arms. Infantry support. Lethal organic fire support. Obstacle breaching. Do you consent? Do you consent?

Yes.

Ears trained on the *plock-plock* of Lyle's boots, I let my vision collapse. Feel my eyes go dead around the edges even as every follicle and nerve ending of my body buzzes with life. My movements smooth out and gain a liquid flow. Running silent and smooth and swift as a tsunami on the open sea.

When I come upon Lyle, it's all I can do to stop.

In a blind alley, the cowboy is leaning against a black town car with its door open, talking to a guy in a business suit. Lyle sees me and winces and at that moment I realize who he's chatting with.

Senator Joseph Vaughn.

The leader of the Pure Human Citizen's Council is taller than he appears from a distance—an athlete. Under his expensive suit, he's muscular. The politician stands next to the car, relaxed and disheveled. He's sweated through his suit. Tie half on. His hair is mussed and his cheeks are flushed.

"No, Lyle," I say. "No."

The laughing cowboy grins at me, shrugs his crow-bitten shoulders.

Lyle is standing here in this alley, chatting with Vaughn like they were old friends. These two should be worst enemies and they're not at all and the meaning of that puts a sag into my knees. Who's paying for all this?

The boss, man, who do you think?

"You're working for the Priders?" I ask Lyle, my voice flat with blank disbelief. "You did this for *them*?"

Lyle stands up off the car, sighs.

"The Brain still alive?" he asks.

I nod.

"Thanks," he says, then turns and I see his eyes have gone dark and blank. My body leaps away before I'm aware of it. Lyle hits the space where I was standing like a torpedo, fists stuttering in the air. His boots scrabble over the gravelly pavement as he gets his balance. He turns back, eyes half closed.

Now I'm between him and the senator.

Lyle smiles, dead eyed. He's given himself up to the implant. Gone all the way into his deep place and put himself on autopilot.

"Whole fuckin' hog, Gray. Level five. World opens up to you in ways you can't imagine."

Lyle throws himself at me like a predator. Like something that our ancestors might have drawn on cave walls by firelight. My body is trying to move, trying to save my life, but I'm tangled up in Vaughn. The politician has grabbed my arms from behind. I twist around to look at him, and he stares back at me with this look on his face like I just shit my pants in church.

"Moron," he says.

Then I'm on the ground. Lyle is on me like a barbed-wire blanket. The pavement gobbles up chunks of my skin as I struggle. But Lyle is too fast, each move part of a series. The cowboy torques a bony elbow across my jaw, and for a moment my mouth doesn't close quite like it should anymore.

Lyle's got me pinned and he's dropping fists on me mechanically. My bruised forearms are up, fending off the bombardment with equally mechanical precision.

"We coulda gone to the stars," he says. "You could have been my brother."

As I start to lose consciousness I catch his face in glimpses, twisted with hate.

"Stop!" shouts Vaughn. "Stop it, Lyle."

It's like shouting at a locomotive. Lyle stops punching and digs his thumbs into my windpipe. Now my arms are so much useless rubber. I'm retreating back to my inside room whether I want to or not. My eyes rolling up, and now I'm looking at the inside of my own skull.

". . . dammit, you animal . . ."

". . . need him . . ."

". . . the fucking plan . . ."

Silence.

I feel something like ants on my face. Stinging and tickling, running around in a blind confusion. It's the blood returning. My vision blooms from tiny pinpricks, expands until I see the buildings looming over me, wavering and dancing.

I'm lying on my back, head bouncing as I cough uncontrollably. Specks of white foam arc away from my lips into the sunlight. The pavement is cool and gritty on my head. Level four is gone, not even a memory. I feel like I've been out for days, but it was just seconds.

Lyle sits a few feet away, arms on his knees. He picks a dandelion from a crack in the cement and twirls it, fingernails rimmed in my blood. He smiles at the flower, considers it. Like nothing happened. But I can still feel his phantom grasp around my throat.

Vaughn isn't calm, though.

The politician wheels around and screams at the cowboy. Walks over to the car and leans on it, catching his breath. Somehow, the sounds don't register in my ears. All I hear is the sluggish pounding of my heart, the crinkled-plastic rasp of my lungs.

"How could you do it?" I croak to Lyle.

He wipes his nose with one swollen fist. Sniffs. "What do you want me to say? Everything's part of a plan," he says. "This is happening all over the country. Right now, today. You could have owned it. But it's all over for you. For me, it's just beginning."

"Why?" I ask, voice breaking.

The pain and hurt I feel are embedded in the question like a needle. Lyle winces at the sting of it, says nothing.

Vaughn kicks an empty can, sends it rattling down the alley. "Get this amp on his way. We've got a lot of work to do."

Lyle's eyes never leave mine. "Whatever you say, boss," he says.

The laughing cowboy drags me onto my feet. I try to swallow through a half-collapsed throat and choke on it. I'm seeing the world through gauze as Lyle shoves me out of the alley. I stand there, swaying on my feet.

"You're letting me go?" I ask, incredulous.

The tang of far-off smoke stings my nostrils.

"Sorta," says Lyle, shrugging. He opens the car door and gets in. Slams it shut on my disbelief.

"You smell that?" Vaughn asks, leaning over the hood of the car. His voice seems to come from far away. "You better run home, my friend. Eden is burning."

The White House Office of the Press Secretary
United States Capitol, Washington, D.C.

Mr. Speaker, Mr. Vice President, members of Congress, I come
to this house of the people to speak to you and all Americans at
a defining moment—as the impact of a volatile new technology
rends at our union and tears at the bonds of human kinship—as our
nation stands on the very precipice of civil war.

Yesterday, a coalition of extremists known as Astra, their bodies
implanted with advanced technology, launched a series of coordinated, premeditated attacks on three American cities.

The attack yesterday posed a direct challenge to the constitutional
rights of Americans to assemble and freely express their beliefs.
Many innocent lives were lost to fanaticism. By choosing to reject
rational discourse and to take the lives of their fellow citizens, these
extremists have abandoned everything except for the will to power,
and they have therefore abandoned their own cause.

I want to speak tonight directly to the hundreds of thousands of
implanted individuals who are peaceful and who bear no ill will
toward our union. We respect your decision to undergo medical
implantation. We understand that over the last tumultuous months,
tensions have run high between implanted and nonimplanted citizens. Debates have raged in our courts, our halls of Congress, and
in our churches and homes. We ask that you be patient. Peace will
come in time.

Tonight, however, we must seek to maintain the compact of our
union that was sealed in the flames of a catastrophic civil war that
took place more than a century and a half ago.

As commander in chief of the Army and Navy, I have directed that all measures be taken for the defense of the American people from the extremists who are in our midst. We will use every resource to hunt these extremists down, turn them against one another, and drive them from safe shelter and into the arms of the law. Likewise, we will not hesitate to use *any means necessary* to protect innocent individuals with implants.

A great task awaits us—a rectification of human nature itself. The continued existence of our union depends upon our success in this endeavor.

We must seek the unity of natural man with the artificial world that he has built—with the technology that can save or destroy him, with new capabilities that can bring about great good or great harm, and with the technological devices that can nourish or starve his spirit.

We must seek and find an ultimate harmony between body and machine, a common ground from which every citizen is free to contribute toward improving the quality of our entire civilization.

This is the search that we begin tonight.

20

GOOD GUY

Smoke is rising from Eden—thin black ribbons braiding them-selves in the sky. I stumble and try to run harder. I'm sucking air in ragged breaths, my throat and ribs and fingers bruised and hurt-ing. The breeze carries the sharp chemical smell of a whole lot of unnatural, man-made shit burning up fast.

Cancer on the wind.

The war has really started now. Jim told me it was coming. *They're just waiting for an excuse,* he said. Maybe my dad even saw a twinkle of it on the horizon fifteen years ago when he healed me and gave me something extra while he was at it. Deep down, they must have feared that one day it would come to this: the new against the old.

Even Samantha saw it.

In my imagination, I envisioned a heroic battle. Guns and guts and glory. Instead, I'm sneaking into a burning trailer park to find a goofy kid and a woman who may have pretended to like me as a favor to her psychopath brother.

I hesitate a moment at the tree line, watching the glint of sun off Eden's unwanted chain-link fence. No movement. Then I sprint across the muddied field, keeping my eyes on the swivel. The spotlighter brawl has left its mark here: wadded-up shirts that got ripped from Priders' backs; glinting debris from smashed-up folding chairs; and that rusted, bullet-riddled generator slumped over like bloated roadkill.

But clear so far.

I climb over the rattling chain-link fence and stop on the other side, leaning against it. At least one trailer is burning for real. I don't remember who lives there. But an honest-to-God blaze is going, with feral tongues of fire roaring up the sides of the yellowed old box. Waves of ash-specked wind surge off the flames, oven hot, tossing the branches of the pecan trees around. The plastic is withering, softening and falling in on itself.

I notice the paint blackening and curling away on the outside of the boxes next door. These trailers are too damn close to each other. At this rate, the whole trailer park will go up.

And there are no police. I don't see or hear any fire trucks. Nobody is around. The authorities must be busy with the riots. The amps must have all run away.

Someone hoots loudly. A familiar-sounding "yee-haw." I curl my fingers into the fence behind me, tense up, and freeze in place.

Three men stomp together through an intersection between trailers. The one in front has a gasoline can and a cap pulled low over his eyes. The other two follow, slouching along with sunken chests and shotguns low and leveled. All their faces are red and sweaty as if sunburned. But it's from the fire. These men have gotten too close to the blaze, and it sure hasn't bothered them any. I can see their feverish grins as they pass by.

They cross the intersection and are gone. An answering hoot echoes from somewhere on the other side of the trailer park. Glass shatters, followed by peals of drunken laughter.

Lucy's trailer is too close to the spreading flame. I unwrap my fingers from the fence. Try to estimate where the Priders are from their catcalls.

I double over and scramble down the main path toward Lucy's trailer. Glancing left and right, I notice lots of half-open doors. I step over clothing and kitchen utensils and kids' toys. Dropped and left behind in the dirt after whatever mass exodus must have just happened.

Maybe Lucy and Nick made it out already. This attack is no surprise; it's been coming for a long time.

I hear a scratching sound behind me and spin around so fast I nearly fall. Instead of the barrel of a shotgun, I see a flowery window covering fall back into place behind a rust-kissed screen. My breath eases out in a hiss. There are still people here in the burning trailer park.

Amps hiding from Priders.

I trot over to the occupied trailer. Knock lightly on the window. "Fire's coming," I whisper. "You've gotta run for it."

Nobody answers.

Someone laughs loudly nearby. I turn to see the round lid of a cement birdbath pinwheeling through the nearest intersection. It crunches into the porch across the street. I press myself flat against the trailer. As the voices grow louder, I count down in my head. Visualizing my fingers. Already going back, eager for the taste of the Zenith in my mind.

Three, two, one, zero—*level four and the world becomes bright and crisp as newly fallen snow.*

Two men stride around the corner, joking with each other. They see me and pause. I nonchalantly raise a hand and wave at a scowling, bearded guy holding a shotgun. He's wearing a sling around his right arm from the last time we met.

Collarbones can take such a long time to heal.

"Hey, Billy," I say. "Long time no see."

The shotgun blast tears a messy hole in the siding of the trailer behind me, but I'm already moving. Head down, allowing the Zenith's tendrils of control to flicker into my limbs. I'm off the ground, on a porch, then beyond it. Running, scrambling on all fours, climbing, and leaping. Sights rush past in fits, fast and slow, playing out on a broken projector.

I hear a woman screaming from the trailer I left behind. That shotgun slug wasn't harmless after all. It must have torn through metal siding and insulation and flesh.

Guttural shouts ring out behind me, met by more hooting coming from somewhere in front. Now I'm on Lucy's porch and headed for the flimsy door, reaching, fingers outstretched.

And then, somehow, I'm on my knees.

The world's gone bright as a solar flare. Overexposed. I'm seeing angels dance, white spots brighter than heaven. I hear the sputtering boom of an explosion in the distance, echoes racing each other between the trailers.

Blinking at the light, I cover my ears and watch. Two doors down, a cylindrical propane tank the size of a doghouse has detonated. It jets a sputtering plume of blue-purple flame, rolling loose over the dirt. The blistering clouds of flame push the tank, swiveling it toward me in vicious inching pirouettes.

I shove myself up and grab the handle of Lucy's front door. The stuttering eruption grows louder. With numb fingers I claw at the door handle. A sudden surge of heat rolls over my back and the world boils as I stumble into the cool trailer.

Before my eyes can adjust, sharp fingers grab my shirt and yank me off-balance. A pair of thin pale arms twists me in a circle and throws me. I bounce off the wall and collapse onto my stomach. Instantly, a knee drops into my back and pins me. A barrage of punches cascade across my shoulder blades. I twist to get free.

"Quit struggling," says a familiar voice. "You're on fire, for Chrissake. Let me put you out."

These are pats, I realize. Not punches.

I roll over and look up into Lucy's face. Her eyes are red. She's been crying recently, but she isn't now. At this moment, she looks sad and afraid and relieved. I want to lay into her, question her about everything Lyle said. I want to give her a hug and kiss her cheeks. I want to curl up into a ball and grieve for Jim.

I do none of those things.

"Where's Nick?" I ask.

The boy crawls out from behind the couch. Puts his arms around my neck. Hugs me awkwardly. He steps back, and I take him by the shoulders and inspect him. The kid's got soot around his nostrils, sweat beading on his cheeks, but he's fine. There is a Band-Aid over his temple.

"Sharks came," he says, simply.

"I know, Nicky," I respond. "You were right."

"We were waiting for Jim," says Lucy. "Got trapped."

I work hard to keep my face empty. My sight hums from the Zenith.

Boom. A hole explodes in the front door. It sounds like the tire of an 18-wheeler blowing out. A shotgun slug moves past my face and keeps going through the far wall. Daylight shines in through both gaps, illuminating fast-moving smoke outside.

"Door's on fire," says Billy, faintly from outside. "Y'all go around. They'll be out the back. I guarantee it."

Smoke is pouring into the trailer. The propane tank must have ignited the siding. Billy throwing gasoline on it probably hasn't helped, either.

No thinking. No time. I wrap my arms around Lucy and Nick, hustle them toward the back hallway of the trailer. We lean together and crawl, coughing through the acrid black smoke already gathering at the ceiling.

Flames are consuming the trailer from the outside in. The sound has changed from a wind-fueled whoosh to a meaty chuckle. I can hear Billy outside, yelling at me over the din of the blaze: "Where you gonna go now, amp?"

I cringe as another fist-sized hole punches through the wood paneling, spraying me with laminated splinters. As Billy reloads, I urge Lucy and Nick forward until we reach the end of the hallway. We crouch together. On my right is the door to the bathroom. On my left is the back door that leads outside.

"Don't go outside until I say it's okay," I say.

I don't have to look out there. I know that on the other side, two men with shotguns are waiting for Billy to flush us out like rabbits from the brush. Lucy tries to say something and I shake my head. I wrap her hands around Nick's grimy little hands. I push them both down until they are lying flat on the floor. Raise a finger—wait here one second.

A shout comes from outside: "Thought you beat Gunnin' Billy?"

Gently I push open the hollow bathroom door. Billy's voice rings loud and clear through frosted plastic window slats. Cheap snowflake-patterned laminate curls up around the edges of the bathroom window, turning yellow from the heat outside. Fake plastic tiles line the floor and walls, blooming with mildew around the shower. A gray cinder block holds up the sink.

I gently drag the block of concrete out, hoist it to chest level. Feel the gravelly bite of it on my chest. I step back into the molded plastic shower stall. Take a deep breath and clear my mind. Let the Zenith speak and listen close because it's important.

Level four. Gun schematics and evasion routes and room-clearing techniques flood into my mind's eye, even teasing the edges of my vision. I stop my trigger finger from curling around an imaginary weapon.

I've got one shot at this and I need to know where my target is standing.

"There's women and children in here, Billy," I shout.

Six inches from my abdomen, the bathroom wall disintegrates and a hunk of solid metal thumps through the siding. Before the slug hits the far wall, I'm pivoting, pulling my arms in tight and powerful like coiled springs—then, I shot-put the cinder block through the cracked window, channeling all my strength and will to survive out into the smoky unknown. The block sails toward that shotgun, the voice behind it, the threat.

Crunch.

Now I hear flames eating and nothing else. There is a piercing crack as the living room roof falls in. Doubling over, I cough into the crook of my arm. Smoke is pouring out of the broken bathroom window, too much for me to see anything outside. In the hallway, two pairs of wide eyes stare up at me.

"Let's go," I say. "Now or never."

Diaphragm spasming and eyes watering, I place a palm flat against the back door. I nudge it open a crack. Any second, I expect the shotgun slugs to come pouring through. But they don't.

Nobody is out back.

The three of us scuttle out the door. Hop down three rotten steps to the sweet, cool ground. We cough into our hands, cheeks billowing, trying to stay silent.

"Ah fuck," says somebody from around front. "Gunnin'?"

Nick hears and cranes his neck, but I plant a hand on his shoulder. Push him forward and keep an eye on the back of his head to make sure he doesn't try to look back. Once you see something, you can't unsee it.

As Lucy and Nick scurry safely away, I drop to my hands and knees in the dirt.

It's just a split-second peek under the burning trailer. Through writhing waves of flame, I see heat shadows roil like ghosts playing. The sight hits me like a camera flash. Gunnin' Billy on his back, laid out on the ground with his arms out, chest heaving. Shotgun dropped and forgotten. There's a soot-stained cinder block lying next to his ruined face. Looks like he caught the corner of it in his mouth. Tried to swallow it. His blue eyes are wide and scared and looking right through me. But he's alive. Two pairs of boots stand around him, placed just outside an expanding puddle of frothy red mud.

"Well shit," says somebody. "Let's get him to the hospital."

Then I'm back on my feet, the heat of the burning trailer curl-ing the hairs on the back of my neck. I wipe dusty handprints on my jeans and run to catch up to Lucy and Nick. Pretend I didn't just see that.

Lucy must see the flat look in my eyes. She grabs me by the shoulders. Pulls me in and stops me next to a trailer.

"Come up, Owen," she says. "It's over."

She massages my shoulders and urges me, rhythmically repeat-ing the words over and over. My eyes close for an instant. When they open, the world is smaller. I feel less alive, all alone without the Zenith to whisper secrets to me. I'm back.

"How'd you do that?" I ask.

"Practice," she says, pulling me forward.

Twisting between trailers, we bang on walls and doors. Shout warnings to empty trailers and to the occasional full one. Faces peek through cloudy windows.

In one slick minute, we clear the trailers and hit the field. Breathing ragged, Lucy pushes me to keep running. Exhausted, Nick climbs onto my back. All three of us hustle for the tree line.

"Jim is gone," I say, and I can't meet her eye.

Lucy misses a step, stumbles, and I steady her. A breeze blows her hair in damp stripes across her forehead. Soot and sweat streak her face, but she keeps breathing through flared nostrils and trot-ting ahead.

"And Lyle started this. Astra wants a war. He let me go to come get you," I say.

Lucy stops running. Looks at me with wide, honest eyes. She's not the girl I thought I knew, but she looks just the same.

"He let you go?" she asks.

"That's not good," says Nick in my ear.

"I'm going to disagree," I say.

"He means Lyle wouldn't let you go unless he had a good rea-son," says Lucy.

"Does it matter—"

A gunshot rings out before I can finish the sentence.

At the tree line, four federal agents wearing Kevlar vests over business suits step out of the brush. Guns out.

"Afternoon, ladies and gentlemen. You, sir, are under arrest for being part of the terrorist organization known as Astra. On your knees!"

And so it ends in the middle of this field. I could reactivate the Zenith and make my move, but the guns are out and I can't risk Nick and Lucy.

So Lucy and I drop to our knees, eyes locked. I thought this woman loved me and she doesn't. I thought we respected each other, but Lyle assigned her to me. Ever since he said those words, the betrayal has been eating me up.

"Lyle wasn't always this way," Lucy says. "The amp did this to him. He wasn't good enough for it."

This is probably the last minute I'll have with Lucy and I don't want to ruin it but I can't help the way I feel. The anger bubbles up from inside. And so I blurt it out.

"Don't pretend to care. I know Lyle gave you to me. Like a birthday present."

Lucy doesn't break her gaze. She considers. Blinks once.

"Lyle told me to talk to you. And I went over to Jim's house because I was afraid of what Lyle would do to me. And to Nick. But I *liked* you."

The four agents are here now. Two of them stay back, Velcroed holsters open, pistol butts peeking out. The other two agents spread out and approach, one behind each of us.

"Am I supposed to believe that?" I ask.

The closest agent steps around me. I feel cold handcuffs slide over my wrists. I'm lifted off my knees with a rough tug on my hands.

"Do you know why I liked you?" asks Lucy.

The other agent helps Lucy up, but he doesn't cuff her. He takes Nick by the wrist. Holds him friendly but tight.

"Why?" I ask.

"Because you stood up for Nick in that field. You stood up for Eden. And none of it worked out and Eden is burned, but it doesn't matter. You tried. You're . . . good. You're a good man."

I try to shrug it off, but her words are warm inside me.

Lucy smiles at me through tears, and I can see traces of Lyle in her features. A glimpse of the person he might have been in a saner world. "And because you're sort of cute," she says.

"Because I'm *cute*?" I ask.

"Sort of cute," she replies, smiling.

"This doesn't count as our date," I call, as my agent shoves me in the lower back. He nudges me toward an unmarked black van. Pushes me against it.

"Let me ride with them," I say.

"You're going to a different place than them, buddy."

"Yeah? Where's that?" I ask.

The voice behind me chuckles. "Elysium."

"Lucy?" I ask, panic infecting my voice.

"Don't worry about us," says Lucy. "Worry about Lyle."

The distance between us is growing. The other agent is leading them toward a car. Its black doors gape open.

"I'll come and find you," I say, craning to look over my shoulder.

"Owen," shouts Nick. "Owen, wait!" The kid tries and fails to wriggle out of the agent's grasp, twists violently, hangs by one arm with his legs sprawled out.

"Use it," he says.

The agent lifts Nicky and tucks him under his arm. He pushes the kid inside the car. As I'm shoved into the van, I can still hear the kid's muffled voice: "Use all of it!"

EXECUTIVE ORDER
14902

- - - - - - -

Authorizing the Secretary of Defense to Prescribe Holding Areas

WHEREAS the successful safeguarding of the nation requires every possible protection against technological threats, be they from home or abroad, and the existence of persons made militarized by implantation technology poses a threat to their fellow citizens as well as to themselves:

NOW, THEREFORE, by virtue of the authority vested in me as president by the Constitution and the laws of the United States of America, and commander in chief of the Army and Navy, I hereby authorize the Secretary of Defense, and the military commanders whom he may designate, to prescribe "safety zones" in such places and of such extent as he or the appropriate military commander may determine, from which any or all persons may be excluded, and with respect to which, the right of any person to enter, remain in, or leave shall be subject to whatever restrictions are deemed necessary.

I hereby further authorize and direct the Secretary of Defense and the said military commanders to take such other steps as may be deemed advisable to enforce compliance with the restrictions applicable to each safety zone, including the use of federal troops and other federal agencies with added authority to accept the assistance of state and local agencies.

21

WHOLE HOG

I'm sound asleep when one of the guards slams his nightstick into my cell door.

"I said wake up, pal," says a deep voice from the other side of the door.

"How the fuck is this guy even asleep?" asks a reedy, high-pitched voice.

The blazing overhead lights never go off in here. I imagine that must make it hard for most people to rest. Me, not so much. Earlier, I dropped into my Zenith and asked my retinal implant to temporarily suppress my visual cortex. You don't get this kind of mind-numbing darkness outside a closed cave system.

I fell asleep in the absolute black, everything stripped away except for that goddamn question blinking in my head: *Do you consent?* Insistent. Steady as my heartbeat. Trying to take me down another level. *Level five. Full sensory networking. Long horizon mission planning. Command and control. Enhanced mobility and survivability. Do you consent? Do you consent?*

Begging me to go whole hog.

Real power is in the connections between things, Lyle said. The pieces are in place but it's up to me to turn them on. Give the go-ahead to let the retinal talk to the neural. Cochlear talk to retinal. The world opens up to you in ways you can't imagine. You have to *see* it to believe it, Lyle said. And then the skinny cowboy made that hyena laugh of his. Threw his head back and let loose like he'd said the funniest thing in his life.

All you have to do is say the word. I refuse.

Bam–bam–bam–bam.

The sudden hammering at the door yanks me out of the deep cave of my mind and back into reality.

I turn my eyes on and blink at the light.

"Let's go, buddy," says a guard, speaking through the slot. "On your feet. Back to the door. Wrists together."

My knees are stiff and it takes a second to stand. Weeks ago, two silent agents put a bag over my head and drove me here in the back of a van. I don't even know where here *is*. I've been in this cage ever since. Pissing in a metal toilet. Eating whatever comes through the slot. Until now, nobody has spoken to me. Nobody has responded to my questions. I've been forgotten.

That nightstick smacks the cell door with an ear-ringing clang.

"Now, motherfucker!" screams the other guard.

Rough hands reach through the slot and ratchet cold steel around my wrists. I stumble forward. Behind me, the solid metal door glides open on oiled hinges. I hunch my shoulders instinctively as a burst of fresh air hits the back of my neck.

"Turn around, asshole."

Two guards stand in the hall, a big one and a little one, framed by the doorway. Both men are wrapped in black armored vests, with kneepads and helmets. No writing and no insignias. The big one has a riot shield clutched against his barrel chest.

I'm standing here, cuffed, my baggy bright-orange jumpsuit hanging off my thin frame. In the weeks since I was captured, I've barely eaten or exercised. My bruises have gone from black to green to yellow. Healing.

The little guard flips up his protective face shield and grabs me by the front of my shirt. He drags me stumbling forward into the hallway. I crane my neck, soaking up the new sights and smells and sounds. Retinal reengaged, I can almost feel the electricity flashing spiderwebs through my visual cortex. My brain soaks up the novelty of information, drinking deeply after absolute deprivation.

Big puts a paw on Little's shoulder. Through his helmet mask I see that he's got worried brown eyes.

"Careful with him," says Big in a deep voice. "They warned us for a reason."

"Check his temple," says Little. "This is just another Autofocus job. A fucking smarty-pants. What's he gonna do, hurt me with his brain?"

Little smirks at me, shoves me forward down the hall. Big hangs back, almost cowering behind his Plexiglas riot shield. He palms his Taser holster with black-gloved fingers.

"Let's just get him there, okay?" asks Big.

Little makes a high-pitched giggle. He prods me in the back with the nightstick, keeping me a few feet ahead, walking down the middle of an empty hallway.

My internal clock says it is one seventeen in the morning.

"Where are you taking me?" I ask.

In response, a wasp sting tap from the nightstick on my ear. It smarts like a bastard. I feel a trickle of blood running down my jawline.

Well, that answers that.

The long, low hallway has the feel of a submarine, running deep and quiet and unknown through midnight seas. Identical steel-plated doors line the walls. Taupe colored, the paint flaking. Each has one slot at crotch level and a slice of mesh-laced glass at eye level.

We reach a reinforced door at the end of the hallway. My breath catches in my throat as Little wrenches on my handcuffs, grinding my wrist bones together. I bite my lip and stop walking, trying not to react.

Little seems like the sort who wants to be provoked.

Big walks around me to clear the way. I notice he leaves a trail of watery boot prints on the hallway floor. It must be raining outside. A rumbling groan of distant thunder reverberates through the hallway. Must be a real hell of a storm to reach all the way in here.

Somewhere, a buzzer emits a quick grinding ring. The noise races up and down the hallway, as if searching for a way out. There isn't one.

The horizon of my life is shrinking down to my line of sight. There are no moves left on the old chessboard. The little guard walks in front of me, cocky and armed. The bigger guard, cautious and wary, is hanging back. The hallway ends ahead in a yawning doorway, fluorescent lights humming on the other side.

An interrogation room.

This is it. All the decisions and possibilities of my life, stripped off and sent fluttering away into nothingness. I can see only one path now. And it doesn't lead anywhere I want to go.

But there's still that goddamn question blinking in my head. Begging me, pleading for me to just say the word. You have to *see* it to believe it. But I don't want to see what Lyle was trying to show me. You go whole hog and you're giving it all away to the machine.

One Lyle is enough.

The interrogation room is a dense cube of space. The air inside is heavy, moves like water, sloshing into my nose and out of my mouth. In the middle of the room, a squat steel table is bolted to the floor over thin, stained carpet. A stool crouches on either side of the table, also bolted down.

And perched on one of the stools is a familiar tall man, graying at the temples, beckoning me lazily with one arm. Today, he looks just like he does on television.

"Take a seat, Owen," says Senator Joseph Vaughn.

Big shoves me into the room and I land on the stool. The little guard pulls out a serpentine chain and threads it from my handcuffs through a U bar welded to the top of the metal desk.

"Sit tight," says Little, snickering.

Vaughn nods, and Big and Little step out. The heavy door closes with a hermetic hiss. I clear my throat and the rough dirty walls chew up the sound and swallow it. I imagine that I can feel far-off thunder coursing through the bones of the building, through the floor, into the soles of my feet.

Vaughn peers at me with birdlike intensity, chiseled face held at a slight angle. He doesn't blink. As he watches, I can feel the information pouring off me in waves: my body language, facial expression, rate of breathing—all of it being absorbed and categorized and assimilated by this perfect-seeming man thing.

I wonder if Vaughn can feel that I'm afraid.

Is it visible over the castle walls of my body? The mayhem of my mind leaking out through trembling fingers? The man sitting across from me is famous for his tendency to orate nonstop for hours, but right this second he is silent as a vacuum. His eyes are so green and still, and God I just wish he would *blink* for Christ's sake.

"You," he says.

Me.

"You have been quite a surprise."

I don't say anything, but Vaughn goes ahead and answers the question that I was thinking: *What did you expect?*

"I was expecting that you'd be more cunning. Defying Lyle couldn't have been easy. I suppose I'd hoped you'd be dangerous in some way, shape, or form. But I suppose not. Look at you. Weak."

He leans forward, palms down on the table, long manicured

fingers outstretched, eyes locked on mine. A row of even white teeth swells from beneath cherry-red lips, lupine.

"Weak. And scared."

"Tell me where I am," I say in a voice that sounds small in my head but comes out so much smaller.

He blinks, finally, mercifully.

"You're in a federal detention facility in Pittsburgh. I want to thank you for joining me all the way out here. More convenient for me than for you, perhaps. I would have tried to visit sooner, but I've been just swamped dealing with the aftermath of some very nasty extremist attacks."

Vaughn leans over, examines my face. "Your eyes are different from Lyle's. Clearer. Honestly, it gives me the shivers when he uses his amp." Vaughn leans back on his stool, relaxing. "He led you down a dark and dangerous road, Owen. Left you there, alone in the night. No one else knows where you are or even that you're missing. You're all mine. And all I'm asking you to do is cooperate."

"What do you want?"

"It's not what *I* want. It's what's best for you and your nation. For your fellow man."

This doesn't sound good.

"You're going to confess your role as the leader of Astra. Admit to orchestrating the timed explosions that destroyed or severely damaged skyscrapers in Chicago, Houston, and Detroit. Admit to training the amp teams who infiltrated those sites in the dead of night using light-sensitive retinal implants. Admit responsibility for killing six thousand three hundred and forty-seven citizens of the United States."

"What? That didn't happen."

He waves his long fingers through the air, miming falling stars.

"I warned them for years. Told the people that someone like you would do something like this. And now you're going to make me the most powerful man in America."

"What did you fucking *do*? You and Lyle killed six thousand people?" I ask, adrenaline lacing hot and cold through my forearms.

"Oh, and you're an angel?" responds Vaughn.

I think of Lyle's little speech. Plants, animals, men, angels, then God.

"Not quite," I say.

Vaughn abruptly stands up. "You crushed a man's face with a cinder block. He happened to be a part of my field organization and a friend of mine. And he would very much like to see you again. If you will not cooperate, then that is exactly what will happen."

Poor Billy. In a hospital somewhere, eating through a tube. The Zenith's question is still there in the corner of my mind. A locked door with the black faceless unknown crouched and hungry on the other side.

"Why do you hate us?" I ask.

"I don't hate you. I pity you. You people can't see it, but you are no longer human. Does a worm know it's just a worm? I even understand that what you are is not your fault. Yet I cannot let that affect my decisions. I have a duty to the children of humanity."

"You bribed Lyle to commit crimes," I say evenly. "Created a fake catastrophe and killed thousands of people. Is that part of your duty?"

"That is exactly my duty. Future generations will retain their humanity thanks to the sacrifices we make. Six thousand today is nothing compared to the countless millions yet to be born. Without me, a generation of children will be cheated of their one and only chance to live out their lives as God intended—as human beings."

Vaughn stops, his eyes refracted with tears. He dabs his face with a pale handkerchief. Some terrible memory seems to pulse under his features, like a living thing, insane and in agony.

"Unfortunately," he continues, gathering his composure, "you've already lost your opportunity. But others haven't."

"I'm not confessing to anything."

Vaughn watches me silently, eyes wide and lucid. Finally he stands, hooks a crooked smile at me. "Deep down, I'm glad it's come to this. There's something I've been dying to share. You aren't the only one I've brought out east. The lady with freckles is very pretty, don't you think? And I hear her deformed son makes up for it in personality."

I can feel my heart expanding in my chest. Things going dull around the edges.

"Lucy and young Nicholas are now residents of the west Pittsburgh Federal Safety Zone, compliments of me. And I want you to picture this scene, amp. On my word, a dedicated member of Elysium enters the safety zone. He drags mother and son out of their beds and into the night for questioning. Beyond the razorwire fence, he puts the cold barrel of his gun into the mother's mouth. And I mean really pushes it in there. He pulls the trigger and sprays her brains all over her own son."

I can't help it and I wince. Vaughn soaks it in.

"Ah, but don't worry," says Vaughn. "He doesn't kill the kid. Instead, he produces a pair of pliers and forcefully removes the boy's implant. And I do mean all of it this time. Digs it out of his overdeveloped brain and leaves him there . . . an orphaned, slobbering vegetable. Now, how do you like that picture?"

I flex my arms against the cold steel cuffs.

"And for your part, well, it's not looking good. The agents here don't have much compassion for you amps. Understandably, I'm afraid. There really have been so many atrocious crimes. So, either you walk out with me to attend your confession or you and your little family face a very different fate. You see—you're either going to be useful, or you're not going to be anything at all."

"No," I mutter, pulse pounding in my ears. "No."

Thirty seconds scrape by. My thoughts hover and dart like mosquitoes. The world has collapsed to two choices. Trust a mass murderer or die. Or . . . open this door in my head. Step into the same dark woods that swallowed Lyle.

Vaughn ambles to the door. Knocks three times.

"I suppose I'll have to inform America that I've overseen your killing instead of your capture. Perhaps instant gratification is better, after all. They're going to love me even more than if you'd confessed, I suspect. Who knows? Maybe I'll run for president."

A gap opens and Vaughn slips out, nods at the guards.

Now, Big and Little stand in the doorway. Little has a nasty grin on his face. Big looks blank and resigned and solid as an oak tree.

"End of the line, buddy," says Little.

I squeeze my eyes shut. In the darkness, I stumble back into the room with the question. The words wait impatiently for me, implacable and alien. *Level five. Full sensory networking. Long horizon mission planning. Command and control. Enhanced mobility and survivability. Do you consent? Do you consent?*

Yes, I think to the beast. *Yes, yes, yes.* I'm saying the motherfucking word. Keep me alive, technology. Come on inside and make yourself right at home.

And something clicks.

I don't feel any different. Whatever I woke up inside my head isn't talking to me. I'm asking it one very important question: How do I live? How do I stay alive in this situation? Please.

But the oracle doesn't speak.

Instead, the answer appears—painted before me like dance moves on a gym floor. Bluish footprints emerge glowing from the tile, flickering slightly between various configurations as the seconds pass by. Next, a swathe of scaly orange-red mountains rises up—a dull reddish tide that burns bright orange in the shape of those watery boot prints. I'm looking at a topographical map of wetness. Mountains of probable slickness.

I blink my eyes, but the additions to the landscape remain. This is coming from me. Nobody else can see this. Retinal talks to cochlear talks to neural talks to executive. I'm telling me what to do. Or the technology in me is telling me what to do. *How is this happening?*

Never mind. I don't care how it works. I just want to live.

"Got fucking dirt in your ears?" bawls Little.

I look down at the U bar jutting from the top of the metal table. A chain rises from the desk and through my handcuffs and back, keeping me pinned. Now a bluish circle emerges to indicate the maximum perimeter based on the chain length.

Can you hurt someone with your brain?

Without thought, I fall into the dance moves painted on the floor. One quick step forward. Little's eyes widen. I pivot to the right but slow. Drag my left foot. Give him time to react to the feint, time to lean forward with that nightstick rising like an angry cobra. Now I twist around the desk, planting my left foot and springing forward. He falls past me, a high-pitched *eek* coming from his black-soled boots on the slick tile floor.

As Little sails past me, I bow my arms out and catch his head under my left elbow. My ass lands on the cold metal desk and I pull my arms up to my chin, pinching Little's windpipe under the unforgiving chain links.

"Hlurgh," says Little, weakly waving his nightstick.

"Back," I say to Big. "Stay the fuck back and I let him breathe."

Little's nightstick clatters to the ground.

Big considers, looking curiously at the twisted snarl on the face of his colleague. I'm breathing hard, but Little isn't making a sound. He's just turning a bright shade of red, eyes squeezed closed. The seconds seem like minutes to me. And they probably seem like hours to Mister "I'm quickly suffocating to death" here, his sweaty head wedged under my arm.

"All right," says Big, flashing me his black-gloved palms. "Take it easy, fella."

"I am willing to crush his windpipe," I say, staring at Big with what I hope is a stern face. I relax the chain across Little's neck. Just enough so he can take a ragged breath.

"Uncuff me," I say to Little.

Little's breathing sounds like gravel being sucked through a straw. He responds sluggishly, fumbles for his keys. I never lift the cold chain from his Adam's apple, and I never take my eyes off Big.

Click.

My handcuffs are undone. The chain drops from Little's neck and slithers away, coiling on the desk. For a split second, nothing happens. Then Little yanks his head up and Big dives forward.

And faster than my brain can process light, those blue lines blink back into existence. Luminous guardrails guiding me toward survival. Just stay on the road, Gray, and you'll live through this.

Two arrowed vector lines shoot away from Little's rib cage. As he drags himself up, back facing me, I reach down and smoothly unfasten his body armor. I yank it up from behind and dump the rear portion over his head. As he staggers forward under the weight of those heavy ceramic plates, I snatch his cuffs out of his belt.

Big charges forward and shoves the flailing Little out of the way, onto the desk. He's too massive to stop. A rhino. Big brings down that nightstick toward my head with both hands like it was a battle-ax, but I've got the cuffs up and waiting. The stick lands between the cuffs and I pull them down toward me and twist the nightstick out of his hands. It hits the ground, clanging like a tire iron. Big lunges at me with his hands, and I pivot away and snap one of the cuffs onto his wrist. The other end I snap onto an ammo loop on Little's body armor.

I dart out of the room. As the solid door swings closed behind me, it cuts off the bellowing of the two guards. I stand in the hallway for a few tense seconds, listening to myself breathe and feeling the storm coursing through the jail walls. I've done the thing I said I would never do.

I've woken up the beast inside my head.

Now it whispers to me in fans of blue light. In glowing mountain ridges of probability erupting from the walls and floor. Schematics of similar detention facilities. Blind spots. Routes and patterns.

I was wrong before. The beast is not silent. It speaks through my actions.

Turns out, the beast says, you *can* hurt somebody with your brain. In fact, you can fuck a person up pretty severely and steal supplies and sneak out of a perfectly secure detention facility—if you've got an okay grasp on the physics of it.

And I most certainly do.

EMERGENCY CIVIL CONTROL ADMINISTRATION
* * *

Instructions to All Implanted Individuals

Living in the Following Area:
Allegheny County

All implanted individuals will be evacuated from the above designated area by noon next Tuesday. No implanted person shall be permitted to enter or leave the above described area after 8:00 a.m., Thursday, without obtaining special permission from the provost marshal at the Civil Control Station.

Be notified that the Civil Control Station is equipped to assist the population affected by this evacuation in the following ways:

1. Give advice and instructions on the evacuation

2. Provide services with respect to the management, sale, storage, or other disposition of most kinds of property, including real estate, equipment, household goods, boats, automobiles, livestock, etc.

3. Provide temporary residence for those in family groups

4. Transport persons and a limited amount of clothing and equipment to their new residence as specified below.

—Partial text of Gen. John D. Meyer's evacuation order

22
UNDER-BRIDGE

"Think you're superior to me?" jeers the dirty-faced homeless guy. "What do you carry, sir? Why are you so *clean*?"

My stomach clenches in on itself. This squirrelly little man came out of nowhere. Outside the federal detention center, I climbed down to the highway next to the river. Under seething skies, I crept along the riverbank until I was out of downtown. Stole clothes from a backyard. Crawled under a bush and wrapped my knees in my arms. It took thirty minutes of teeth-gritting concentration to come up from level five. Eventually, I fell asleep with the trash and leaves. Somewhere along the line, I ended up in the neighborhood of Polish Hill.

Tattered relocation posters are plastered everywhere. A whole lot has happened in the weeks I spent locked up. Lives have changed forever. It's hard to grasp the fact that we have always been one executive order away from this.

Most of the row houses here are boarded up in plywood and squeezed together suffocatingly close. Each house split from its neighbor by a narrow three-story-tall slat of darkness. The bum must have been crouched in the gap-toothed void between abandoned homes. Hiding. Or waiting.

The amps who lived here have now been sequestered away like a virus, cut out of the heart of the city and dropped in a petri dish so they can't infect the rest of the population. Traumatic surgery, leaving this hemorrhaging hole in the center of the neighborhood.

Buildings, whole blocks, collapsing in on themselves without enough occupants inside to give them a purpose.

The hobo jabs a stubby finger at my temple and throws words like rocks. "I said what're you *endowed* with, buddy? What foul gadgetry yet lingers in your nog? What's your *frequency*?"

He creeps closer, hisses, "Are you with me or against me?"

"I don't know what you mean," I sputter. My hands rise up defensively, awkwardly filling the space between us. But the blue-eyed squirrel man bobs just out of reach.

The little guy is an amp, I realize. A nodule perches on his temple like a cancerous mole. He is standing too close to me, his lips moving too fast. His eyes are too pale—a clear, disturbing blueness that somehow floats apart from his dirt-smeared face.

"With me? Or *against me*?" he shouts at my face. *"With me or against me!"*

He's loud and shrill and he moves too fast, but he's an amp. My own kind. So I take two steps back and I put out my hand. "I'm Owen," I say.

A sudden smile breaks out on the man's face. He dives forward and grabs my hand in both of his. Shakes it up and down with gusto. It's like nobody has shaken this man's hand for years.

"Peregrine," he says. "Name's Peregrine, friend. But I've adopted the simple moniker of Perry on account of the laziness of idiots and impertinence of the fools who infest this burgh like a swarm of lice-ridden plague rats."

"Okay," I respond, gently pulling my arm back. Perry focuses intensely on my face and speaks in rapid-fire bursts. His sentences are studded with ten-dollar words.

"You'll notice I'm loquacious and you'll rightly surmise it's on account of this medical implant lodged here in the old dusty cortex. I love the taste of words, sir. And each *logos* spawned from my lips, sui generis, mind you, carries the ambrosial tang of an exquisite candy. And I'm afraid that I've got *quite* the sweet tooth."

He flashes bruised teeth at me.

"A gentleman such as yourself will understand that my intellectual curiosity is piqued by that telltale seal of otherness that stamps your temple and marks you as a fellow *amp, as they call us.* And at the risk of appearing obstinate and demanding, I'd like to return to the previous line of questioning in which I implored you to share the nature of the gadgetry cocooned within you."

"You want to know about my implant?" I ask.

"Cocoon," he purrs, eyes half lidded. "Oh, now that's a good one. Ex-quisite."

"Uh, Perry?"

His eyes flutter open, like headlights flickering on. "Sir?"

"It's for epilepsy," I say.

"Ah, the shakes. A woeful fate, indeed. But you're not alone, friend. The United States government cured many a pal of mine. The schizos, the alkos, and the bipolars. Even cured my own indisposition toward the mental muddle of autism—with a heaping dollop of paranoia for flavor. But, praise God, the taxpayers fixed those of us under the bridge by the miracle of modern science."

He flinches at the sound of his voice echoing. "How much did they cure you?" he whispers.

"How much?"

"Well, they can cure you a little or a *lot*, can't they?"

I think of my father and Jim. The discussion they must have had when I was just a boy. I remember the flashing dance steps on the ground as I sidestepped that guard.

"They cured me a lot," I say.

He considers me briefly, then digs out a worn plastic ruler from under his filthy coat. He dangles it over the cracked pavement.

"Put your fingers around this but don't touch," he says. "When I let go of it, pinch your fingers together."

"Okay."

"Sheep fucker," he says, then drops the ruler. My fingers pinch by reflex, even as Perry's strange words hit.

The little man grabs my wrist.

"Hold it. Right there. Don't move a muscle." Perry bends over and inspects the ruler. His lips twitch as he does the math in his head. "You caught it at zero point zero seven centimeters. With the speed of gravity, seven milliseconds. Visual reaction time . . ."

Perry looks at me, rubs his hands together greedily.

"Why, you *have* been cured a lot."

Perry's eyes go to my maintenance nub, then he glances up and down the empty street. "I don't doubt your veracity a whit, young gentleman. Only the brainiest amongst us yet walk the streets unmolested. What with these confounded roundups."

"Roundups?"

"Indeed, sir. How have you ever managed to fall truant to that information—"

"I've been in jail."

Perry waits for me to continue. I don't.

"Fair enough, then," he says.

"Where are they taking the amps?"

"Why, to the under-bridge, sir."

"Under what bridge?"

"The bridge is the fair shore where many of us once lived in peace—before tasting the apple, you see? The bridge dwellers dissipated, it's true. Set sail for the shores of normalcy. Bewitched by that flirting specter of gainful employment.

"But lately, a great exodus from Mundania has begun. Under government mandate many a bridge dweller has returned and more. Countrywide they've come to the central repository. By train, by plane, and by hoof. The amps, sir, have come home to the under-bridge."

Lucy and Nick.

"Do you mean the west Pittsburgh Federal Safety Zone? Can you take me there, Perry?"

"A wise notion, sir," he says. Then the little man smiles up at me, a glint of anticipation in his eyes. "You'll find that twisted folk linger out here. Some were amped before the technology was ripe, you see? These leftover amps are fierce and *rotten*. Under-bridge is the safest place to be, sir."

As the sun sets, Perry leads me through the forgotten fissures of Polish Hill, down narrow alleys where our shoulders brush sweating concrete walls. Over weedy lots where the grass is ingrown with ancient trash. Down endless rusty railroad tracks.

We stop briefly in a back lot where trash bins squat in the shadow of a looming megastore out front. One arm hooked over a trash can, Perry roots for stale bread and continues his monologue. "Lucky, we are. Yes, sir. Lucky to live in this cutting-edge era of progress. When men can aspire not only to be well and healthy, but to be *better* than well. Better than healthy. If you ponder it, Owen, why, it's clear that you and me are technological marvels of the modern age!"

Finally, we reach the deteriorating Washington Crossing Bridge. A few hundred people mill about in what looks like half a campground and half a swap meet. The stained concrete is layered with blankets and sleeping bags and bulging plastic sacks. Windblown empties rattle over the concrete, barely audible under the muted hum of conversation and the sporadic roar of traffic overhead.

Perry throws an arm around my shoulder, gestures to the mesh-covered belly of the towering structure overhead. "Welcome to the under-bridge."

Weeks of scraggly beard cover my face, but I keep my head down anyway. It has become a habit. I try to shush Perry and take in my surroundings.

National Guardsmen in camouflaged gear ring the shaded area under the bridge. Their eyes are veiled by shining new riot helmets, watching everybody and settling on nobody. Long black batons hang on their hips, rifles hanging from chest straps. Side by side, the men might as well be statues. They aren't looking through us but past us.

Hundreds of Pure Priders mill across the road, watching the under-bridge.

Beyond the bridge, a crumbling warehouse the length of a football field squats on a vast paved expanse. Coils of barbed wire have been thrown haphazardly over the cracked cement in a wide ring around the building. The area inside swarms with men and women and children. I make out a game of baseball; they're using torn cardboard for bases. The massive warehouse doors gape open. Thousands of people shuffle in and out.

This must be the safety zone. And where I'm standing is the processing station. Amps are coming here voluntarily, just to escape the wrath of angry Priders.

A ragged column of amps wait in line to enter. Men and women, each with a maintenance nub, holding sleeping bags and backpacks and garbage bags stuffed with clothes. Dragging suitcases and trunks ahead a foot at a time as the line sluggishly creeps forward.

A guardhouse at the front gate processes the families. Just beyond the processing station, beyond the fence, ragtag shops are set up, built out of plywood. Newcomers are buying and trading for food and first aid kits and blankets.

The people on this side of the fence are either bargaining with one another or in line. Dozens of kids mill around. Some stay near their parents. Others travel in packs, carrying sticks and shepherded by stray dogs. The kids are dressed okay: clean clothes, new shoes. And now that I think of it, most of the dogs aren't strays. A golden retriever with tags pads by me, bushy tail slapping against my legs.

As I stop to take it in, Perry shuffles nervously.

"How long has this been happening, Perry?"

"The recall order went in three weeks' past. After the attack. Locomotives materialized here more than a week ago. Spilled the bulk of the amps."

"Are there other camps like this?"

"Another half dozen, at least. They say Central Park accommodates over twenty thousand. Corralled the Daytona speedway entirely. Probably only ten thousand here at the under-bridge. These personages are the stragglers," says Perry. "Tried to stay out and learned the hard way what's best for them."

"How long are they keeping people here?" I ask Perry.

"Why, until they're safe," he replies, nodding at the street where Priders roam. "Now come along with me. I want to introduce you to someone."

I take a deep breath of the musty air and feel the vibration of the bridge traffic overhead rattle through my chest. To my left, I notice a man peeing against the wall, wobbly kneed and singing. The soldiers watch impassively. Barbed wire glints in the light of the setting sun.

Lyle's plan is stalling. The amps aren't fighting. They're obeying.

"Come along now," says Perry. He eyes the guard station desperately. Then his face darkens. He focuses on something just over my right shoulder. He speaks without looking at me: "Come, sir, let's absquatulate," he says. "Right quick."

Perry jabs a thumb into the air to motion me to follow and I see that his hands are shaking. I glance over my shoulder and spot a small misshapen head attached to a crooked torso moving toward us, balanced on what look like black stilts. Emaciated black arms hang menacingly from the torso's sides.

It's the wire man. The nightmare shape that nearly killed me in Detroit.

People scatter before the lurching gait of the man thing. I watch a father usher his two children away, losing his place in line without a thought.

Perry grabs my arm and tries to tug me away. "Let's motivate," he whispers. "That's Mr. Cordwainer and he'll busticate us for a lark, sir. You'd best give your full credence to that fact."

The wire man's head lolls in our direction. A pink stripe crosses his brow, a gash that's healing slow. I make eye contact, and there is an instantaneous shock of recognition between us. Perry whimpers and stops walking.

"Too late now," he whispers as the monster staggers toward us. "Cordwainer is quicker than a jumping spider. If he has to give chase, it'll go worse. He's an angry man. Word is he used to peregrinate via skateboard until Uncle Sam granted him new legs. But he didn't stop there, did he? Got the arms amputated, too."

The wire man stops before us and twists his body off-kilter to aim his shrunken, crippled head at me. "Hello, thirteen," it says, lisping toothlessly over the words. "Thought you might come through here. Been waiting for you."

"Cordwainer?" I ask.

The creature's eyes slide over to Perry. "Yes, that's my name," it says. "I see you've made a convenient friend."

"Simply, uh, simply, took him on as a parergon," sputters Perry. "Escorting my companion and his personalia safely through the willowwacks—"

"I didn't know about Lyle," I say, trying to focus on Cordwainer's face, to ignore the rest of that horrible mess. "I didn't realize what was happening . . ."

But Cordwainer is staring at Perry.

"What's in the pocket, Perry?" he asks.

Perry pulls his coat on tighter.

"I would have saved Valentine if I could," I say.

I glance sidelong at the soldiers, but they stare right through us.

"Empty your pockets," slurs Cordwainer.

Perry just gapes at him, his floating blue eyes wide and round with terror.

"No?" asks Cordwainer. Then, smooth and fast as a riptide, the wire man lunges and grabs Perry with one spider arm. His other arm flies forward and back three times. One, two, three punches and then the celery-stick crunch of Perry's cheekbone caving in. Jams his claws into Perry's pockets and rips out the contents in a swirl of papers. He drops Perry wailing onto the cement.

Perry begins to crawl away.

Reaction time. It's defined as the length of time between sensing a stimulus and responding to it. I caught Perry's ruler quicker than a snake strike. That was fast. This is faster.

I ball my left hand into a fist and hurl all my weight into a short, vicious left hook. Cordwainer is already dancing back, but the punch connects in his solar plexus, in the precise spot where a bundle of wires plunges beneath his skin to interface with the motor nerves embedded in the muscles of his belly.

Cordwainer's legs drop out from under him like somebody flipped a switch. He falls forward and wraps his coat-hanger arms around me. "Stop," he hisses, hanging from me, his legs twitching like half-squashed bugs. "Stop and look."

A crumpled piece of paper lies at my feet, rocking slightly in the phantom breezes from unseen cars and trucks whining across the bridge overhead. My own face stares up at me in black and white, a crude photocopy.

IF YOU SEE THIS MAN . . . it reads.

I let Cordwainer steady his feet.

"You're faster than last time," he says.

A few dozen people shake their heads at us, muttering. Kids whisper to each other and point, pantomiming the fight. Perry continues to crawl away.

"He was leading you to them," says Cordwainer, pointing at the guardhouse at the front of the line. "Your photo is in there. Twenty more yards and these soldiers would have taken you. If you want inside, sneak in."

"About Valentine—"

Cordwainer stops me with a wave. "Val is gone, but those of us who are left can still try to keep the peace. Lyle was right that there will be a new world. Just not the one that he wants."

"Thank you," I say.

"Be careful," says Cordwainer. "The reggies are massing and they are angry. Soon, they may be angry enough to strike. And then everyone in this place will die."

Associated Press

Crowd in Florida Demonstrates at "Safety Zone" as Backlash Grows

By DENNIS JAY

DAYTONA BEACH, FL (AP)—A violent and perhaps predictable backlash is spreading across the nation as details emerge about Astra—the extremist amp organization that planned and carried out the attacks in Chicago, Detroit and Houston.

Police from Daytona, Florida, and several nearby counties turned back 3,000 Pure Pride marchers—some blatantly displaying holstered arms—as they tried to march through the front gate of the Daytona Speedway Federal Safety Zone late last night. Hundreds of demonstrators were arrested, said Daytona Police Chief David Wilson. There were no injuries and demonstrators were kept outside the main entrance of the Daytona International Speedway.

Meanwhile, a law enforcement official in Pittsburgh, speaking on condition of anonymity, said the FBI has made a breakthrough in its search for the mastermind behind the attacks by following leads provided by the Pure Human Citizen's Council, an anti-implantee organization that has been targeted by extremists in the past. Head of the PHCC Senator Joseph Vaughn is scheduled to deliver a speech to a massive audience in Pittsburgh tomorrow afternoon. He could not be reached for comment on whether the speech is related to the reported breakthrough.

23
POTENTIAL OUTCOMES

Since the sun dropped over the horizon, the tower spotlights have been strafing every twenty seconds or so. Plenty of time. You'd think the guards would be focused on keeping amps from sneaking out. Instead, they're watching for the Priders who threaten to flood inside.

I'm crouched on the weedy bank of a hill overlooking the west Pittsburgh Federal Safety Zone. Sweating and mosquito bitten, I'm too far away to feel the breeze that sweeps in off the Allegheny River. I can see the wind, though, in the harmonized flapping of drying laundry that hangs on a twanging confusion of nylon cords. Inside the massive, softly glowing warehouse, the murmur of thousands of people sighs out across the cooling cement plaza. The sound washes over my face like warm breath.

Lucy and Nick are somewhere in there, compliments of my friend Vaughn.

A milling throng of amps spills from the hangar doors and crowds the pavement. They ignore the glazed stares of military police. The amps move slowly, talk in hushed tones. They seem oddly quiet and solemn, victims turned into judges.

On the crumbling street a hundred yards farther up this hill, through the gaps in trees, I see a line of several hundred human gawkers. Some are curious kids on bikes, staring down with wide eyes. Others' eyes are narrow, swimming with vile intentions. I wonder how many guns have been quietly loaded and now swing heavily in pockets above.

It's not clear to me whether the warehouse down there is a prison or a fortress.

A shiny new coil of barbed wire meanders around the perimeter of the facility, only five feet away from where the cement turns to brush. Three hastily constructed wooden towers rise, spaced out behind the razor-sharp wire and linked by high fences. I can make out the dark silhouettes of military police. The slender barrel of a rifle and the wink of its scope. On the ground, a few widely spread military policemen saunter along.

I take a deep breath and do what Lyle taught me to do. Focus on my goal up front. To get past the sharp fence uninjured. To avoid the men and lights and guns. Most of all, to *not hurt anyone*. Lucy told me I'm a good guy. But each time I turn on the Zenith, there is always the chance I'll surface with blood on my hands.

Three, two, one. Zero.

I fall backward into the blackness behind my own eyelids. Surrender control to the implant. Whole hog.

I am still, even as the world and all its data shimmer around me.

Hidden paths and tiny objects and environmental information starburst into colors and light. Retinal and cochlear and Autofocus blend together into a symphony. The heat differential on the pavement. Density of the barbed-wire coils. Even the sweep of the spotlight collapses out of time and falls into a visible pattern. I can see where the light is. I can see where it will be.

And then my legs are moving. The muddy hillside slides away under my feet. I hear the gentle ticking of my shoes on the pavement. The knee-high coil of barbed wire jerkily approaches. It's clearly been unwound from a spool and hastily thrown off the back of a truck. One spiky loop is snarled up, uncoiled; it gleams at me like a tunnel of light.

A bare instant after the spotlight glances overhead, the serpentine blades loom up at me. I'm leaping that flat spot in the wire, sliding across the weedy pavement on the other side.

I vault onto the chain-link fence and climb. The metal bites into my fingers and then I'm catapulting myself over the razor wire on top. The pavement rolls with me when I touch down on the other side.

Five seconds later, I reach the back of a tar paper shack at a dead sprint. I'm running on my toes for silence and sacrificing control. I hit the side of the flimsy building with a smack and lean against it, gasping for breath. Sweaty palms pressed hard against rough wood.

Okay, turn it off now, I'm thinking to myself and it's starting to work. Take control from the amp. Turn it off. *Off, off, off.*

The colors have gone dull and faded when this young soldier walks around the corner of the shack. He whips his flashlight up. Aims it at my head. The beam of light hits the surface of my face and I swear I can feel the individual photons bouncing off me, bouncing back into his retinas and triggering a shudder of surprise.

My scraggly beard hasn't fooled him.

I don't think about how to respond. That's just the problem. The technology does it for me, and by reflex the world outside is moving again. That flashlight grows brighter. A surprised adolescent squawk escapes the soldier as the heel of my palm tags his windpipe. A moment of vertigo as the flashlight spins in the air. I can feel myself spinning with it in a gentle arc. Ground turns to sky turns to ground.

I catch the flashlight, crouch, and gently set it down. Then I leap.

Now my right arm is in a viselike V shape, closing in tight

around the soldier's neck. It blocks the surging, panicked pulse of his carotid and jugular. The back of his head is pushed against my cheek, and I can smell the sweat in his hair. I smell his shampoo and I'm trying so hard to will my arm to stop, but it's like trying to focus your eyes on something too close to your face. I can't haul myself up out of this hole in my mind. Through gritted teeth, I scream at myself, at my own tightly locked arms.

The soldier goes loose and limp. He makes a little snorting sound from deep in his throat. I can see his face is relaxed and serene as a doll and I know that now he is dying. Each tenth of a second without oxygen takes him closer. The urgency of this knowledge floods my body with new adrenaline. My grip begins to shake. With a whining grunt behind my teeth, I force my arm to open. A bit and then some more.

The spell finally shatters and the Zenith deactivates.

I lay the soldier gently on the ground, pull his body into the shadows. He is unarmed. Just a billy club and a radio. The sickly colors around me finally recede and the patterns of death and destruction shrink back into the earth.

Leaning over, I check the soldier's pulse. Sluggish, but he's alive. He'll likely wake up inside twenty minutes, confused. And then this place will be on lockdown.

Standing, I turn and stride away.

In half an hour they'll be tearing the under-bridge apart looking for me. But as of right now, I am a prisoner. Just an amp like any other.

I walk quickly, trying not to draw attention to myself.

The warehouse roof soars overhead, hazy with distance and smoke from portable stoves. On the ground, people are crammed in together everywhere. Capsules of privacy grid the landscape. People crouch behind walls made of cardboard boxes and inside tents or hastily constructed shacks. They are resting and cooking and reading books in lawn chairs. The adults are marinated in boredom. The children are in constant motion.

Most occupants are amps, but not all. Plenty of reggie families are here with their amped relatives. Husbands following wives and vice versa. Mothers and fathers dragged into this situation by their littlest and most vulnerable family members.

I find a maze of hanging tarps and curtains suspended by drooping twine. I peek behind them, finding only strange faces. It's been fifteen minutes already. My head is clouded by the urgency of this search. The closest thing I have to family is here. If I don't find them before Vaughn does, I don't want to know what may happen.

Then, I hear a familiar giggle.

Striding down a winding aisle between cots, I peek behind a government blanket hung up to form a partition. When I push it away I find my favorite people on opposite ends of a cot, sitting cross-legged and wearing pajamas, playing cards under the high rusting bones of the warehouse.

Nick and Lucy.

The instant Nick sets his piggish eyes on me, he leaps off the cot. Grabs me around the neck and hugs me for all he's worth. Without a counterweight, the cot tips Lucy backward. Her cards fly into the air like confetti. Nick in one arm, I dive forward and catch Lucy around the back. We all land in a heap on a blanket, feeling the bite of the cement underneath, like a reminder.

I give Lucy small starving kisses.

Nick mimes the kisses, making fun, and I push his small face away with my free arm. Between kisses, I try to explain. Priders could rush the warehouse any minute. I've got maybe ten minutes to get us all out. Before the military police come looking for me, searching bed to bed for the intruder.

Lucy grabs my arms and sits me down on a plastic milk crate. Nick watches us expectantly.

"How'd you get in here?" he asks.

I hesitate, and they stare at me in the weak light, worried. The warehouse thrums with conversation like waves murmuring against a dock. I can still feel prickles of sensation on my face from the soldier's flashlight.

"I used the Zenith. All of it."

Lucy puts a hand over her mouth. Nick leans forward, eyes bright. "What's it like?" he asks.

"Like . . . being a ghost. Watching somebody else's life. Seeing events unfold precisely according to a plan that nobody told you."

"Like destiny," muses Nick.

Destiny. I think about how it feels to fall down inside my own head. The potential outcomes of my actions laid out in colored stripes on the ground. Dance steps painted in invisible ink. Could I choose to do something else? I realize I haven't tried.

"I've got to get you both out of here. Right now."

Nick and Lucy don't move. I'm not getting through to them, so I continue.

"Vaughn won. He used Lyle to spark an atrocity so bad that it made places like this. Camps where amps are separated and regulated. The feds took me to Vaughn, but I escaped. Not before he threatened to kill all of us."

Lucy frowns. "Lyle wouldn't let anybody use him," she says.

"It doesn't matter," I say. "Vaughn wants us dead and I've got about three minutes to get you out of here."

"And then what?" asks Lucy.

"Then we run. Stay alive."

Lucy takes my face in her hands. She turns my head and I see. Dozens of amps stand around us. Peeking over the tops of blankets and towels and shower curtains. Standing tall and grim and stone-faced. Some have their children. Many have crude weapons fashioned from whatever can be scavenged: furniture, tools, lawn equipment.

"We're all part of this, Owen," Lucy says. "There is no other life right out there. No place to go. It's not safe to be alone. In here, we can look after each other."

"But it's not safe—" I say.

"Jim died for these people."

An electric current seems to sweep across the warehouse floor. People are chattering to each other in hushed voices. In quick furtive motions parents are corralling their children, folding their valuables into backpacks.

"The guards are coming," says Lucy. She pushes a backpack into my hands. Inside, I see a few granola bars, some clothes, a few stray dollars.

"You've got to go," Lucy says. "Nick and I can hide here. Nobody will let anything happen to us."

"If someone asks you to go with them for questioning, you say no. Don't go with *anyone*. Always stay with . . ." I stop. Looking into her face, I already know what she's capable of. How strong she is. I grab my backpack and squeeze her in a quick half hug. I nod to Nick and touch his shoulder.

"I'll fix this, okay?"

"Vaughn?" asks Nick.

"I'm going to stop him from hurting you. Once and for all."

Article XIV

All *persons* born or naturalized in the United States, and subject to the jurisdiction thereof, are citizens of the United States and of the State wherein they reside. No State shall make or enforce any law which shall abridge the privileges or immunities of citizens of the United States; nor shall any State deprive any person of life, liberty, or property, without due process of law; nor deny to any person within its jurisdiction the equal protection of the laws.

24
SIMULATIONS

At level five, there is constant movement in stillness. Especially in stillness. There are so many potentials in the quiet moments before action.

I catch up with Vaughn outside his PHCC offices near the University of Pittsburgh. My old neighborhood. The buildings and telephone poles are plastered with signs about Vaughn's Pure Pride speech later this afternoon. From a cab, I watch the front door of his building until the man himself finally emerges. Four gray suits shuffle him into a generic black SUV.

I dig money out of my backpack and hand it over to the cabbie. When he looks at me, I turn my head on instinct to keep my nub pointed away from him. We lurch into traffic, following Vaughn for a few miles. Finally, his car pulls off the road.

The gray suits let Vaughn out at the front gate of the Allegheny Cemetery. The facade of the place is centuries old, built to look like a castle with battlements of brown sandstone. Beyond the gate, rolling hills sprout tombstones that are linked by shady cement paths under ancient trees.

Senator Vaughn goes in alone.

I pay the rest of my fare and take a walk up the street. A block down, I jump the winding stone fence. Then, I track Vaughn through the woods.

I've been thinking. Lyle may be a weapon, but Vaughn is the person who pulled the trigger. Even if Lyle were out of the picture,

Vaughn would keep going. He'd find another weapon and use it. There is only one way to stop him.

Three, two, one, zero. Level five consent and I'm in.

Pacing between the trees, a series of attack simulations come to me. I can't stop them. My Zenith is talking to retinal. The two collude, slicing up my vision with crisp blue lines. The beams crisscross, meander down the stone path along high-probability approach routes. If the target comes this way, do this. If he comes that way, do that.

The choice is mine, sure, but either way, it's kill, kill, kill.

Shadows play through the chattering leaves overhead, dappling Vaughn's suit as he crosses a hill about a hundred yards away. Incredible to think this man single-handedly engineered a national crisis. Made a whole country afraid of amps. Capitalized on it to outlaw the technology and imprison everyone who has it.

Some small sound alerts me to the presence of a bodyguard. Without seeing him, I change route to flank. Place my steps one by one, quiet and deliberate.

I close my eyes, but the blue lines are still there—rolling Gaussian hills, superimposed over a faded image of the path as I last saw it. The faux scene plays out on the backs of my eyelids, borrowed from my memory of seeing it, even tilting and moving when I turn my head.

That would be cochlear talking to neural talking to retinal.

Shit, I'm carrying a lot of plastic in my head. A scrapyard of high-tech, all of it communicating and collaborating. Hundreds of subprocesses running alongside each other to figure out what's happening, already happened, or is going to happen very soon.

My target keeps moving: Senator Joseph Vaughn. Six foot one. Forty-four. Graying at the temples. Snake eyes. Absolutely human through and through, and damn proud of it.

In a few hours, Vaughn will orate to the world. He will stand on an ornate wrought iron balcony jutting from the sheer lime-stone face of the Cathedral of Learning. On camera with his black wire-rimmed glasses and clean white teeth and a pure gold American flag pin on his lapel.

When he speaks, his words will bury me. If he announces my capture and escape, there will be no refuge. No way of proving my innocence. The crime is too colossal—it blots out all details by its existence.

Vaughn pauses to look at a grave. Leans over it, hands behind his back. The tombstone is white marble.

I crouch next to a tree. Put my fingers against the bark and feel every whorl and crevice in minute detail. Every one of my senses is alive and trained on one goal: killing the unlucky man standing over that tombstone.

A gray suit strolls past in the distance, but the bodyguard doesn't go near Vaughn, keeps walking instead.

It's pretty likely that here in about sixty seconds, I'm going to bury my skinned-up knuckles into Vaughn's soft gut as I work my way up to crushing his windpipe. Mathematically speaking, there are an infinite number of ways to kill him with my bare hands. Combat algorithms rip through my vision, indicating exactly where I should stand. How to pivot. Which vertebrae to shatter and how much force it takes. Pressure points and bone-cracking leverage.

Whole fucking hog.

I *want* to hurt him for what he's done. I want to gouge out his natural eyes and break his natural arms and legs. Puncture his natural organs with his natural ribs. Until Vaughn's definition of a human being came along, me and Lyle and Samantha—we weren't amps. We were people.

Someday, we'll be people again.

The phantom movements I'll make are already itching through my hands, a series of reflexive twitches. Every approach and outcome pair are broken down to physics and equations and meat. The grass swarms with six-inch-tall figures, glowing blue and visible only to me. Implant generated, the dummies grow out of the shadows and engage each other in a variety of high probability mock-combat situations.

Twitch, twitch, snap. Twitch, twitch, snap.

One of the tiny golems silently bends back the virtual fingers of its diminutive enemy, breaking them one by one. I shiver, hoping that scenario doesn't happen. It looks painful as hell, even virtually.

Is this really you, Owen?

Am I a killer? I don't know. It occurs to me that my body operates almost entirely without listening to my opinion—balancing, daydreaming, and healing itself, not to mention breathing and digesting food and a million other little things. I'm not sure how much control I really have anymore. How much control did I ever have?

I scan the periphery for gray suits.

Nobody is around. Vaughn is alone, crouched at the tombstone. His back is to me, perfectly vulnerable. I slowly rise, and the grappling dummies fade.

Now, I attack.

Trees and hills accelerate to a gray blur around me as my vision closes in on blue boot prints rising out of the soil. My legs are pumping, palms slicing the air as I gain momentum over the damp grass. My arms pull back, hands collapsing into fists like neutron stars.

As I make my final leap, my eyes register the tombstone. My retinal keys in. It's carved in the shape of a cherub, lying down, wings folded and sleeping. Three words are inscribed on it that detonate in my mind: *Emma Camille Vaughn.*

Those first two letters: *EM.*

My heels dig into the ground and I grunt with the exertion of keeping my fists by my sides. I'm a foot behind Vaughn, catching my balance, and it's suddenly, deafeningly still and quiet in the cemetery. The sound of my breathing rakes across the chattering chorus of windblown leaves overhead.

Vaughn speaks, on his knees. He doesn't turn around.

"If you're here to kill me, go ahead," he says.

With an effort I stand up. Blood rings in my ears.

There is a new flower next to the tombstone. A simple yellow daffodil. An older flower is in the grass next to it, still yellow.

"She was six," says Vaughn, still facing the grave. "Six years old. It's hard, really, to explain how little and sweet she was. My Em."

Elysium. *Em.* His baby daughter's name.

Beneath the child's name, in small block letters, is the simple message: HUSH MY DEAR, BE STILL AND SLUMBER. ANGELS GUARD YOUR BED.

"Elysium," I say. "Heaven. Where heroes go when they die."

"My inner circle. Friends who know why I fight. *Who* I'm fighting for."

Vaughn wipes his face and his hand comes away wet. He isn't acting. Was never acting, I realize.

"We had the implantation done privately. It was all my idea. My wife said wait. Said we should let the technology mature. But the doctors told me Emma was going to learn slow and that didn't fit into my program. I had the access and the money and I thought I had the answer. And for a few months, I did.

"It was an infection. She started vomiting and we thought she had the flu. We took her to the hospital, but it was too late. She was so *little*. Such a sweet little baby girl in her hospital bed."

Vaughn's head bows.

"That doesn't give you the right to start a war," I say.

The man turns, looks up at me for the first time. He wipes away tears and snot with a carefully manicured hand. One of his knees is stained with dirt.

"I'm not starting a war," he says. "And I don't intend to."

"You hired Lyle to kill the other Zeniths."

Vaughn blinks at me, frowns. "What's a Zenith?" he asks.

The politician is hunched over, hair mussed and cheeks covered in tears, and he has a look of real confusion on his face. He honestly doesn't know. Vaughn doesn't know what's been happening.

I'm backing away from this kneeling man, finally realizing.

Somebody is building a new world.

The laughing cowboy.

"It's Lyle," I say. "It's always been Lyle."

Someone shouts from the woods. In my peripheral, I see a gray suit coming, knees flashing as he runs. Gun winking at me.

I've got a goddamn ace up my sleeve that's been waiting there for ten years. Since the birth of Pure Pride. Wait until I show them what I got. Then *they'll know war.*

Vaughn is the ace.

"He's going to kill you to start a real war," I whisper urgently, backing away. "The safety zones aren't his goal. He just needed to put the amps against a wall. So they'll fight. Cancel your speech. You need to hide. You need to *run*."

"You're mistaken," says Vaughn. "Lyle belongs to me. Not the other way around."

I can hear footfalls now. The wheezing grunt of a linebacker hurtling through space. Too far away to catch a Zenith, but no time left.

"Please," I say to Vaughn.

And then I am motion. The trees swallow me up.

Q&A: The US "Amp" Problem

The president of the United States has declared a state of emergency, going so far as to create "safety zones" to protect hundreds of thousands of citizens with neural implants from violent demonstrations.

Implants of this sort are in common use throughout the European Union, medically and electively. So why are they causing such a row in the US?

What is an "amp"?
The derogatory term refers both to a neural implant or to an implanted person.

Why are Americans debating?
An emotional debate has raged between those who say the technology is vital for medical progress and those who say it creates an unlevel playing field for those who do not have the implant. Scientists and people with disabilities have claimed that neural implants can cure disease, but many middle-class voters and religious groups are opposed.

Why has the debate turned violent?
Government funding of brain implantable devices has been blocked and the US Food and Drug Administration (FDA) recalled the most popular type of implant. Discrimination against implanted individuals was legalized. Some implantees responded with a series of violent attacks. American pundits believe these attacks may have provoked an even more violent backlash from regular citizens.

25

BAD GUY

I get inside the Cathedral of Learning by scaling the back side of the building. The front is guarded by police and mobbed by demonstrators. But whole hog, the soot-stained concrete wall is alive and writhing with virtual handholds, friction estimates, and climbing routes. My fingers are steel claws. It takes three minutes to solve the tower wall, thirty more seconds to wriggle in an arched window.

If anyone saw me, it's too late to matter.

And there are plenty who could have. I can feel the roar of a thousand people outside rumbling through the structural bones of the building. The lawn out front is packed with Pure Pride supporters. A thousand pairs of eyes turned up toward a double wood-plank door perched above a three-story arch. It leads to a wrought iron balcony big enough for one man and a nest of microphones.

Senator Vaughn stands there now, framed in ornate stonework.

I sprint down dim hallways, praying that Lyle hasn't beaten me here. I'm faintly aware that I'm gasping for breath. My chest heaves as I negotiate cramped corridors, trying to reach the room that leads to that iron balcony.

Finally, I spot the door at the end of a hallway. There's a piece of white paper taped to it. PRIVATE, it says.

Some minute vibration in the floor causes me to freeze, throw my back against a wall. A gray suit crosses farther down the hallway, patrolling the building. I watch him, holding my breath, letting my eyes taste the shadows.

The guard doesn't seem upset or panicked. Lyle isn't here yet. Nobody must have reported me climbing the wall yet, either. There is still time to save Vaughn's life. Time enough to stop Lyle from triggering a civil war.

In a fuzzy way, I realize that I can *see* the sound I'm making. Every careful step I take closer to the door sends a ripple racing over the tile, like splashes through a puddle. Each quiet breath I take dissipates quickly to silence. Surgically planting each foot, I manage to creep closer while eliminating the ripples of visible sound.

This is the only door that leads to Vaughn, and it's under constant surveillance. Well, almost constant.

Gray suit paces a few more feet, turns. The door is unwatched for a split second. Observing the smooth, relaxed muscles in gray suit's neck, I leap across the hallway. As his muscles contract and his bald head begins to turn, I knife the door open with my fingers and ease my body through. A gaze estimate appears like a spotlight projected from gray suit's eyes, racing down the hallway. It lands on the door as it closes the last few inches.

A soft snick and I am in the empty room.

I crouch and listen as gray suit approaches. Watch the rippling light from his footsteps swell under the door. He nears, stops. Slowly, the doorknob turns as he checks it. Turns all the way, pauses, then lets it flip back.

He keeps walking.

Now I allow myself to breathe. This room is a stone alcove. The carved ceiling folds into itself over the polished marble floor. The far wall is dominated by arched wooden double doors that lead to the wrought iron balcony and to Vaughn.

I'm too late. He's already giving his speech.

A line of light runs between the doors. From the other side, I can hear Vaughn speaking. He enunciates each word into the microphones. This is it: Vaughn is outside delivering his master stroke. If he claims to have identified the villain behind Astra, well, there's nothing I can do about it now.

From the sound of it, I'm only hearing the tail end of the speech.

"I do not stand before you today, I stand *with* you," says Vaughn in a measured tone. His magnified voice echoes against the hard buildings outside. "We who are gathered here today, made in the image of the Almighty, stand *together* in naked defiance of martyrs and terrorists.

"*I* stand with you, arm in arm at the edge of the abyss. And together, we stand stronger than any man-made steel ever beaten in a foundry. And though vicious extremists may lash out at us, we continue to stand together firmly, without fear, and with the knowledge that we stand for America.

"And that is why, mere blocks away from the medical laboratories where this grave threat to our nation was born, and mere blocks from where it will soon be eliminated, I ask you all once again that you *not retaliate*. We have the amp problem firmly under control. Violence will not right the wrongs. It will not solve our problems. And it will not best serve the interests of our children, those born and those who have yet to join us."

The air reverberates with the dull impact of thousands of dutifully clapping hands. The temblor builds slowly, growing until the shadowed room itself hums as if it were on a launchpad. A few angry catcalls pierce the applause as it begins to fade. But judging from the general response, Vaughn's message seems to have been accepted.

"Thank you," says Vaughn. "God bless America."

And the crack of light splits in two.

Joseph Vaughn stands before me, a stark black silhouette against bright gray Pittsburgh skies. A great writhing mass of humanity spreads out behind him like a cloak.

Before I know what's happening, I've got two fistfuls of his shirt and I'm yanking him inside. I kick the double doors shut, muting the clamor outside. Drop my forearm under his chin and ram him up against the wall before he can make a squeak.

"Where's Lyle?" I ask.

He snarls and I notice he's bitten his lip. Those white canines peek out at me, dipped in blood. "Don't know, Mr. Gray," he says. "He and I are done. Our transaction is complete. He performed his duties and I paid him handsomely."

"Why didn't you name me as head of Astra?"

Vaughn eyes me greedily. "Because you had escaped. But now here you are. Lucky me."

His eyes go to the door and I know he's waiting for those gray suits. It's a good bet they'll show any minute. But the guys with walkie-talkies are the least of my worries. They're only human, after all.

"You've got no idea what's about to happen," I whisper.

Vaughn struggles to straighten himself against the wall. He pushes against my forearm with a soft palm. I don't let it budge. "I would suggest that you get your fucking *amp* hands off me," he spits. "You think your little friends in the camps have it bad right now? Do you have any clue what those people out there would *do* if I were harmed?"

I relax my grip, but keep him pinned. Keep my eyes inches from his face, watching every expression that sweeps over his face.

"That's exactly why Lyle is going to kill you," I say.

Vaughn shakes his head.

"Lyle Crosby and I built the Pure Human Citizen's Council together from nothing," he says. "Pure Pride was an idea that he and I hashed out in a basement nearly a decade ago. The organization runs on *fear,* Gray. Fear needs violence. Pure Pride required the intellect of a great man and the bloodlust of a savage. Now let me go or I yell."

I uncurl my fingers from his shirt. When I speak, my own voice echoes in my ears. "You think that you used Lyle against his own kind," I say. "But you've been used. He won't stop."

Vaughn laughs in my face. Hot breath rolling over my cheeks. With a sharp tug, he yanks my arm off his chest and I let him. He steps back and wipes the blood off his mouth with his hand. Looks at it and shakes his head.

"We've worked together for a decade. The man hates himself, pure and simple. And there's no way out of it. The implant changes your brain patterns over the years. A little nudge here, a nudge there. Even if Lyle were able to remove the technology and still function . . . he would never be a man again. He knows that. It's why he never wanted it to happen to another person. And that was a guarantee that I could provide."

Vaughn pulls a white handkerchief out of his breast pocket and dabs at his lip. "We've got the research shut down and seized. Control over the doctors. The existing amps are corralled and imprisoned. We won. It's over. Lyle Crosby got everything he wanted out of our arrangement."

I hear a familiar acid chuckle behind me. Stepping away from Vaughn, I slowly turn around. My eyes devour the light, analyzing.

Lyle.

Leaning across the open doorway like a butcher knife buried in a kitchen table. He's wearing black jeans and a wrinkled cowboy shirt with pearl buttons. There is a smear of blood on his chest. A gray-suited body of a guard sprawled at his feet. In his right hand is a dead-black Glock .44 semiautomatic pistol. Index finger inside the trigger guard. He casually reaches up and scratches his temple with the slide of the gun. The fluorescent orange sight dot hovers, mesmerizing.

"I wouldn't say I got *everything* I wanted," he says. Lazily, Lyle extends his arm. Pulls the trigger without the slightest hesitation.

Three, two, one, go.

By the time the bullet leaves the barrel of the gun, I'm moving fast as a reflection in the mirror. I feel the light of the sudden searing muzzle flash blaze across my retinas. Tiny meteorites of gunpowder residue impact my cheeks and forehead as I lunge forward.

The bullet passes by. Not meant for me.

Twisting, my palm closes across the slide of the gun. The brass cartridge arcs past my face, end over end. The bullet itself is ten feet away, vaporizing a hole in Vaughn's expensive suit, tearing through the meat of his pectoral muscle, shattering a rib and a clavicle, and spraying the wall behind him with pieces of his shoulder blade.

As I tear the gun from his hands, Lyle depresses the magazine release with his thumb. Then he lets go of the gun altogether. The magazine, pregnant with rounds, drops away.

Vaughn staggers with a plume of red mist erupting from his chest. His knees hinge drunkenly and he falls. The side of his face audibly slaps the tile wall. A wet, coughing bark grates out of his mouth as the weight of his body meets the ground. The head of the PHCC and second-term senator from Pennsylvania lies still.

I land and roll with the empty gun in my hand. The ejected magazine is too far away. With a tug from both hands, I disengage the slide and smack the top of the gun against my palm, popping the barrel out. I land in a crouch, pieces of the Glock raining around my feet.

Vaughn screams hoarsely, face buried in the crook of his arm.

"Aw, quit your crying," says Lyle, a feline smile curled into the corners of his mouth.

"You promised I could turn him in," gasps Vaughn. "You promised."

Lyle clucks his tongue. "Listen to yourself. You used to be so put together. When I found you, boy, you had balls. Now you're just a sad, fat, old reggie."

I'm on my feet. Circling toward Vaughn. Hands up and ready for when Lyle attacks.

"Help me," says Vaughn.

"He wants me to help him," Lyle says to me, rolling his eyes. With one eye on me, he steps over Vaughn and spits words at the sweating, bleeding man.

"You were never in control, genius. After I leaked the existence of Echo Squad and got us disbanded, I did a nationwide search to find a guy just like you. What happened to your daughter was such a *sad* story. I constructed the bones of the PHCC for you. Told you what you wanted to hear. But, goddamn, how could you not know by now? You never did figure it out. I only built you to *destroy you*."

"No," says Vaughn, and he is crying now. "No, we did it together."

"I made you more than a man. I made you a *symbol*. You're the most human human there is, boy. And here in a minute, when I toss your screaming ass over that balcony and you go splitter splatter in front of the ten million zealots we created? Hoo boy. *Then* a real war's gonna start."

"What about the amps?" I hear myself say.

"We trigger a life-or-death situation and *force* them to fight. Force them to overcome."

"They'll *die*."

"Maybe. But you gotta understand, Gray. In this world, I'm a broke-dick dog. A tool to be wielded by another man. But in the new world? Shit, I'm a warlord. A barbarian king. Free to spread my dominion over this nation. Who knows, man, maybe the world."

"You're going to get five hundred thousand people slaughtered."

"Aw, I'm disappointed in you. You're looking at the little picture, Gray. You think Europe is going to allow a genocide? Rest of the world is already using implants. In China I hear they're state issued, for Chrissake. This thing is gonna go global quick. And we'll be heading the charge."

"Help," calls Vaughn, who then crawls about six inches toward the door before collapsing. The politician has got his useless arm pulled up tight under his chin, cradling it with his good arm and stretching out his expensive suit jacket. Beads of sweat glisten on a dime-sized bald spot I never noticed. Blood is smeared on the marble.

Lyle watches Vaughn, amused. "Help? Ain't no help. I got your dead bodyguards stacked like cordwood in the hallway, dipshit," says Lyle.

He winks at me, then continues: "Remember your little friend Samantha? She and I seen the same thing. She went and got her panties in a knot and jumped off a building. But I took the bull by his damn horns. We live once, buddy. One time. That's all we get. And I intend to make my mark. I mean, look at us."

Lyle strides to the balcony. Throws open the doors and gazes out over the thousand murmuring demonstrators. Even from here, I can feel their collective heat shouldering in through the doorway. Lyle turns to me, silhouetted, and his eyes are shining—finally, really alive.

"Who among the world of men may judge us, when we are as angels to them?"

Vaughn stirs from the floor. Looks up at Lyle with scared eyes. He's pale. His right arm is twitching uncontrollably.

"Autofocus was meant to help people," I say. "It was meant for good."

"Well, hell," says Lyle. He doesn't seem to notice Vaughn anymore. "I'm beyond good and evil. And it ain't too late. You should join me. With the shit you got upstairs, boy, we could split the world in half. I know you ain't a killer, but the best generals never are."

Lyle puts out his hand for me to shake. But I'm already listening to my Zenith. Dropping levels. On an express elevator to the planet core.

Three, two, one. Three, two, one. Three, two, one.

"Don't you do that," says Lyle, smiling. His hand snakes out toward me and I'm not there. "Where you headed, buddy?"

I'm going deeper than I've ever been. Sinking through the levels fast and smooth like a stone through water. Lyle backs up onto the balcony. A confused murmuring comes from the crowd as they spot the cowboy. His face is shrouded in black and he is dangerous as electricity, and having him only feet away puts a sickening fear into the pit of my belly.

Lyle speaks, words coming out in a torrent, a hoarse whisper that pulls me in. "Kill him with me, Owen. We can make a new world together. *Ad astra cruentus.* To the stars, brother, both of us stained in blood."

I feel the vibration from deep inside me, vocal cords flexing, each minute movement of my tongue as it crafts the word from a gasp of air.

Never.

And in my head, I hear my father's voice. My sight fades as he speaks to me. The familiar sound of him floods my mind with memories and it puts a stinging blur of tears in my eyes. *I gave you something extra, Owen. Level six. Freedom from suffering. Full executive extinguished. A conduit to your soul. Thought to action. I love you, son. I trust you. Do good. Do you consent? Do you consent?*

He left this message for me. All this time. My father.

Do you consent?

I consider it for a fragment of a second.

Yes.

The Zenith awakes.

The room explodes into flowing, scintillating paths of murder and battle. Shining gossamer strands that represent the vicious arc of fists and blunt trajectory of knees. Dense probability maps rise out of the floor based on tiny variations in its surface, routes toward cover, light reflections. Every glowing wisp of probability and vector streak of light slashes a path toward Lyle's darkened face.

Every level before this has been a reflection of this glory.

For a handful of milliseconds, I simply stand in awe of the implant-generated vista. I never knew anything could be this beautiful. Somewhere, my true eyes are going dead and blank in the face of this overwhelming splendor. This must be what a cheetah sees, sprinting seventy miles an hour, fangs out, inches from sinking claws into writhing flesh. Every object humming with life—a flickering corona of data with only a single purpose: to help me survive a fight with Lyle Crosby.

The muscle-priming routines snap into action like a mousetrap. Each movement of my initial feint and stuttering leap toward Lyle pulses through my body as a reflex action. The skinny cowboy charges at me, anticipating my first three feints, but my last change of speed and direction catches him centimeters off guard.

His hardware is running hot but not as hot as mine. We hit like bullets colliding. He stumbles back and I pin him against the balcony railing.

Before an audience of thousands.

"Where are you?" whispers Lyle.

Our arms intertwine, thrashing in short purposeful bursts. Attacks and parries at the speed of the nervous system. Watching it unfold, I see so many arm configuration probabilities radiating from our interlocked limbs that we look like Indian gods. Each brutal exchange digs us into a deeper, more intricate grip. When I snap his ring and middle fingers backward, breaking them both at the first knuckle, he barks a hyena laugh, tendons straining his throat.

But the fight is already over. Gruesome efficiency. An equation solved.

Our arms are locked up like a stuck drawer. Lyle's side is wedged against the railing. Behind him, the crush of a thousand bodies presses in on us. All the infinite ghostly arm position configurations have collapsed into this single incontrovertible lock. Almost gently, I press my forearm over Lyle's neck. He struggles, twists his sweaty head back and forth. Trapped between iron and flesh.

We both know he has a near-zero probability of escape.

Lyle's eyes are shining like oily pavement after a thunderstorm. His tanned face reddens, darkens as the oxygen is cut off. Blinking just to focus, he grunts, "You're not a killer."

My forearm remains steady as bedrock as the words dissipate. Lyle looks confused. Sort of hurt, like I just called him a bad name.

These days, a single man can do more than his fair share of evil. The technology makes each of us so much more. This skinny cowboy could kill millions. And all he has going for him is raw grit and anger and the will to dominate—and that white-hot spark of science fueling it all.

I wonder if I am any different. I wonder if it even matters.

"We've all got a killer inside us," I whisper, and I bear down with my forearm. Lyle's eyes widen as his throat collapses, as the arteries and airways close for business. A surprised smile briefly plays over his mouth and his lips part. But no words come out.

Lyle's black eyes close for the last time.

I watch his still face for a long minute before I let his body fall at my feet. People in the crowd below are confused. A woman screams. And something moves inside the room. Vaughn. He's propped himself up on one elbow. Face sheened in sweat, he smiles at me and speaks with a bloodstained tongue.

"They'll never believe you," he says.

I hear shouting in the hallway, footsteps growing louder. My skin is buzzing, vision wavering. Staggered, I lower my hands onto my knees and double over. I can't say quite why it feels this way, but I'm thinking that I just killed my best friend. Or my brother. Maybe myself.

Vaughn's sweat-slicked face is pinched with triumph as he lies back, his strength completely exhausted.

But his smile fades as I reach up and pinch shaky fingertips around the nub on my temple. My retinal video has a cache of the last twenty minutes. I know this because I watched Nick learn it the hard way.

"No," says Vaughn.

I give myself one deep breath, take hold of the port, and close my eyes.

Then I rip it out.

Pittsburgh Post-Gazette

"Pure Pride" Rocked by Criminal Investigation

PITTSBURGH—In the last several days, the Pure Human Citizen's Council (PHCC) has lost substantial backing, including from the AARP—one of the nation's most powerful lobbying groups.

Support has waned to historic lows with the revelation that at least some of the recent internecine violence was caused by mercenary outfits allegedly hired by the PHCC itself. Civil rights proponents have long claimed that Pure Pride rhetoric borders on hate speech and encourages discrimination. Now, some are even claiming that the tri-city attacks were bankrolled by the anti-implantee organization.

The president of the 90 million strong AARP, Dr. Sven Sorenson, sidestepped the allegations and recent arrest of Senator Joseph Vaughn, saying simply that "the majority of our membership agrees that the promise of brain implants as a medical technology outweighs the threat."

Meanwhile, emboldened civil rights leaders have been calling on other unions, community-based organizations, corporations, churches, student groups, and individuals to also officially withdraw support from the PHCC in a show of solidarity with "implanted individuals who just want their lives back."

EPILOGUE

We're all of us on islands. That's what Nick says. According to the chattering kid, everybody, whether they're an amp or a reggie, is on one kind of island or another. Millions of islands, millions of sharks. But billions of bridges. It's the connections between the things that are important, he says. More important than the things themselves.

Nick has a new backpack and that same old faded Rubik's cube. He's pacing my shadow as we cross the field to the government prefab where school is held. The goofy kid doesn't hold my hand anymore, but he stays close just the same.

We're rebuilding Eden.

Time seems to move slowly in the humid Oklahoma summer. At night, we sleep on cots in air-conditioned government prefabs. They're lined up in the field outside Eden like dominoes, crushing the memories of spotlighters into the dirt. Every day they clear more husks of burned trailers away. Scorched patches left on the ground like bad memories.

I thought about going back to Pittsburgh, but my people are here. The people who need me, and the people I need. My own kind, as my father once said.

In the end, it was the technology that saved us.

By the time the ambulance came, Vaughn could barely speak. Ashen-faced, he struggled and gasped and managed to accuse me of trying to murder him. I didn't resist. Losing my port left me nearly comatose, splayed out on the ground next to Lyle's corpse.

The cops must have arrested me because I woke up cuffed. Vaughn went into critical care. For a minute, it looked like Lyle was going to get his wish. People were scared and angry and inches away from civil war.

But Vaughn survived. And so did my prosthetic memory.

I waited in the hospital under police watch while they played back my retinal cache and realized what had happened. Cochlear picked up pretty good sound, but even so my lawyer brought in a lip-reader to decipher the video. The prosecution had its own lip-reader, too.

But my case never went to trial.

After that last standoff went viral, Vaughn's life changed quickly. From what I understand, they arrested him while he was in the hospital. And what with him being the head of a domestic terrorist organization with splinter factions spread across the United States . . . well, he didn't make his bail.

Still, he's a hero to a dangerous few.

Nick runs ahead of me and joins a couple other kids in front of the prefab that serves as our schoolhouse. It's odd, but he's got friends now. Smart ones who can keep up with him. A couple of them are waiting with Rubik's cubes of their own. Nick isn't shy about telling the tale of his escape from Eden. He's a half-pint legend now.

I open the door for Nick and his friends. Follow them in.

Inside, thirty-five pairs of eyes stare up at me. Thirty-five nodules on temples, some decorated with glitter and neon lights and others just left alone. The kids sit on government-supplied folding chairs around three mismatched tables. There are no recognizable grade levels. The difficulty of the material has to do with your implant and your natural intelligence. Age is immaterial for these amps.

I lay my books out on an old kitchen table and take a seat. Lucy is already at the table next to mine. The little girls of her class are sitting close to her, hands folded and eyes trained on their teacher like small predatory birds. They are eager to learn. Lucy is patient and caring and she never underestimates her students.

I reach across the aisle and take Lucy's hand. She gives my palm a squeeze and her grasp is strong and warm. Nick raises his eyebrows at me and I just shake my head.

"Okay, class," I say. "Today, we're going to study government. There aren't enough books, so those of you with modded retinal implants should scan the pages and then share with your neighbor."

Humankind needs technology.

It's the one thing that we do better than any other animal. We communicate, cooperate, and make tools to extend our reach. Every new tool changes us. As we grow, sometimes parents find they can't recognize their children. The old fears the new, and the two threaten to destroy each other.

Our technology is what makes us strong. And it's what makes us dangerous.

Before the implants, plenty of these kids were a little slobbery. A little slow. Now they're faster, smarter versions of who they were. They're on their way to becoming altogether new types of people. It's frightening. But the landscape of our lives evolves in lurches. There is no stopping and no going back. There never was.

We just didn't know it.

I've heard it said that technology makes a good person better, and it makes a bad person worse. That's okay with me. I say we keep building new versions of ourselves, keep exploring the unknown, and keep growing.

We're gonna be fine. Different, but fine.

Because most people are good. Right?

ACKNOWLEDGMENTS

I owe deep thanks to many people who helped this book in all kinds of ways:

The students and faculty of the University of Tulsa and Carnegie Mellon University for sharing (and continuing to share) their knowledge and expertise.

Ron Randall for a couple of great illustrations and a quick turnaround.

My many friends and experts, including Donnell Alexander, Ryan Anfuso, Mark Baumann, Ryan Blanton, Colby Boles, Paul Carpenter, Taylor Clark, Courtenay Hameister, Matt Holley, Jonathan Hurst, Brian Long, Philip Long, Brett Lundmark, Amalia Marino, Shelley McLendon, Alex Nydhal, Geoff Shaevitz, David Spencer, Cynthia Whitcomb, Timmy Williams, and David Wilson. And my absentminded apologies to anyone else whom I may have forgotten.

My parents, Dennis and Pam, who are in the fabric of everything I write.

Special thanks to my editor, Jason Kaufman, for insight and a long walk in the park. As always, deep gratitude to my agent, Laurie Fox, and manager, Justin Manask, for their unflagging enthusiasm and support.

And finally, all my love always to Anna and Cora.

ABOUT THE AUTHOR

DANIEL H. WILSON is the author of the *New York Times* bestseller *Robopocalypse,* the young adult novel *A Boy and His Bot,* and the nonfiction titles *How to Survive a Robot Uprising, Where's My Jetpack?, How to Build a Robot Army, The Mad Scientist Hall of Fame,* and *Bro-Jitsu: The Martial Art of Sibling Smackdown.* Wilson earned a PhD in robotics from Carnegie Mellon University. He lives and writes in Portland, Oregon.